WITHIN CESSATION

NOIR HAYES

Enjoy his slip into madness.

Noir Hayes

This is dedicated to my fur baby, Bella. I wish that you were curled up next to me when I finished this book.

Special thanks to Dani and Jacquelin for all your help with edits and suggestions.

CHAPTER ONE

"It's great, Tatum, it's really great," Jackie pushed her lips into a grin, but it seemed forced.

"But…?" The younger male asked, his eyebrow pressed into an upward arch.

"Aren't you afraid it's a little… cliché?" Jackie asked as she threaded her fingers together. Tatum watched as her hands rested on top of his manuscript and Jackie's eyebrows matched his - pushed up. He knew what that damn word meant, and he also knew that she might as well have lit the damn story on fire.

"Cliché?" Tatum let out a small huff that was immediately concealed with a slouch of his shoulders. He struggled to swallow the spit down the correct hole, the cough confusing his airways. He tilted his ears towards his shoulders and felt his bones hunch forward, back rounded over. He also couldn't stop the childlike sigh that came out of his mouth before he could put a stop to it. Annoyance, which quickly switched to anxiety, resulted in Tatum chewing the shit out of his cheeks. He only stopped when he tasted the metallic twinge of blood, which prompted his jaw to release its prisoner. As he sat there, unable to get comfortable, the only thing that settled was the burn of his raw cheek. He was a grown man, a thought that prompted him to turn his 'C' curved spine into a straight line. His shoulders were next, to which he pinched and rolled them back.

According to his mother, there was nothing more appealing than a man with excellent posture. He could remember the excitement he felt when he sent his mother the photos of him at his first red carpet appearance. Instead of words of praise which he expected, the phone call turned into a fifteen-minute lecture, in which she had nothing nice to say. According to her, his shoulders were hunched, his hair was messy, and he looked unprofessional. Tatum knew that if she could, she would have sewn his shoulders together to stop them from rolling forward. As a kid, she went as far as sticking a sewing needle in him each time he slouched. At a certain point, his back was covered in the annoying red marks. People asked, of course, but his mother was quick to pass it off as acne. This was a time in which child abuse wasn't as sensationalized and serious as it is now. Had she done this in current times, her ass would've been thrown in jail. Back then? People simply shrugged it off. It was hard to believe that he was now thirty-two, certainly not growing any younger, but those moments from his pre-teen years were still so vivid.

"No," he said lowly as the memories flooded in. He wasn't that boy anymore, and his resentment towards his mother was something that got buried with her. He was a grown man and now was not the time to have a bruised ego. His mother wouldn't have liked the self-conscious side of him, either. She would have told him that if he felt so insecure then he should go to his room and not come out until his manuscript was the best that it could be. She would have told him that his pitch merely wasn't good enough, that he should be embarrassed.

"It's great, truly," Jackie back peddled, but Tatum didn't believe her. Did she sense his spiral of self-hatred? "But I fear that it's all been done before. Right now, you have a decent starting point, but what makes it different?" Jackie mirrored Tatum's straight spine and pushed back shoulders. He intertwined his hands around his knee and cleared his throat, a sad attempt to conceal a frustrated grumble.

"Well," Tatum wasn't prepared for this question. He expected her to tell him it was brilliant, to skip the part where she read the first draft, and to give him the book deal he deserved. "It follows a female lead, one that's younger, at that. She is quiet and keeps to herself," he started, to which he noted Jackie's all but pleased expression. Her eyebrows, threaded together, created the small bulb of skin between her eyes. Her once smiling face pushed into a frown. He once again felt the frustration that bubbled in his chest wall. Couldn't she just be grateful that he came to her with forty pages of content? Couldn't she appreciate the way he constructed twenty-six letters in different and unique ways? Was nothing good enough for her?

"Well, different for you. There was a time where all young adult novels had a strong female lead. Every book or movie had their females step out of the shadows that they lived in. They were no longer the sidekicks, they were the leading ladies. Before we knew it, every woman could wield a bow and arrow or shoot a gun with perfect accuracy. Each year there was a new badass to admire, and a new woman for teens to look up to. It was quite inspiring. So, this female lead idea of yours is nothing new." She looked at him and her right ear tipped towards him, expectant of Tatum's response. When he didn't have one, Jackie continued. "Your characters in all your books, to this point, have been male-driven. They've been the strong and dominant, never afraid to step up and take charge. I can understand the feeling that you need to change, trust me. Your characters, whether they were the leads or supporters, all shared the same character trait. They were all carefully constructed male stereotypes," she pointed out, even though Tatum wrote the stories, so he knew this already. The continuation of her comments felt relentless, and it was the kind of conversation that caused him to have an all too firm grip on the chair's armrest. He stared at the wooden desk and wondered how hard he'd have to smack his head off of it to knock himself out. She was saying the same thing over and over, a repetition that ground his gears. Not to mention the low blow that came with the word *stereotype*. As if he didn't hate the books already.

"My *one* book series," Tatum corrected. He felt the familiar ache and pressure of a tension headache, the kind that had a heartbeat behind his eyes. He expected this meeting to relieve all tension in his body, but he was wrong. It only made things fester and grow. He was rigid as he threaded his fingers together to stop the desperate clench of his fists. This movement lasted a short moment before his hands rose to the side of his head. He imagined his pointer and middle finger crushing through his temples, anything to give him a sense of relief. He wondered if anyone had done that to themselves, even if it was accidentally. However, he wasn't sure what kind of idiot could accidentally crush their skull. He'd have to tuck that idea away for future use.

"I know you're trying to recreate yourself," Jackie didn't seem phased by the psychotic tendencies taking place in front of her. Instead she rose to her feet and turned her back on Tatum, "Coffee?" she asked as she lifted the pot.

"I just... don't like being known as the romance guy. I need something different. When I wrote *The Devil's Bride*, I never expected it to turn into *The Devil*, *The Devil's Child*, and *The Devil's Revenge*. I mean, fuck, I wrote those books to break into the writing world, you know?" Tatum sighed, "Coffee would be great," Maybe that would ease the headache.

"People love *The Devils* saga, though," Jackie said as she put on the fresh pot of coffee, "If you were to write a final book in the series, I'm sure we could get you a movie deal or some kind of television show. It has been ten years since your last book, after all. People loved that series, I'm sure a new book would not only get the interest of your old fans, but new ones, too. People would brush off the old books and start to read them all over again, people would bid for original and first editions on Ebay. What is your sudden resentment towards the saga, anyway? It's a brilliant piece of work and people love it." God, if he had a dollar for every time he had that said to him.

When he finally called Jackie after their several years without talking, he half expected Jackie to tell him to go fuck off and delete her number, but here they were. The same place they started this journey a decade ago. If he believed in some higher power, he'd thank whomever that was for Jackie's generosity. Ever since their last work together, he watched from the shadows as her clients rose to success while the buzz around *The Devil's* saga slowly dissipated. People forgot about the devil, and they forgot about his bride. They forgot about Tatum Hyland, too. He didn't blame them, whenever you pour your money into an author and get what he gave them in *The Devil's Revenge*, he'd be uninterested, too.

"I just want to write something... outside of some Devil's love story. I mean those books were years ago and they were juvenile. I mean, you may as well have made Edward from *Twilight* the devil and you would've had the exact same story, give or take. Besides, isn't it you that always says change is good?"

The struggling author argued with his agent before he narrowed his eyes, "Wasn't it you that called my characters stereotypical?" He crossed his arms. Maybe when he called, she expected a new extension of *The Devil's* story. Perhaps that's what this whole thing was about. But he couldn't milk that series any longer. He wasn't a sell-out. There was no saving the shit show he created in *The Devil's Revenge*. No, that story needed to die and remain forgotten.

"Tatum," Jackie sighed as the coffee scent filled the room, "Change is always good. However, it would be best if you weren't trying to change just for the sake of it," she bent over to pull a small carton of vanilla creamer from the mini-fridge. "And I said they were carefully constructed stereotypes. The basic reader hardly noticed, I'm sure. Most people are drawn to ordinary because they are used to it. If you get too bizarre and niche, people become less interested. I'm just trying to make a point." Her tone was firm as she looked at him. For the first time in all his years of sitting in her office, he felt like a student who was sent to the principal's office. He squirmed under her green eyes and tried to look away, tried to focus on the coffee, the creamer, or anything else for that matter.

"Take this work in progress. The story is somewhat decent, the characters are basic… it has a good start and a good skeleton, just re-evaluate what you need to make it different. And not just different to Tatum Hyland, but to the entire world of readers." Jackie poured some coffee into a blue mug and handed it over to him.

"I wouldn't tell you to rewrite if I didn't think it had potential," Jackie smiled, and this time, her teeth were exposed. Her mouth was wrinkled in the corners, from years of smiling, Tatum assumed. All her success and she had yet to fix the crooked bottom tooth. There was something poetic about the way she rose to fame but remained the same. Some of her clients, ones that grew bigger than Tatum, moved far away and deep into the city. They lived in penthouse apartments with beautiful views. Some of them over inflated their lips with fillers and went under the knife so often that they no longer looked the same. He liked to think that he and Jackie stayed true to themselves and to their small town, in the same office that seemed to lack air conditioning.

"You think that if I could just magically pluck an idea out of my head, I wouldn't have done so?" Tatum sipped his coffee and the liquid burned the tip of his tongue, and the roof of his mouth followed. He cringed and pulled away from the mug that was hot everywhere other than the handle. He slid it onto the coaster-less wooden desk in front of him and crossed his ankle over his knee. God, he hated that stupid statement. He licked his teeth at the thought and then ground them together, nearly nipping his already burned tongue and almost biting his already raw cheek.

"Tatum," He could tell by the way her hands clenched and the corners of her mouth twitched that her patience was running thin. She kept her fingers threaded together and she leaned forward, elbows now resting on the manuscript. "The first four chapters of your novel follows a college student in the zombie apocalypse. Tell me… what makes it different and what would make a reader pick it up?" Jackie prompted.

"It follows a college student, separated from her family, lost and confused," Tatum replied, "Forced to figure out how to survive on her own." Didn't they already have this conversation?

"What is making it different, though?" she asked, "Imagine someone standing in front of the hundreds of zombie apocalypse movies, comics, and novels… What is going to make them pick it up?" she asked.

Tatum's hands moved to press through his hair. He tugged at the brown locks and then released as he leaned back in the chair, arms crossed, "I don't know," he admitted, "I just don't want to write love stories anymore."

"Then don't write a love story," Jackie shrugged, "Write this badass apocalypse story but make it different… make it unique," she said to him. The same old talk, rinse and repeat." Dig deep and come back to me with something different," she slid the manuscript over towards him, "I know it's in there."

Tatum sighed and grabbed the small stack of papers. The coffee on his fingers stained the white pages and he looked over at her, "Okay," he finally declared, "I'll come up with… something."

"I know you will." Jackie reassured, "and I look forward to it." As Tatum placed the coffee mug down on the desk once more, Jackie shook her head at him and waved a finger, wedding band glistening in the light. Her hand pressed forward on the mug. Tatum heard it side across the wood and once more, Jackie grinned at him.

"Keep it. Don't want any coffee to go to waste, and if you have it, it'll give me all the more reason to get you back into this office."

Tatum left the safety of the coffee-scented office and made his way to his car. As he moved through the lobby, he ignored the receptionist telling him to have a nice day, and he tossed his manuscript into the trash. Tatum climbed into his car, the temperature all too hot for his proper attire. He shrugged out of the stiff sport jacket and tossed it into the passenger seat among all the other trash, plugging his key into the ignition. He quickly pulled out his phone and sent a quick text to the only person who has managed to keep him sane."

Can we meet soon?

The reply was just as quick as he had sent it.

I've been dying for some shopping – meet me at Target now?

See you in ten.

Wandering around a Target was probably on the bottom of things he'd like to be doing, but he couldn't turn down seeing Ellie. If he didn't go with her now, he would just sit on his couch, stare at his computer, and slowly watch his sanity drift away. He'd watch the stupid blinking cursor dance on the screen, mocking him. He needed to get out of the house, and he knew inspiration could always find him in the most unlikely places. The drive would only take ten minutes, but Ellie would find a way to beat him there. He drove in silence, radio turned off and the only sound being the car's air conditioning as it struggled to blow cool air. The vents resembled that of a weak hand dryer in a bathroom that hadn't been updated in years, and the air that did come out smelled of dirt. Everything seemed to bother him as he drove, hands clenched on the steering wheel and his teeth ground together. By the time he reached Target, he could spot Ellie's white Mercedes as he drove the wrong direction in the parking lane, down an up lane. He swung his car awkwardly next to hers, and all he could see was the top of her head as she looked down at her phone. She didn't look up as Tatum moved to her side of the car and knocked on the window, which seemed to startle her, the phone nearly flying out of her hand.

"You scared me!" he heard through the muffled glass. Whenever she stepped out, her keys clung and crashed together, her lanyard struggling to keep up with the number of objects that hung from it. He had tried to warn her it was only a matter of time before the weight broke her key off in the ignition, which he promised not to help her with when it happened. He joked that she better not call him to break the news and ask him to come and save her.

By the time her beat-up Converses hit the ground, her arms wrapped around his neck in a hug. She smelled of roses and some kind of cinnamon, both scents fighting for dominance. Most days, it was overbearing, but today it was comforting. Most people had a wife or a sibling to turn to after a hard day, and he had Ellie. Despite the fact that her hugs weren't always wanted, he let himself melt into her firm hold for a moment. He took in her scent, her touch, and tried to lock it into memory. He stayed there until the electricity that came from her became too overbearing, to which he finally pulled away. He took a long look at her, took in the image of her all too long brunette hair as it flowed way past her shoulders and nearly to her hips. Her eyes were green in appearance today due to the band t-shirt that she wore that was a hideous puke color, even though Tatum was certain that the shirt was at one point his. With this thought in mind, he looked at his friend, who was easily a foot shorter than he was, and he dreaded the question that was about to come out of her mouth. He could feel it in his bones, and part of him already regretted even telling Ellie about the meeting. Had he just asked her for coffee, they could have went to their favorite place in town, they could have sat and enjoyed each other's company, and he wouldn't have to resurface his anger and frustrations about today's meeting. His arrogance had gotten to the best of him, to which he talked to Ellie about the meeting long before he should've. He truly expected it to go better than it did. Was he stupid to assume that the meeting would go great?

"How did the meeting go?" she asked as her green

eyes looked over his face. Part of him wondered if she had come up with an extravagant conclusion already. He wondered if she was just as bad as he was, already expecting news of being published within the year. He really didn't want to disappoint her. Was it weird that he wanted her validation more than he wanted Jackie's?

"Let's wait to talk about that... I'm still digesting it all," Tatum said with a small sigh as he let Ellie loop her arm around his elbow. She was the one that walked him like a dog, never once allowing him to fall more than two steps behind. If that were the case, she would just drag him along and complain about it the entire time. That was what Tatum did, he avoided any and all confrontation and he tried to avoid making Ellie uncomfortable or in any way angry.

"I'm happy to be part of your digestion process," Ellie said to him, "I really shouldn't be doing any shopping, but here we are." Ellie raised her arms in a gesture towards the large brick building. "Come on," she relinked their arms together and started to walk into the store.

"So, is this your way of telling me that Jackie hated an idea or something?" she broke their silence as she merged to the left and began to flick through the multiple hanging shirts. As soon as she left his side, he felt the weird sweat that lingered in the crook of his elbow.

"It's not that she didn't like the idea... she just picked the shit out of the technicalities. But that isn't anything new for Jackie," he said to her as he rummaged through the notes app in his phone, beginning to scan half-baked ideas that had gone there to die. They were still riddled with typos from the moments his fingers moved faster than his mind could process. They sometimes could not even be understood, but he kept them there, all the same, hoping that he would someday understand what his brain tried to tell him. Nothing sparked joy, and nothing turned into something more profound. At the thought, he tucked his phone into his pocket and crossed his arms.

"What kind of technicalities?" she asked, distracted. For a moment, they walked straight but very quickly veered off and to the left yet again, and her hands rummaged through another display of shirts.

"Said it was too cliché."

"And is it?" Her thin eyebrow was arched upward at him, her hands stalled as she caught his eyes.

"Is a zombie apocalypse story too basic?" He wasn't sure if he wanted to hear her answer, as his ego had already been beaten down a few levels. He shifted on his feet and then crossed his arms, not wanting to be a hostile little boy. He needed to remind himself that the opinion of Jackie *really* didn't matter much. If he wanted, he could take the idea and there would be someone somewhere that loved his ideas. So why was he getting so hung up on one opinion? Was it his love and respect for Jackie?

"Maybe," Ellie was casual in her motions. "You'd have to do something to make it more interesting." Of course, that would be the young woman's response. He couldn't be angry at her for the painfully oblivious and mundane attitude of it all, but that didn't stop the hiss that escaped from between his teeth. Ellie wasn't a writer or an artist by any stretch of the imagination, so maybe the thought of coming up with an interesting idea felt mundane to her. Tatum bit on his lip as he tried to repress his irritation.

"You sound like Jackie," Tatum said as he thumbed through one of the stands of clothes. Everything would more than likely fit his smaller frame, as Ellie often stole his more obscure clothing, but he wasn't here to shop. Maybe he was here in hopes that Ellie would give him the inevitable burst of inspiration. Perhaps he was here to distract himself from writing. Rejection brought out the worst in him. It made him want to throw his arms up and say to hell with it all. It made him want to light his manuscript on fire and go into hiding. Childish, sure, but who *actually* liked rejection? Who walks into a room or turns in a paper and thinks, *"You know what would make my mood soar right now? A good old red X of a rejection!"* The answer was simple: No one wanted that.

"You guys both act as if I can just pull an idea out of thin air and make it great." He said, stubborn like a child.

"Maybe it's because we have a point, idiot," Ellie stuck her tongue out at him. "You men, none of you can admit the fact that women can be right, even if it's once in a blue moon." She rolled her eyes. "I didn't say to pull an idea out of your ass or to conjure up

19

some kind of spell. You asked if a zombie apocalypse was boring and I said to switch it up. What more do you want?"

He would be lying if he said he didn't care for and love Ellie. Maybe it was the way she was brutally honest, just like Jackie was, but he always appreciated her tender tone and way about life. There was a mutual liking between them, a certain sexual tension, but they had never found one another at the right time. Maybe it came down to the timing in which they loved one another, or maybe it was something dumb like never being what the other needed. Ellie found her sense of worth by fucking guys in dirty, run-down bar bathrooms. She had downloaded and re-downloaded Tinder about ten times in the past year, and she always claimed it was for entertainment purposes. Part of him believed her, but the other half knew that she got a boost in confidence in loser guys telling her she was pretty.

Tatum on the other hand, only found comfort in superficial romances - the kind only found in secret bedroom whisperings and hookups. Outside of sexual contact, Tatum wasn't one to be seen holding hands with a lover, wasn't one to go on dates with his arm slung around a shoulder or a hand on his partner's thigh. He didn't need to find his confidence in that of others. Or maybe that was a lie. If he thought he was so brilliant, why did he seek validation through Ellie and Jackie? They were two people out of the billions that could pick up his book and read it. Would everyone think it was too over done? Or would it be the next *The Walking Dead*? Every idea was pretty much the same at its core. No idea was truly original through and through.

"I don't know," Tatum said as he scraped his fingers through his brown hair with a huff, a solid thud hitting against his chest wall - anxiety pulsed in his body and everything hurt. From his chest to his head, then to the neck and shoulders. He was tense to the point that he was rigid and always had headaches. He needed this to work out. He needed his idea. Tatum Hyland needed to rise from the ashes, and he wasn't going to do that by sitting in a Target store, aimlessly plucking through clothes and objects. He really shouldn't be here, as it was just more opportunity to spend money he didn't have.

"Hey," Ellie said as she grabbed his wrist, which pulled him out of his self-obsessive thoughts, "It'll all work out. You'll get a great idea and it's gonna be awesome." she said to him. "Just don't break into the nicotine addiction too early, yeah? You'll have plenty of sober insanity to suffer through to fuel your desires." She smiled once more at him as she let go of his wrist. "I'll be here every step of the way, okay?"

He wanted to believe both Ellie and Jackie, both seeming to hold out hope for him. Or was it an unreasonably high expectation? He didn't know what they would think if he were to fail, scratch all ideas, go back into hiding for another ten years. People would surely eat up any book he wrote then, right? He would have twenty years to have practiced and tuned his craft to a fine science. He may even have some credibility on Twitter. All it took to make it in that place was a holier than thou attitude and a way to say things with confidence. However, if he waited another ten years to figure it out, would forty-seven be too old to be on Twitter? Would it be too hard to figure out an algorithm and to find his section of the internet? He couldn't be sure. No, he needed to hold out hope. He could do this. After all, his two favorite girls said he could, right? They believed in him.

And Tatum could only hope that Ellie would stay true to her word. He hated to admit it, but he needed her, and he couldn't do this alone.

CHAPTER TWO

From one writer to another, Jackie should know better. She should know that ideas can either hit you like a freight train or miss your stop. They don't slow down for anybody and it's hard to change what you've been dedicated to. He had his main character figured out, and he had a general idea as to how the story would end. He had a few character ideas that the readers would meet throughout the journey, and he already had actors and actresses picked out for the inevitable movie or TV deal. How was he supposed to change it all now? He tried to think of a new and unique idea, as this one clearly wasn't cutting it, not in Jackie's eyes. Not in Ellie's eyes either, apparently.

But what was he supposed to do to come up with a good idea? His mind raced back to his conversation with Jackie, which prompted his feet to move before he could process it. He pushed through the back door and wandered into the yard behind his house, grass overgrown and pushing past his ankles. The way the green tickled him was in no way pleasurable, and the man found it slightly annoying. It bothered Tatum, but not enough for him to do something about it. Tatum has his eyes set on one thing only. He moved to the giant oak tree in his yard - the only tree or decoration back there, and he stared up at it for a long time.

He stood there, hands on his hips, and he waited a moment before his eyes started to scan. Tatum studied the architecture of the tree. He examined the surface, starting where the moss grew at the bottom of the trunk. His brown eyes moved upward, to where the moss had tapered off. He studied the pieces of bark peeling off and the chunks of the tree that were missing. There was a sheet-like white layer of wood exposed amongst the brown bark, and he wondered if that meant the tree was dying or thriving. He contemplated whether the trunk would be smooth to touch at its missing pieces or prickle at his fingertips. He moved to touch the curves and the valleys before his eyes wandered upwards and towards the arm and fingerlike branches. They cracked and groaned as the wind hit, a few leaves fluttering down towards him. He blinked as an orange-hued leaf nearly landed on his head, before it joined the others on the ground, a big suicidal pile of branches and colors gone to die.

Every author had their process. Whether it was a cabin in some hidden away mountain that they could use strictly for writing, or whether it was a certain room in their house. Some people still wrote with pen and paper, others wrote on their computers, others on their phone. He hadn't really picked up a pen in what felt like years, and the thought of plotting felt foreign to him. He had forgotten what a good idea felt like, he hadn't felt the rush to get his ideas out of his head and onto paper. His life had been a whole lot of nothing in the past ten years, and now with an idea so close to him, he wanted nothing more than to take it and run with it. He never once had a certain writing process, no random or stupid traditions. He didn't require a certain paper or cigarette to be held between his fingers, he didn't worry about the little details that settled the compulsions, he always just had ideas and he wasn't used to working for these kinds of things. So, here he stood, under his tree. He tried to remind himself that inspiration could hit in the unlikeliest of places, but he had nothing.

As he stared, the process started to frustrate him. All he wanted was an idea. He wished that his brain had the idea like a branch, one with fingers, merging and growing into several concepts. He wanted the idea to hit him, just like the way dead branches hit the ground so unexpectedly. He didn't know if he wanted that figuratively or literally, as a good bump to the skull could potentially give him the idea he wanted. All the better if his neighbors find him in a pool of blood and had to rush him to the hospital. He was sure that once word got out about Tatum Hyland being in the hospital, his book sales would rise. Everyone loves a tragic comeback story, right? He could come out of the hospital and tell everyone that once he's fully recovered he will release a new piece. He would tell the press that he was very excited about it, and he'd watch his popularity skyrocket. But first, he needed a damn idea.

His fingers found the temples of his head and he gave the muscles under his fingertips a squeeze. There was that thought again, the one where he considered crushing his head. If he had the strength, would he? How cool would it be to be known as the guy who crushed his own head like a grape? "No!" he yelled. He needed to knock it off. He needed to be present and aware, not knocked unconscious. Besides, his neighbors never bothered him before. It's not like he has any family, so Tatum knew he'd just lay in his backyard in a pool of blood, limbs trapped under a huge tree branch. No, he needed to do this traditionally. Good old brainstorming and plotting. That's what all the good writers suggest, right?

He knew he could pick up a book of the classics and listen to their 'on writing' tips. He would be littered with thousands of rules, the dos and don'ts. But who needed that and who listened to it? Who were these righteous people to tell him what was right and what was wrong? How did they know and how many people followed their lead? People on Twitter would probably tell him that there was a formula, and to just practice writing prompts, but that wasn't what he wanted. He didn't want Scott49382 to tell him what was bad versus good, the right way or the wrong way. Just like he didn't want the girl with dog emojis in her name giving him advice. Maybe it was righteous, the way he looked at others in the community, but he didn't care. He didn't need writing prompts and journaling. He wanted ideas. He wanted them handed to him on a platter.

He wasn't used to working for the ideas; they used to just come to him. Whenever he wrote *The Devil's Bride*, the idea came to him out of the blue. So out of the blue, in fact, he had nowhere to write it down. He could remember the vivid details of the blaring horns and near accidents he caused as he swerved back and forth. He remembered the noise the strips on the side of the road made, a warning that told him he was about to fly into a ditch. Back then, cell phones weren't a thing. Sure, in college he had a flip phone, but you couldn't write novel ideas like he sometimes does now. This was back in the time where you accidentally hit the Internet button and nearly broke the keys on your phone to take it back. Internet access on a flip phone wasn't a thing. Not unless you wanted to get charged for that shit. Now, if he were to get an idea, he could steer with his knees and twiddle away with his thumbs. That probably wasn't the safest bet, but he'd rather die in a car accident as opposed to forgetting an idea. Morbid thinking? Maybe, but he needed an idea. No matter what it took.

It was then he realized just how crazy he looked. Crazy old man Tatum, just stood out in his back yard staring up into a tree. As he remembered he had just yelled at himself out loud, he groaned as the defeat hit him. He felt the pressure build behind the eyes and his vision blurred as he moved towards the back door that he forgot to shut behind him. He walked into the kitchen and his eyes scanned every surface. What word, phrase, or object would trigger an idea? Maybe the college student is an amputee? Would making her have a knife for a hand at some point in the novel be too offensive? Was that too *Nightmare on Elm Street*? Today, he knew most ideas were offensive, or one idea was too much like something else. If one idea sounds even remotely similar to some book, you are scrutinized for stealing ideas. It didn't matter what the intention was or how unique the actual story is, once you were deemed an idea stealer, there was no coming back from that shit. This thought caused him to lean against his table and he felt the damn thing buckle against his weight. That was what he got for buying a table off Craigslist back in a time where things were good, but he wasn't willing to spend money on a decent table. Now he truly did live paycheck to paycheck, none of that by choice. Funding was low, his income hardly existed anymore. He'd be lucky if one person a week was even buying his book; the royalties being nonexistent. Thank God for freelance work, or else he would be living in a ditch or dead by now.

He scratched the stubble on his cheek as he looked around the kitchen once more. Could she be in a pack of college students, all trying to survive? The more the survival kicked in, surely the angrier and more anxious the group would become. How long until one snapped? Until they all snapped? At the thought, Tatum swiped the table's contents onto the floor with all the other garbage and grabbed a pen. Scribbling a note onto the notepad, he stepped away to look at it.

Zombie apocalypse… turned survival of the fittest?

At those words, he let out another groan of frustration. Isn't any apocalypse already the survival of the fittest? At the thought, he crumpled up and discarded the paper. The trash can was two steps away, but the sliver of paper still landed on the floor. He has meant to take the trash out for two weeks. Now it was just embarrassing and a heaping pile of take out containers and discarded novel ideas. He pretended to not see the ants that crawled on the floor and on his walls in lines. He'd get around to cleaning eventually, but it wasn't on his priority list. It wasn't second on that list, either. He knew, ultimately, he wouldn't be cleaning anything until he saw an ant the size of his fist rummaging through his trash. He also wouldn't do anything until he saw a rat. Even then, his motivation to take out the garbage was questionable. Why would he waste his time on such a stupid mundane thing?

He moved to the sink, the only part of his house that was clean, and ran the water. No water was ever cold enough as he splashed it into his face several times. Once he felt more aware, he wiped his face with a towel that had a pungent sour smell to it. Times were hard, and the only thing that called out to him right now was drugs and alcohol.

The thought of his dealer, Ryland, came into his

head next. A few drugs could reach the part of his brain he couldn't scratch. A lock on his bedroom and leaving him with only the drugs, his notebook, his laptop, and some beer. If he didn't lock himself in, he ran the risk of wandering off in a state in which he was a danger to himself and to others. He ran the risk of wandering out of the house without shoes on and straight into a line of traffic. No, a good lock on the door and he wouldn't have anywhere else to go, no one to bother. He'd leave himself a few empty bottles so that he wouldn't even need to leave the room to take a piss.

That was all it took for *The Devil's Child*. It was just a few psychedelics and several hours alone in a room. He could do it all again. A simple call and a few hundred dollars would give him an arsenal. It could let his demons rest and the creative flow pulse in his body. He wouldn't need to force an idea into the grooves of his skull and brain. The drugs would just bring it out of him. He would see his characters in the shadows on the walls. He would be scared shitless of some of the things his mind could conjure up, sure. Was it worth the nightmare fuel if it gave him a solid book idea? He shook his head back and forth before he dug around in the fridge and found a bottle of beer. He quickly chugged it down and felt the bitter liquid move smoothly down his throat and get caught in his stomach. Alcohol mixed with the coffee from earlier was never a tasty concoction, so he tried to get the coffee taste out of his mouth. He swished the alcohol around, feeling the acidic liquid on his tongue before he swallowed. He didn't even like beer.

He plopped his smaller frame onto the couch and pulled the laptop out from under it. The computer was only under there for a few hours, but he had to blow dirt and ants off the top of it. He watched as a few fell to their deaths, the others trying to steady themselves on his laptop lid. The laptop creaked as he pulled it open, the screen about to snap off its hinges at any moment. He typed in his password and the bright screen strained his eyes. His eager fingers adjusted the brightness to his liking before he pulled open the Word document.

UNTITLED - ZOMBIE APOCALYPSE IDEA

Without thinking, he pulled backward and deleted the entirety of the document. Sure, it was only forty pages total, but it was one now. One blank page. A new start. Now the daunting white screen stared back at him, with a flashing straight line, no words following its lead. He stared until his eyes burned and tried to get back to the place he once was. He was so eager to show Jackie his work - but now he stared at nothing. What was once something was squashed in one meeting and his ego took a hit. Tatum Hyland didn't get rejected. His debut novel was a *New York Times* best seller.

"She hates it," Tatum grumbled as he stared at the page, eager to be written... err... typed on.

"Come on," he said as he took a drink of his beer. He hit himself on the side of the head as if it would create an idea on impact, "You got this," he said out loud as he sat up and looked at the screen once more." You got it," he tried to reassure himself.

His fingers tapped on the side of the mouse pad. They drummed to an imaginary beat and his head pulsed as it searched his brain. He wasn't sure how long he stared before he found himself slamming the laptop shut, harder than anticipated. He knew the next time he'd open the computer that the damn thing would creak and crack louder than it already did. It would flash vibrant colors, jumping from one extreme to the other for a split second, and then it would return to normal. Right now, though, he didn't care in the slightest. Flashes be damned, he wasn't doing anymore writing tonight. He tucked the computer under the couch once more and his hands found the TV remote. He laid back on the lumpy pillows and flicked through the options on the television. Like clockwork, a zombie movie was on channel 543. He watched with eager eyes and chugged down more of the hard liquor.

"Aren't you afraid it's a bit… cliché?" Echoed on a loop in his head.

"She doesn't know what she is talking about," Tatum huffed, "I could go find another publishing house," he was sure that an agent there would be eager to release a new debut novel of Tatum Hyland, best-selling author who was on break for the past few years. They'd eat it up, right? He could see the headlines now; Tatum Hyland - back now and better than ever!

His phone let out a startling chirp, which caused

Tatum to jump. With an increased heart rate, a solid thud in his chest walls, he pulled his phone out from his back pocket - a text from Ellie.

How is the writing going?

At least six emojis were included in her message, a smiley, a heart, a different smiley, and a pink heart. He didn't care to note the other useless things in the message. They were both in their early thirties, having grown up in a time long before emojis and smart phones were a thing. While he felt like the grumpy old man of the pair, with his hatred of emojis and anything deemed too extra, Ellie was the complete opposite. The girl loved her bar hopping, her emojis, and her dating apps as if she was a teenager again.

Bad. And it's not.

Okay, maybe it was a bit dramatic. Tatum, at least, could see that. However, Tatum couldn't force himself to have a conversation about whether he was getting any writing done. With that thought, he shoved the phone back into his pocket and looked up at the TV screen. The zombie movie seemed fitting, as ultimately, that was what he was writing about, and his eyes watched the scene unfold in front of him. What started off as a single character slowly turned into a massive horde of zombies, and he watched as the guy or girl somehow started to dominate the scene. He watched as the sawed-off shotgun was swung around, bullets flying, and he watched as the guy pulled the machete from its holster and drove it down the center of the zombie's head.

It was blood and guts, and most frustrating, it was all the same. He had seen the same move a thousand times before: a character is overwhelmed and as good as dead, only for them to remember they have several good weapons at their disposal, and a close call ends with a sharp object cutting a zombie's head in half. It had been done before, but did the director's bosses tell them that their idea was too cliche? Why could they get away with it, but he couldn't?

Everything frustrating him to his core, he flicked the TV off and threw the remote onto the table in front of him. He sat up straight and found himself hoping that the silence would bring him some kind of greatness. When that didn't work, he looked around at his empty apartment. Well, nearly empty. Scratches of paper, much like the note he wrote in the kitchen, covered the floor. Half written-in notebooks cluttered the hallways and half-read books sat a few inches after that. He had all these creative outlets, and absolutely nothing to inspire him.

"Fuck this," he decided as he stood up on his feet. Tomorrow would be a new day, a better one. Isn't that what that manifestation stuff was all about? You put into the universe what you wanted to get out of it? Maybe he'd try that in the morning. Meditation, manifestation, and maybe a dream would trigger some untouched moment.

This thought in mind, he sighed and moved into the small bedroom. First, he dug through the messenger bag and pulled out his notebook. The back of it got ripped off a long time ago and some of the springs were unraveling, some even cutting his hand from time to time, but he refused to get rid of it. It was his idea notebook, the same one he wrote the beginnings of *The Devils* saga in.

He always sat that notebook and his favorite black pen on his bedside table. It seemed fitting that the pen was nearly out of ink, some of the letters resembling that of dashes as opposed to full letters. He kept the same notebook next to him for years, hundreds of different ideas scribbled in different areas.

Part of *The Devil's Bride* was scratched up in the margins, *The Devil's Child* making appearances up and down the sides of the paper. Some of the ideas merged, not able to be read come morning. It had been something he's done for years, keeping a mode of writing as close as possible to his bedside. If he were to get an idea or would need to write down a decent dream, the notebook was there for him. He didn't have to be blinded by a phone screen and he didn't have to fumble around - it was just ready for him.

He looked at the start of his notebook - the eager sloppiness of new ideas written so long ago. His fingers moved over the curves of a pen that once moved so quickly that the ink smudged. The ink ran in streaks across the page and he was sure, when these things were written, it was across the back of his right hand. His fingers carved the ideas that brought him the fame he so desperately wanted back then.

With each flick of the page the memories came

back - legs thrown over the bed, messy hair, hands barely awake enough to write anything - no less aware enough to make sense of the madness in his mind to put them down on paper. Each idea that appeared was always a movie in his mind. Those movies were attempted to be written in half-aware words and uncertain blinks, unable to tell if it was real or just some dream. With each flip, the ideas became more spread out. The once long stream of ideas became things with question marks and uncertainty. With each flip, he found more fragments of papers now ripped out. He could sense the frustrated artist from here. He flicked until he reached the last page he had written on, not remembering what came of the idea before he opened it up to a new one and set it on his bedside table.

He sighed, unbuttoned the stiff dress shirt, and tossed it onto the floor with the heaping pile of clothes. He worked on trying to get the pants off his lanky legs, and with a stumble, he fell onto his bed with a flop. He grumbled as he shook his legs violently in attempts to get the stupid pants off his legs. Sure, standing up, unbuckling his belt, taking out one leg and then the other, would be easier. It'd take less time. Hell, had he done it that way, he would be undressed by now. But he chose flailing around like an idiot instead. Once the leg restraints were off and his legs were free, he didn't bother to get up anymore. Instead, he laid on his back and looked up.

He focused on the swirls and the bumps in the ceiling and wondered if he could find an idea written there. He searched each curve and each uneven surface, but once more wound up empty. He wondered if his past self, if the characters within him, had written an idea up there, one that he just wasn't seeing. Taking this approach, he flipped so his head hung off the foot of the bed, his feet propped against the headboard. His neck ached in this position, but maybe he was looking at it all wrong. He stared until his eyes were dried and his brain hurt from not only the suspension, but from the forced pressure. With a small throb, he felt as if it was his brain begging him to rest for the night. As he started to give in, he could only hope that the release of sleep would bring him an idea to wake up to.

He wanted to dream. He wanted the subconscious mind to breathe a new form of life into him, to give him something to write about. He would have settled for nightmares, and even for a night terror, but nothing came. Instead, he didn't dream that night. He didn't toss and turn, and the colors didn't coat his eyelids. He slept firmly and soundly, but not much more than that.

When he woke up in the morning, he had a moment where he had forgotten where he was. His bedroom orientation was a bit wayward, as he was now upside down. His head wasn't on his pillows and his neck ached with stiffness as he searched for his phone. He had to power it up and once it did, it buzzed loudly with a notification.

Oh no :(. I'm sure it's not going as bad as you think.

Want to meet?

He didn't know how to tell her that he hadn't even written a word. He didn't tell her how he had hardly slept and he drank a shit ton of booze. He didn't know if he'd tell her that he deleted forty pages worth of work. Instead, his fingers moved to send a text back.

Your place. See you in 30.

His eyes glanced at the small clock in the corner of the screen which informed him it was later afternoon. He truly didn't mean to sleep as long as he did, as he had a lot of work to do, but here he was. As he started to become more aware, as things became more certain, he started to wake his body up. His thumbs moved slowly and ached with each extension. Damn carpal tunnel. He cursed as he threw his legs over the bed. His brown eyes landed on the notebook and the empty page that stared back at him. His fingers fumbled through the pages - all great ideas gone to die. It felt like some of them just wanted to commit suicide as soon as they were written by his pen. He assumed, bad ideas were better than no ideas, but all the outcomes brought frustration to his body. All outcomes started and ended the same - a whole pile of nothing. An entire list of things that would never find the light of day. He needed to stop whining, close his notebook, and use his time with Ellie as a distraction. Trying to write was just giving him a headache and he needed to move on.

He slowly thumbed through his shirts and settled for a vintage The Decemberists band T-shirt. Much like Ellie had worn his shirt yesterday, he wasn't certain as to whether he had bought this shirt himself or if he had taken it from someone else. If he accidentally stole it, he wondered if the person missed it, if they thought about it often. He wondered if they looked at pictures of the shirt on their body and then asked themselves where the shirt disappeared to. He brushed these thoughts aside, not ready to lose his mind considering the deep complexities that came with life and friendships. No, Tatum was trying to get up moving, and wanted nothing more than to get to Ellie's.

He shrugged the same pants from yesterday, which still laid crumpled on the floor. He didn't care about the wrinkles, as he was a struggling writer, and assumed he could just fit the look. As he pushed a toothbrush into his mouth and held between his lips more than he scrubbed his teeth, he ran a quick hand through his hair. God, he was starting to look old. He had the wrinkles that formed around his mouth in a downturned fashion. Opposite to Jackie's evidence that showed years of smiling, his showed the years of frowning. There were signs of stress that loitered around his eyes, and his cheeks weren't as slender as they once were. His once chiseled jaw had rounded out, his eyes that once were always searching for new inspirations had gone dull. As he spit the mostly watered-down toothpaste into the sink and brushed a hand through his dark hair. He noted and tugged on the curls that were starting to make an appearance, the kind of curls that he used to have in high school.

Once he was done trying to pull off the starved artist look, he would need to get a haircut immediately. He knew Ellie would offer to do it, as the woman knew he hated any kind of social interaction – especially the kind that dealt with strangers touching him. Once he was done having an intense moment of vanity, he moved into his bedroom and fumbled for the familiar notebook once again. He pushed it down, the book drowning amongst the pens and trash.

Ellie's house was only a fifteen-minute drive from his place. The girl was no better off than he was, but her area of town was a bit better. A bit closer to the nicer shopping mall, a bit closer to Krogers, and way closer to their favorite movie theatre. She lived in a neighborhood that was quieter than his - one that was mostly old people as opposed to younger families with their kids, but their grass was still a lot shorter than his. He drove past each one, confident that most of the grass in these lawns wouldn't go past the tips of his shoes. Ellie's house was out of place, she loved it more than anything else. It was red brick instead of white paneling. The black curtains and window shutters darkened in comparison to the blue ones that her neighbors had. Her mailbox was still leaning to the side from when he was drunk and hit it while trying to get to her front door. Still, to this day, he had no clue how he did it, as the thing looked as if it was taken out by a truck, not a person.

He walked up to her front door and he knocked twice, shuffling back just enough even though the thing swung inward as opposed to outward. Whenever she opened it, Ellie was in her natural glory. Her long hair had still been pulled back and her makeup was long removed. She wore a shirt that he was sure was his, and sweatpants that belonged to neither her nor him. She wrapped him in yet another hug with a small giggle on her lips.

"I got your coffee started," she said as she moved him inside, the door shutting behind them. She walked through the living area, her feet light on the carpeted flooring and her eyes on him as she nearly stepped backward. She moved expertly through the foyer and then through the small living room before they reached the kitchen.

It was dated, Ellie refusing to change it as she enjoyed its charm. The lights were too yellow and the chairs, he felt, hadn't been changed since before the house was hers. He couldn't judge her too harshly, as his home was in shambles, and he took a seat in one of her chairs, nonetheless.

She placed a mug in front of him and then a container of French vanilla creamer and a small cup of sugar with a spoon. He enjoyed his coffee black, but he needed a boost of energy. Or was it morale? He wasn't sure. He still accepted the coffee nonetheless, and he moved to take the mug in his hands. His eyes took in its color, this one a speckled green that said the name of a university that Ellie didn't attend on the side. He assumed it belonged to an ex-boyfriend of sorts, one who didn't care to take his mug back home. He got lost in the thoughts of this mug, his eyes focused in on the wording, which made him think of

Jackie's cup which still sat in his backseat.

"How did it go last night? After we departed?" Ellie's words brought him out of his train of thought, and he lifted his brown eyes to look at the woman across from him. She was stirring her coffee now, the liquid nearly white in color. He listened to the spoons scrape against the bottom and then the click as it hit the sides.

"You mean after I stared at a tree for a long time? Or after I contemplated getting in contact with my old friend that happens to be a drug dealer?"

"Hmmm, Tatum Hyland, you aren't allowed to go on acid trips without me." Ellie pointed a finger at him before she stood and pulled a toaster strudel from the toaster. He watched as she squirted the white icing onto the sugary pastry before it was lifted to her mouth, the steam visibly burning her face and her lips.

"Okay, come with me then." He chuckled as he leaned back, his coffee in his hand as he watched her try to conceal the betrayal of the food that burned her.

"Yeah, right." Ellie smiled. "Could you imagine me on some kind of trip?" She rolled her eyes. "I'd be a panicky mess and you'd be stuck with me until it passed," she said to him with a huff. "Anyway, I suppose you can tell me about it once you finally sat down at your little computer and started to write."

"I deleted the whole thing," He replied as he lifted his own cup to his lips and took a long sip, the hot beverage not phasing him.

"You what?!" she asked, green eyes bulged so wide that they might just pop out. "You didn't."

"I did. Jackie didn't seem to be sold on it, what would a fresh start hurt? It was only forty pages. I guess I just figured a new start would be the best thing," he said to her with a huff, the chair hurting his spine. "Forty pages is nothing, my dear." That was a bold-faced lie. Forty pages were close to three days' worth of work for him. It was worth several hours, days, and weeks.

"I can't believe you." She laughed, but Tatum didn't return it. He looked at her for a long moment before a casual shrug rose to his shoulders.

"I just... wasn't feeling it. It didn't even feel like a good foundation, Ellie. Now I'm writing this whole story knowing and feeling like it's all been done before. A new start just... felt right."

"Mmmhm," she hummed as she took a sip of her coffee, "You never told me this idea that you think Jackie hates so much. All I heard about it was that it dealt with a zombie apocalypse, but I'm sure there's more to it than that."

"Is me wanting a fresh start not a good enough reason to not like it?" Tatum defended himself, but he watched the way that Ellie's eyebrow raised upward, almost expectantly. She too lifted her mug to her mouth, albeit cautiously. She still hadn't touched the sugary pastry since that first traumatizing bite.

"It follows a girl in an apocalypse. She's a college student... across the country from her family. Forced to survive on her own," he explained as he tapped his fingers on the table a few times. He let the silence settle between them before he shifted and then he settled again, his posture pulled away from her.

"Okay, so yeah, it's a bit cliché," she said to him.

"You haven't even read it... and you don't know what I could do with the story... what twists it could take." He protected himself and his work, defensive habits up. Writers could front the fact that they wanted criticism all they wanted, but most would feel a need to defend their work. There was only so much hiding that could be done behind words and phrases like," Your writing just isn't for everybody and that's okay!" The truth sucked and the internet was nothing short of ruthless. Maybe he would be in higher spirits if, for now, Ellie lied straight to his face. She could always tell him it sucked later, right?

"Okay, smartass, since it's so good, why did you delete it?" she asked him, never flinching from his sometimes colder tones. She would stand toe to toe with him if the situation required, both stubborn assholes at heart.

Tatum didn't know the answer to her question. He felt the fury and uncertainty rise in his bloodstream and he felt the way the idea gnawed somewhere deep in his stomach. He felt it just at the tip of his tongue, but it never passed the threshold. He looked at her for a long moment as he chewed on his cheek, chewing until he tasted the bitter blood that dripped onto his tongue. He licked over the sensitive pulled open flesh, the touch of his wet tongue stinging the now open wound.

"I don't know," he finally admitted to her as he huffed, his fingers rubbing at his face.

"Maybe we have a point. Right now, your idea is fine, Tatum. But I don't know where you're headed with it… I don't even think you know." She leaned forward. "Because the Tatum I know, when he had an idea that he was really excited for? He would have the book description written out, and three other ones in case one sentence didn't sound right. The Tatum I know would have a list of books and movies to compare his book to. Right now, you have nothing, do you?"

She was right, Tatum had nothing. He knew deep down that there was nothing but forty pages of nonsense, only forty pages of talking in circles.

"This sucks," Tatum declared, a large huff pushing through his body. He felt his elbows slouch forward and then his shoulders moved next.

"Tatum," Ellie reached across the table to hold his hand in hers. "Look at me when I tell you that this idea will come to you when it's meant to, okay?" she asked him. "Maybe make it a girl that has a big ass boot on her leg or something. Make it so that she was supposed to die at the start, but now she is outliving her other friends. Make it so she outlives the athletes. Make it so that no one bet on her horse, and now she's the one laughing." Ellie smiled at him.

"The idea will come when it's ready to and the idea isn't going to drop into your little man brain until it's ready." She smiled at him. "I love you, Tate. So, I want you to promise me that you aren't going to do any-

thing drastic… unless you let me know about it first."
A smile poked out from the corners of her lips, something that prompted a chuckle in Tatum.

"Alright," he smiled, "I promise."

"Good. Are you done being a self-conscious prick now? Can we please eat some food and forget about the world?"

CHAPTER THREE

"So, you mean to tell me, in an apocalypse, you aren't going to try your damn best to survive?" Ellie asked as she took a sip from her glass of water. At first, she claimed she would drink water so that she wouldn't get sick off the booze, but she was three glasses in, and the woman showed no intentions of standing up. He wasn't even sure if her refrigerator held the alcohol Ellie liked - those all too sweet twisted teas. He was sure she would add more sugar to them, something she always denied, but he knew Ellie better than himself.

The pair sat on her couch; the sun having gone down a long time ago. They hardly had any lights on in the room, Ellie only finding the motivation to click on the small lamp to her left. It projected a little glow onto their two bodies, most of her smaller frame covering the light. The conversation had gone from writing to life to school and to the apocalypse. He wasn't sure what sparked the conversation, but he also loved seeing Ellie get fired up.

"I'm not saying that. I'm just saying that I'm not gonna be going out of my way to loot and murder everyone. I'll try to live and survive, sure. But am I going to be seen running around in the blistering heat or the freezing cold to live? Of course not. You can bet your ass that I'll lay down in the field and accept death if it comes down to it." Tatum had taken advantage of his struggling writer card as he sipped from a glass of whiskey. It was his second glass, even though Ellie claimed she wouldn't allow more than one.

"I call bullshit, Tatum Hyland. You liar." She rolled her eyes. "You mean to tell me that if we're this bad-ass duo, that you're just gonna lay down and die?" She lifted the glass to her lips, condensation running down the side.

"A liar, huh?" he asked with a smirk, " Who says I'd want your slow ass holding me back, anyway?" he asked as he sat up straighter, feeling the slightest buzz of warmth in his bones.

"A damn liar. And we both know in a dead sprint, I'd leave you behind in the dust." She giggled as she too sat up, her legs tucked underneath of her. They shared part of the love seat now and they both were on their respective cushions until Tatum lifted his hand to shove her shoulder.

"Fuck off, we know that you're dead weight when it comes to surviving," he teased her. "Remember, I used to save your ass in all those video games." He pointed a finger at her, a chuckle bouncing off his lips.

"Video games and real-life aren't the same thing!"

she gasped as she moved closer and pushed him.

"You're full of shit." He laughed as he looked at her. "Forget it if you're even minorly inconvenienced." He waved her off jokingly before he stole a glance at her, a smirk tugging so hard on his lips that it hurt his cheeks.

"You're the actual worst," she laughed at him. "We'd both go loot an alcohol store and get drunk off our asses until the zombies broke the doors down and you know it. You'd be no better off than me, mister." She pointed a finger at him.

He couldn't help but chuckle. "Yeah right, Ellie, I'm a professional. I would never do such a thing." He held a hand over his heart in mock hurt before he chugged the rest of his whiskey, already standing to fill his glass again. "Speaking of drunk, when are you gonna have a glass? Or are you going to force me to get drunk alone?" he asked as he turned to look at her. "Or are you planning on taking advantage of me?"

"There's actually something I've been meaning to tell you, Tate."

"What could that be, Ellie?" He chugged another glass down before he even came back to his seat. "You aren't attracted to me or something?" he slurred with a smirk on his face. Their physical contact had never gone past a few drunken kisses and make outs, although they had a few close calls. Ellie was always of the sounder mind, always too scared of messing everything up if they were to sleep together. Tatum had to admit that there was always a small sliver of hope with each night he came over to her house. Was he wrong to think the way that he did? Was there ever a real scenario in which a guy and a girl could be friends without any sexual tension? He didn't believe it. He and Ellie had been friends for more than ten years now, having met at a punk rock concert. Tatum, in Ellie's eyes, had saved her from the crowd surfer that was about to come barreling onto her head. Tatum didn't have the heart to tell her that he had his girlfriend at the time on his left side, Ellie having been on his right. He somehow managed to pull the wrong girl out of the way. He never heard the end of it from his ass of a girlfriend whenever Ellie wanted his number to properly thank him. Since then they've had the never-ending stream of almost kisses and hookups, neither of them having the balls to do anything about their attraction. Ellie would tell him they were better off as friends, and she would say that she didn't want to ruin things. It was the same song and dance time and time again, and maybe they were better off as friends, but Tatum's mind didn't want to admit that truth right now. "You're falling in love with me?" he asked her, a smirk in the corner of his mouth. He could blame this on his drunken antics, right? Of course, deep down, he knew that drunk thoughts were subconscious sober ones, but he swallowed these admissions down.

"You're such an ass," the laughter didn't rise to her cheeks, she hardly looked up at him whenever the cackle moved past her lips. A stone-cold sober Tatum would've noticed this and immediately demanded to know what was wrong. He wasn't sober though;

he was slightly buzzed and the fuzz in his head didn't help his judgement.

"You're... hmmm," he began to scratch his chin in attempts to guess what words were going to come from her lips, but nothing was happening in his somewhat clouded mind.

"Pregnant," Ellie told him quietly, her eyes not meeting his.

"Funny joke," Tatum said as he leaned back against the couch, his arm draped along the top. "Seriously, though. You going back to school or somethin'? Are you dating that asshat again?"

"I haven't spoken to Seb in over a year." She rolled her eyes, "And I couldn't afford school, anyway." She said to him with a bite of her lip. "A one-night stand. Can you believe it?" she asked him. "All my friends can hook up with any guy they want at any time and never get pregnant. The one time I do it, though? I don't know what I'm going to do," she laughed dryly.

He saw her lips moving, but he didn't hear anything further. That was it. That was the connect he had been searching for - that he had been longing for. He didn't miss his stop on the train - the train came barreling at him and hit him quite hard. He wasn't going to have to jog a block to find it again. It was right there in front of him. Ellie was his living, breathing, talking muse. This was it. It was what he wanted and what he needed. It was what he contemplated using the drugs to find. It was what he hoped the tree branch would knock into him. He needed this connection - he earned this. It was the one thing that plugged into all the other ideas. Yes, this was it. This was his unique twist.

"Ellie," he breathed as he took her hand. "It's brilliant," he took a long breath and felt the tension leave his shoulders. "You're fucking brilliant, Ellie." Tatum stood and, without thinking, grabbed both sides of her head and pressed his lips onto hers.

"Tate, I don't understand," Ellie was caught off guard, her eyes bulged outward again. There was a shake in her voice and tears that lingered in her eyes as she looked at Tatum. He stumbled on his own two feet, grabbed his bag, and nearly forgot his shoes by the front door. He moved so quickly that Ellie didn't get to tell him how it wasn't safe for him to drive. She only heard the jingle of his keys and the rumble of his engine.

There wasn't a moment in which he stopped to consider his state of mind. He wasn't sober, but he had it in him to locate his keys, slide on his shoes once he found them, and plug the keys into the ignition on the second attempt. He knew that the nine to fivers had all gone home for the evening, children more than likely weren't playing in the streets due to the fact that they were either in bed or eating dinner. The only person at risk was himself, and ultimately Tatum didn't care whether he lived or died. It was all about this idea, he focused on that as he drove home. He was unable to remember whether he drove ten miles under the speed limit or above it - or if he did either of the two. Whenever he got home, he made sure to have his eyes scan over his rusted over truck, not noticing any new dents or scratches to the panel.

He worked out a quick text to Ellie, one that didn't make any sense to neither him nor her, and he turned off his phone as he moved through the front door. He hadn't locked it - he never did, as he had nothing to lose, nothing worth stealing. Part of him always wished it'd get robbed, as he was smart enough at one point to get most of his shit insured. If any of it went missing, he'd just get it back, but no one broke into their houses around these parts. His neighborhood was too quiet.

He needed to get his idea onto paper or onto the screen in the modern terms. He needed the words to flow freely from the tips of his fingers. He needed to get it out before it was lost to the wind and before it was wiped clean from his memory. He could only hope that these words would make sense in the morning or when he came to, he could only hope that he could see the vision as clearly as he was seeing it now. He needed to get it out of him. He needed it to be released. He'd talk to Ellie later. He'd be a shoulder to cry on, he'd reach out to her and go with her to all her appointments. He'd be a true gentleman, the one that would be a pseudo father to her daughter or her son. Hell, would Ellie even keep the kid? No, he didn't have time to dwell on that. He needed to write.

Ellie would understand. She had to understand, didn't she?

UNTITLED CHAPTER ONE

"What are the rules?" Chelsea asked, knelt onto the floor as she fastened the bag around her daughter's small body. Her child's tank top was nearly too big, a gap existing underneath her armpits. Finding children's clothes that fit properly was near impossible - and that was even before there was an apocalypse at hand.

Pebbles cut into the exposed skin on Chelsea's knees and shins, grinding and moving with her skittish movements. She looked over her child, pretending as if she didn't notice the bruises and cuts that lined her fragile skin. What was supposed to be a clear white canvas was something that looked as if it had beat to hell and back. Her child's canvas was just in rough of shape as Chelsea's was - the cruel world unforgiving.

"No words," her daughter spoke quietly, the shake and stutter still being worked out.

"Not a word," Chelsea repeated as she placed a gentle kiss on her head. The child's hair reeked of dirt and grime - showers were a thing of the past. She smiled sympathetically towards her child - never going to remember bubble baths and rubber ducks. Her child would probably never feel the warmth of a bath or the steam of a shower - it just wasn't their world anymore. Her daughter would only know washes of the body in murky lakes. She wouldn't know the feeling of a hot bath after a day of playing in the snow. Her daughter wouldn't sip from chocolaty hot chocolates that left behind foam mustaches. She wouldn't get lectured just for eating the whipped cream. That wasn't their world right now, the once familiar was a thing of the past. This was their new regular. Their new good day. Their world was extra harsh winters and little to no civilization. It was overgrown grass fields with yellow and dying leaves. She would know no meadow and know no slide too slick and too new for her small body. She would get the rusted left-overs and stories of what used to be.

It was just their world now.

"How high do you think you can count this time?" Chelsea asked as she brushed the blonde matted hair from her child's face. It stuck to the side of her scalp slick and greasy, sweat clinging to sweat. Tomorrow's focus would be locating a body of water to both drink and to bathe.

"Twenty-five," Jillian said to her mother.

"I'll bet you can get to thirty, what do you say?" Chelsea smiled.

Jillian giggled, her voice always forced into a whisper, another rite of passage taken from her child. "Dats too high," There was no shriek in her voice, no shrill of laughter. Merely quiet voices coming from her child's body.

"I'll bet you can do it," the young mother encouraged as her hand stroked the child's prominent cheekbones, "I'm gonna lift you up now, okay?" Chelsea said as she rose to her feet and lifted her daughter on her hip. Jillian didn't reply, she didn't even nod her head, she just obliged to what her mother was requesting.

Chelsea sighed as she pushed up on the ceiling tile and watched as the world of darkness opened to them. Her daughter was all too light, so light that if this were normal times, she would have CPS called on her, but that didn't make this any easier. She was balanced on a shelving unit and forced to deadlift her daughter up above her head and into a small ceiling area - something her boyfriend would usually do for her. The thought of him created a bitter feeling in her throat and a burn deep in her stomach. She tried to push these feelings away as she looked at Jillian with a gentle smile. Her arms had been aching for days, but her child's safety was the most important thing. Her boyfriend had a different view on that, but that was part of the reason he wasn't here with them anymore.

"You be quiet and don't come down... even if I get into a lot of trouble, okay?" Chelsea whispered, movement beginning to pick up outside,

"You always keep counting. Right in your head," she tapped the small child's temple twice with her finger, "I'll be so fast and I love you," she whispered before she slowly slid the ceiling tile back into its proper place.

The blonde hopped down from the shelving unit and brushed her fingers through her sweaty and matted hair. Her fingers got tangled and they pulled, which resulted in her head tugging backward slightly. She glanced around the quiet and abandoned convenience store and tried to take in the moment. Getting herself into the stupid convenience store was hard enough and adding a small child to the mix felt impossible. They did it though, they always did. The moments in which her triceps ached with exertion and her low back screamed at her - they did it. Her child couldn't be to blame, she grew up in this world. She wasn't a child born in the apocalypse. Chelsea simply wasn't fucking her boyfriend in the light of the campfire. Chelsea wasn't waddling around pregnant as her child lived in her stomach, while her boyfriend murdered all the bodies. No, Jillian was a pre-apocalyptic child. Before the outbreak, the girl, much like most, had a normal life. She had a life of bubble wands and questions about bugs and the wonders of the world. Now she was forced onto her mother's hip, forced to be dependent on her for survival in ways that weren't normal. In ways that went further than providing food, water, a home, and nurturing.

She had no opportunity to have a rebellious stage, had no time to make friends that would ultimately be a bad influence on her. Her daughter wouldn't have the chance to sneak out of the house to go to parties, to have to throw up all her alcohol before she knew her limits. Her daughter would never get callouses on her fingers from swinging on monkey bars. She'd never feel the thud of her knees against rocks. These were experiences that were robbed from her, but maybe it was for the better.

Her daughter lived in this world and knew no other. She wouldn't read in school about the good times. Her daughter would have survival worked into her bones, second nature, and that was all that coursed through her body. Innocence lingered in the hairs on her head and under her dirty fingernails, but a rough around the edges look followed everyone in this world. Her daughter, once an infant, would know no different. She would only know survival of the fittest and she would never get lectured for not sharing her food. She would know to run and never stop, and she wouldn't know of a time where you could walk hand in hand with a lover.

As Chelsea scanned the store, she could

remember a time where empty shelves were a rarity. In her time, the only empty shelf would be when the store had cherry Pepsi instead of Vanilla Pepsi. Diet instead of regular. She remembered when a store with the power out was flooded with back up lighting. Now they were lucky to see a flicker of light. Back in her time, midnight runs to the gas station were normal, despite the things that went bump at night. Now nighttime runs were death sentences. Now they were things you did in dire situations, something you did when you had no other choice.

Chelsea moved through the mess and rummaged through the broken glasses and knocked over shelves. This place was looted a long time ago, probably back when things had just broken out and when the world still was uncertain about what was going on. With each step came a different crunch, even though her heels were lifted, and she walked on her toes. She searched under the cold and flu sign, only to find empty shelves and boxes - but no medication. Through weeks, she's learned not to dwell on the losses, but to just move on. She no longer felt disappointed when she came across trashed stores and houses, as she has wasted far too much time on frustrated tears. About to cut her losses, pull her child from the ceiling, and move on, she stopped when her eyes found something. She spotted a holy grail - a small package of protein bars.

They were smashed to bits under a shelf - but any food was good for her. She tucked her fingers under the unit and tried to lift - but the structure was three times her size and body weight. She felt it was more likely that the damn thing would grow legs and walk away before she was able to lift it, but she worked tirelessly anyway. Her boyfriend usually did the hunting and the gathering. If he were here, he would have had this thing lifted, he would've probably tried to bench press the damn thing to prove some kind of point. Part of Chelsea had wished she had taken him up on his offer to do some weight training. Back then, though, she was obsessed with thinning out, not bulking up. Man, she regretted her decision now.

She sighed as she tried to work on another angle. She climbed over the unit and pulled on it, which only caused a strain in her back. Yeah, her muscles didn't agree with that one very much. She huffed as she slid, fell on her ass, and decided that she wasn't going to get anything done this way. She climbed back over and started to wiggle the box out from under the shelf. They had to come out eventually, didn't they? Maybe they'd be nothing more than a smashed up, flattened tire of crumbs, but that was better than anything they had right now.

She wiggled the box a few times, and the box cracked and got flatter with each little jiggle. She felt as though the unit got heavier, trying to steal the box and keep it for itself. She wasn't sure if five seconds had passed or fifteen minutes, but her hairline was soaked with sweat and she felt the water drip down her chest and past her sternum. She was close now, at the halfway point, and she pulled harder and faster. Just as she was about to feel its release, she heard a voice.

"Stand up, turn around slowly, and I won't shoot you in the back," a voice barked. It belonged to a female, one who must have come in when she was making all the noise in the world. The woman wasn't there whenever she had climbed over the unit, that she knew, because Chelsea could only hope that she would've seen someone standing in the doorway.

Chelsea was stuck in a position where she was a sitting duck. Hair thrown over her shoulder, crouched over, and fingers jammed under a shelving unit. She was ready and basically asking to be shot, so much so that the voice felt as though it was a million years away.

Chelsea cussed to herself as she felt the familiar feeling of fear wash over her. If she had any contents left in her stomach - she'd be shitting her pants right now. Her heart thudded slowly, her blood was cold, and a cold sweat started to rush over her body. She had no other choice but to do what she was asked. The shotgun on her back has been out of ammo for weeks, which only left her with a switchblade as a mode of defense. She stood slowly and she eyed the protein bars. Those probably cost her life.

"Listen, I just want-" she began but was cut off.

"Shut up and turn around slowly," the voice was cold, authoritative, even. The thought caused Chelsea's mind to wander, when was the last time she saw a uniformed police officer? Were all of them safe, tucked into an underground bunker with the rich and political figures? She wouldn't be surprised.

"Are you deaf? Turn the fuck around. Last chance."

Chelsea did what she was asked. Her arms rose above her head and she did a small pivot. It was then that she came face to face with the woman. Before she could take in the stranger's image, her eyes lifted upward and towards the ceiling. Ultimately, she'd much rather her child die of starvation than how she was about to go out. She didn't want to fight off a horde, only for her child to be bitten or murdered by ruthless humans. Would Jillian hop down, wander into the cruel darkness of the world without her mother? In that case, how long would she last? How long until a body ripped her to shreds? How long until she was picked up by a group of strangers that promised her food only to torture her and eat her meat? How long until she was robbed of her pink princess backpack and until they found the fruit snacks that survived the apocalypse thus far?

God, she couldn't think like that. Death was a part of their life, the world chewing you up and spitting you out at a much faster rate now more than ever. Chelsea couldn't go on living if she witnessed her daughter's death, parents weren't supposed to bury their children. Maybe it was selfish to think, but she'd rather die long before her daughter and be unaware of her ultimate fate.

She just prayed that her daughter wouldn't make a sound, wouldn't attempt to save her mother, and wouldn't wander out into a world of violence and hatred.

She couldn't help but wonder - in a world filled with violence and hatred, would they take mercy on her daughter?

CHAPTER FOUR

It was brilliant. A young mother left for dead by her deadbeat baby daddy. Leaving her with her four-year-old daughter. It was the perfect concoction of loneliness, strength, love, and survival.

Tatum knew that it had all the potential for sequels, movie deals, and television deals. He could see it now - his name back in the lights. The lights they were in all those years ago. He would never have to charge absurd amounts on Fiver, doing work that people could do for free if the writers looked in the right place. Maybe it was fucked up that he took advantage of those that didn't know that beta readers and light editing could be done for free, but he had bills to pay, his own mouth to feed.

Once he was home, he ensured that his phone remained off. He couldn't afford to be pulled away from his work by the ping of a text or the blaring of a ringtone. Of course, the only person that called or texted was Ellie. Sure, his friend was pregnant and needed him, but she would figure it out. He'd write a few pages and then go back over to her house, be a shoulder to cry on. He just needed to get the ideas out of his brain and onto his paper. He could write and change as soon as it was down. If he didn't write the ideas now, they would dissipate into nothingness. He knew Ellie would understand. She had to, right?

With the first snippet written on his computer, he was on his feet, laptop closed and tucked under the couch like a dirty secret. He started dinner, his light feet dancing around the kitchen, despite the lack of music. He moved effortlessly as his body worked over the stove, his free hand reaching into the bag of cheese curls. Once crunchy and fluorescent orange, the snack was now stale, and the artificial color flaked off. He wiped the cheese fingers on his pants and then on his chest, uncertain when he chose to take his shirt off. Those same hands moved to fumble for the remote, turning on the small TV that hung from his cabinet. The picture was fuzzy, and the sound was shitty, but Tatum's brown eyes watched as a woman sat at a desk with the other news anchors, all watching her intensely.

"The number of deaths has risen in the state of California and are growing in surrounding states. Health officials are still uncertain as to what is causing the death rate to skyrocket so suddenly, but neither the CDC nor the government has made an official statement."

"Many people have reported those seemingly losing their minds have had no symptoms, they just seem to suddenly burst into aggressive episodes."

"Maybe we shouldn't use terms like 'losing their minds,'James, as there is probably a scientific explanation as to what is happening."

"Yeah, but how do we know-"

Another channel covered the same story - it was just another set of news anchors sitting behind the safety of their desk and their news station. He wondered how these people felt, talking about the world, their world, as if it was some faraway country in make-believe land. Did they feel safe in their own little studio? Did they sit behind barricaded doors and bulletproof walls?

He stared at the news for a moment longer before his fingers located his phone. It took a minute to turn back on, a delay coming each time his phone gained service and another text buzzed through. He swiped past the notifications that showed three missed calls from Ellie and a few texts and his fingers swiped for the app that featured the bird on a blue background. Once he found it, he lifted the phone so that it could scan his face to allow him entry, and then he pulled the screen downwards to refresh his feed.

He sighed as he swiped around for a bit and found the news apps and articles he was looking for. This wasn't a growing pandemic. It was a series of murders. Murders in the grizzliest forms, bad enough to gain the media's attention. He sighed, shaking his head as the likelihood of a long and happy life decreased due to the loss of sanity of those around him. He closed the app and then moved to look at his texts

- something he was avoiding like the plague.

Hope we can meet soon....

Did you at least make it home okay?

He knew she deserved a response and that he should probably give it to her. Ultimately, he couldn't ignore the girl forever. She was his best friend, and he had kissed her right before he left, that much he remembered. God, how did he get home last night? Was it morning? Was it night? He couldn't be sure. He looked out the window in his kitchen, the night sky still dark. He must not have been writing that long, but long enough that his buzz was now gone. He'd have to continue drinking, but first, he needed to text Ellie. He looked at the time again, uncertain as to whether he zoned out for thirty minutes or thirty hours. It was always a guessing game. Ellie, right behind his book, was his number one priority. He knew that she'd likely be happy that her situation created a new idea for him - a good one, at that. Hopefully, she would forgive him if Tatum agreed to dedicate another book to her or name a character in the book after her or her child. He figured that would make up for it. After all, fame would often make humans happy - even if it were the slightest bit of recognition in the public eye.

He sighed as he drank back some more of the Smirnoff and noted that he'd have to go buy another bottle if he wanted his writing to stay consistent. Of course, writing brought out his insanity more and more, along with his drinking problem, but that was the price he paid for being a decent artist. What artist didn't have an intense problem of sorts, anyway? He couldn't think of one.

His thoughts, once more interrupted, by a call. He sighed as he looked at the contact name and he wasn't surprised when he saw who it was. He hit the answer key, muted his television, and held the phone up towards his ear.

"What's up, Ellie?" Tatum asked as he moved to stir more of his noodles, the phone pinched between his ear and shoulder.

"I saw you read my text," Tatum loved Ellie, honestly, but she was essentially the obsessive girlfriend... even though she wasn't his girlfriend. Was she? Did the fact that he kissed her change their standing? No, of course it didn't...the kiss was a friendly one. Lots of people kissed their friends out of pure excitement, right? Right?

"Was just getting ready to reply," Tatum lied to her, "I just wanted to apologize for how I stormed off. You're...condition... gave me a brilliant idea that I couldn't lose," he said to her, "Sorry if I came off as insensitive to what you are going through," he said as he started to make the Alfredo sauce. He felt like some after school special, to which he brought more alcohol to his lips and past the threshold of sobriety.

"I'm glad I could be of help." The difference between yesterday and today was something that nearly rubbed him the wrong way. He caught his negative train of thought and cleared his throat. If he cared for Ellie as much as he thought he did, he needed to be better.

"How about I come over for a bit? And I promise if you let me come over, I won't leave super abruptly... we can even continue our previous conversation." Tatum offered, "Let you read the first snippet... before it even gets into Jackie's hands. I'm making some Alfredo now and I can bring some over... I'd offer to bring wine but..."

"Alfredo and some reading sound great," Tatum could sense the brightened tone through the phone, "I'll see you soon. Text when you are on your way over," Ellie said and then he heard the click of the phone on the opposite end.

He knew he had to be better for her. She was now his muse, after all. Without her, he probably wouldn't have gotten the idea, which would lead to a whole different butterfly effect. It all came back to Ellie, her condition, and the fact that she chose today to tell him. Would he have gotten the idea if he skipped going over to Ellie's house this morning and told Ellie he was busy? Would he have told Jackie to fuck off, gone rogue, or found a new publishing agent? These were things he'd never know, as he was on a new path now. It was a path to success, Tatum knew this. Every success story came with humble beginnings, either that or it was some tragic story that made someone rise from the ashes. Hell, who knew that his friend being knocked up would give him the best idea?

While he waited for the noodles and sauce to finish, he found himself climbing onto his countertops.

He rose on his tiptoes, expecting to find a hidden cupboard with even more Tupperware containers, but he came up empty. When he found a container that would suffice, he hopped down and poured the piping hot contents into the Tupperware. He watched as the sides filled with steam and the scent of the Italian drifted up into his nostrils. He closed it up tight and placed a piece of garlic bread on top of the lid before he shoved his own piece into his mouth. Six were left behind, having left behind those that still had a frozen frothy layer of cheese on top. He knew that he wasn't going to put them away anytime soon, meaning the pieces would be glued to the pans by the time he did decide to clean up. He'd have to buy all new pans at the rate he was going. The ants that loaded onto his laptop were about to have a field day with what was left behind. He was in a good mood, so much so that the thought of ants prompted the thought of finally hiring an exterminator to clear them out.

He tossed the notebook in his bag and then his laptop. With the bag flung over his shoulder, garlic toast getting soggy in his mouth, and food in his hands, he made his way outside and towards his car. It was raining now, which added to the soggy bread that was causing slobber to dribble from the sides of his mouth. He fumbled around outside, not expecting the rain, and climbed very quickly into his car for safety.

He shook out his now damp hair and pulled his phone out to send a quick text to Ellie. He let her know he was on his way and he'd see her soon, and his pointer finger and thumb twirled the dial on his all too ancient stereo in his car. The stations, more fuzz than they were music, took some searching before he settled for an old rock station. Even then, his frustrations grew due to the horrible radio quality, and he missed at least half the second verse of Sympathy for the Devil due to the poor quality. It was more crackles than it was the Stones as they hummed in the back.

Sympathy for the Devil was a classic, and one of his all-time favorites, which he felt was ironic. Of course, he was trying to escape *The Devils* saga, but a song with the word devil in the title was bound to come on his shitty radio. He tapped his fingers to the all too familiar beat and lit up a cigarette as he drove.

Whenever he pulled up to her house, a half-smoked cigarette hung from his mouth. As he unloaded the food and his messenger bag from the car, he cursed as he realized the lip accessory. He assumed smoking around a pregnant lady wasn't all that great of an idea, so he tossed the cigarette to the ground and watched the rain put it out. His foot was half lifted to step on it, but the drizzle killed the spark as soon as it made its appearance. Leaving Tatum looking like an idiot with his knee now pulled up near his hips. His ankles were exposed to the cold air, getting splashed with water as he lowered his leg and stepped on the cigarette for good measure.

He knocked twice on the front door and Ellie seemed to be waiting as the door opened almost as

71

soon as his knuckle left the door. Her face looked paled over, cheeks prominent, and hairline beaded with sweat. She had changed her shirt but wore the same sweatpants. Her hair was still pulled back, but the long tendrils escaped their restraints. Much like Jillian, he could see the grease that made her hairs stick nearly to the side.

"Breaking into the cigarettes a little early, aren't you?" Ellie asked, "You usually don't get into the cigarettes until your second edit." Part of it was accusatory. After all, he had just promised her he wouldn't break into drugs or anything. Now here he was, however many hours later, already sucking cancer down his throat and into his lungs. He truly didn't like smoking. It made his lungs flare up and his coughs painful, but maybe it was an aesthetic thing. Perhaps he liked the thought of when his life was made into a movie that the actor smoked a cigarette. Jesus, if his mom knew that, she would have gotten in her car, driven the eight hours it would've taken her to get here, and she would've beat his ass. There was no doubt about it.

Ellie knew him and his writing methods better than anyone. She was the female version of him, if only he were a better person. Ellie was pure inside and out and somewhere deep down the woman only wanted the best for him. Was it love? Admiration? He couldn't be sure. Maybe going through this phase of life would help him figure it out. Maybe this was what he needed in both his writing life and his romantic life. Maybe it was Ellie all along. If he hadn't dedicated himself to Chelsea's and Jillian's names, he'd go as far as putting Ellie as the true survivor in his book. He couldn't jinx himself, though. It was Chelsea and Jillian and the mysterious redhead. They were his trio, his trinity of muses. It was then that he realized he hadn't spoken to Ellie and her accusations, a prompt that made him sit back and clear his throat.

"I feel like my entire writing process has been grabbed by the ankles and shaken upside down," Tatum replied to her as he moved towards her kitchen. He unscrewed the Tupperware lids and emptied her helping of Alfredo onto a paper plate. Next, he made himself up a plate, minus the garlic bread, and moved to join her at the kitchen table. She sat, legs crossed underneath her, and scrolled through her phone. Her eyes only met Tatum's whenever he put the plate down in front of her. Maybe there was a part of him that could get used to this, that could get used to a life with Ellie, day in and day out. He looked around the room in attempts to imagine this being his place, to imagine having a child running around here. Would he baby proof everything? Put rubber tips on the corners? Or would he let his kid fall, get hurt, and get up? He needed to stop. This wasn't his kid. He didn't even know if Ellie was keeping it. Them? He didn't know the proper pronouns right now.

"Thanks," she said as she locked the phone and put it face down on the table, "Smells great," she commented as she took a plastic fork in her hand and spun a few noodles around it.

"So, before we get to my writing," Tatum shoved a forkful of noodles into his mouth and took a moment to chew, "Let's talk about you." He said as he looked at Ellie, his new muse. Whenever he looked at her, despite her only being a few years younger than him, he still saw her as the girl he befriended in middle school. While he had made Chelsea a young mother, Ellie was the age in which most women had started families. In their town, where the young adults started having children early, most of the kids they graduated with were two to three kids in. Hell, most probably considered the rip age of thirty-two as being too old to have your first child. With this thought in mind, he took another long look at her. He continued to chew the remaining noodles as the creamy substance covered his lips.

"What do you want to know?" Ellie asked as she pushed the noodles from one side of the plate to the other.

"How do you feel about your... condition?" Tatum always had a lack of words, despite being a writer. Words were just a different combination of all the letters in the alphabet, but he couldn't find the right mix. It was a curse, as it got him into a lot of trouble, especially when it came to people with their sensitive feelings.

"Well, I tried to tell you that today, but you stormed off," Ellie said as she sucked a noodle into her mouth. He cringed at her slurping, and he swallowed before he spoke. Yes, it was time for him to explain the reasoning behind being such a jackass.

How long ago was that? Jesus, he was so thrown off, he needed to know.

"Well," Tatum licked the front of his teeth before he replied to her, "I'm here to listen now."

"It's just frustrating... because my friends can have unprotected sex every single day of the week and they never get pregnant... the one time," Ellie had a blush color raise to her cheeks, which caused Tatum to raise an eyebrow at her. For someone who was very much pregnant, he found it odd that the topic of sex made her uncomfortable. These were the subtle reminders that Ellie was very much a grown woman, but still rather high school in her emotions and the way she thought of things. It was a confusing con-coction of details and little quirks about Ellie, and he wondered if he should include that in Chelsea's character traits. He wondered if Ellie knew the way in which her mannerisms were giving him all the inspir-ation and fuel he needed to get this novel written.

"And you're upset about it and you don't know whether or not to talk to the guy, right?" Tatum asked, another fork full of noodles jammed into his mouth.

"Right," Ellie agreed. "Well, that... and I just feel so lost as to what to do." She sat back, no longer lifting any food to her mouth.

"See? I listen, just... don't make it obvious," Tatum said with a smile over at his friend. "I think you'd be a great mom, you know," the darker-haired man said, "Especially because, you know, the character in my book has a child and she's a great mom." He tried to reassure her.

This created a laugh from Ellie as she shook her head back and forth, "No way," was all she was able to say.

"No way what? That my book follows a young mom or the fact that you'll be a great mom?" Tatum asked.

"Both," Ellie replied once she stopped laughing, "Your characters in your books can be strong as hell, Tatum," Ellie pointed out, "I'm not one of your characters... I'm a living, breathing human. I'm real... and I feel things and have so many... struggles."

God, what was it with these people? Was Ellie attempting to say that Tatum's characters were surface level? Nothing short of a robot with a name? And what was that about having other struggles? Sure, none of them lived and breathed in the real world, but they were about as real as everyone else. They may not be driven by the stress of work drama or pregnancies, but they could be if he wanted them to. No, he couldn't get into this right now. Not whenever Ellie was so fragile.

Tatum laughed and shook his head, "The girls in my novels are princesses thinking they need to be saved... Chelsea? She's so different. So bad-ass... she has a little girl and is in the middle of the apocalypse," Tatum explained to her, "And not like Judith in *The Walking Dead*, or Carl, even." He quickly elaborated, "I'm talking a little independent badass... one that doesn't remember a life before survival. One that has surviving built into her bones. All while not

understanding what is happening, still not understanding how unsafe it is to wander too far from her
mother."

"And my pregnancy announcement brought that
on?" Ellie asked. To say that was an understatement,
Ellie had to know this, didn't she? Did she not know
she was the living and breathing example of a muse?

"Hell yeah it did!" Tatum explained, "I know your
situation is less than ideal, but think about it... if
you were to have a baby and four years from now, the
apocalypse breaks out. What are you doing with your
kid?" Tatum prompted her. "We talked about what
we would do... but never what we would do if we had
a kid with us. One that we would be forced to keep
fighting for. I mean, it's one thing to accept death as
a single bachelor and bachelorette and to not give
a fuck. But to be surviving for the mere purpose of
someone being there for your child?" he grinned and
waved his hand as he elaborated. "There is nothing
like it, I'm sure," he said as he looked at her, admiration twinkling in his eyes.

"I mean, shit, maybe you can help me think of the
kid's name. Or maybe your child can have the name
of a character in the bestselling book I'm about to
write. How cool would that be, your kid having the
name of a badass character before it was cool? We
could even have him, or her, make a few red carpet appearances. People eat that shit up, Elle." He slammed
his plastic silverware onto the table. "See?! I knew
this idea was destined for great things. I'll even let
you have a cameo in my movie."

"You're a big dreamer, Tate. You always have been. It's one of your most admirable qualities." Ellie remarked with a grin, "I will hold you to it, no cameo needed, but I would love to be your date on that red carpet."

Tatum smiled at her words, "Hell yeah!" he said to her, "And then we can have drinks... once you aren't with child of course," he grinned as he scooped the last bit of his noodles into his mouth.

"Oh, I am already longing for the taste of some hard lemonade. You have to promise to have some in my honor." Ellie smiled as she looked over at him, the hand holding the fork still playing around with the noodles like a child. She nibbled on the garlic bread and he watched as the crumbs fell from her mouth to her plate. The conversation that followed wasn't about life's mysteries. Ellie didn't even offer to read his beginnings - the whole reason he came over here. It was short and cut off - conversations that ultimately meant nothing of value to him. He would hold the ability to take anything out of a conversation- whether it was the way someone spoke and stuttered or if it was the way their mouth twitched or certain twangs fell off the tongue. He watched for Ellie's mouth to tug at the corners, for her fingernails to scratch with uncertainty, but things were cut off. Things were bleak, pale gray, no sparks of color. Things were tense and awkward, a combination that put Tatum on edge. He wasn't sure what transpired between the two of them, but they were dramatically different. It may have only been twelve hours ago that they were talking about their post-apocalyptic plans. Did they still want to be survivors together? Did all that change? What did he say that changed that?

Once he stared at an empty paper plate, he leaned back in his seat, patting his stomach. He glanced down at the plate, the paper coated in grease and fork marks, and he admired his hard work. "I do make damn good Alfredo," he said as he looked at her. He wanted her to come at him with the typical Ellie remark and to tell him the food sucked, that the sauce was too runny.

Ellie nodded her head in approval, but she continued to stir the noodles around on her fork. She looked disinterested, to say the least, and Tatum frowned.

"You don't like it?" Tatum nudged his head towards the nearly full plate. Usually, Ellie would eat him out of house and home, giving him a run for his money. This, like most of the evening, was weird. It didn't sit right and something deeper was brewing.

Ellie shrugged her shoulders, "I'll blame it on being... with child," she giggled sweetly, but there was a distance that lingered. In the time that they had coffee until now, so much seemed to twist around in Ellie's mind. There was a distance that was prompted, and Tatum couldn't finger as to why. She never struggled with mental health issues, that much he knew as that was all his area, but she was different. Not just a pregnancy kind of different.

Tatum shrugged his shoulders, "I wish I could say

I understood, but…" he trailed off as he collected his plate, "I'll put it in the Tupperware and you can keep it in case you get a craving for it… just as long as you promise to give it back," he smiled, "It was the only container that I could find with a lid to match it," He laughed.

Ellie nodded her head as she leaned her head into her hands, "Sounds great," she said, but her smile was weak. She twisted her brown lock around her finger before she rolled out her shoulders. "Sorry, Tate… I'm just not feeling it," she said with a huff. "Rain check?" she asked as she stood to her feet, already moving Tatum towards the door, hand on his low back and pushing him forward. Aside from her hug this afternoon, this was the first physical contact they've had in a long while, but this was unwanted - and not in the hugging kind of way.

"Sure thing…" Tatum said, having to toss his fork into the garbage can. She moved him out the door so quickly that before he knew it, he was staring at the wooden door once more. Rain trickled down his face, wetting the plate he still held in his hand. The damn paper bent and got soggy in his hands and he was left to wonder if he could leave it on her front porch. She did basically kick him out, after all. What else was he supposed to do? Did she even realize what she just did to him? He bent down, placed the plate off to the side, and started the jog back to his car. The rain was heavier now, the sky a darker and angrier gray. The moon didn't shine through the layers of clouds that coated the sky, and he could hear the ticks of rain against his windshield. The thunder grumbled and groaned at him, the firework-like flashes only miles away.

He sighed as he began his drive home, taking his time as the rain splashed onto the windows. He supposed he could always make his apocalypse story take place in extreme weather conditions. Hurricane season or below freezing weather. Who didn't love the thought of frozen zombies? He could do a part where the zombies swam at an Olympic level, grabbing ankles and biting people underwater. He chuckled at the thought and continued to drive until he reached his dreary house once more.

He supposed, since Ellie essentially kicked him out, he would force himself to write. He sighed as he flicked his do not disturb button on, placed his phone face down, and started to write.

UNTITLED CHAPTER TWO

The woman in front of her sported a gas mask that wrapped around her head. Her long red hair fell in tendrils, knotted at the ends. She wore green pants and black combat boots, the original kinds and not the name brands, and her fingers held a bow and arrow. It was pulled tight, ready to shoot Chelsea in between the eyes, Chelsea assumed.

"Listen," Chelsea said once more, "I just want a pack of protein bars jammed under that shelf," Chelsea pleaded, "You can take half of them… I don't care. I just really want those peanut covered snacks and I would much prefer not having to die for them," she begged as her fingers continued to hold the knife in her fingers.

"You kept your back turned towards me and didn't even hear me come in. If I wanted you dead, you would've been already. Don't be stupid," the woman lectured Chelsea as she hooked the bow onto her back. "You on your own?" The woman asked as she moved over towards the shelf. At first, Chelsea believed that the woman would steal the protein bars and take off.

Instead, she used her strength to pull the stand up. "Get your damn protein bars," the woman grumbled, holding the shelf's weight with ease. Chelsea watched the way her muscles were defined, creating creases in her arms in which Chelsea lacked. The stranger held the stand up like it was a small cardboard box, so much so that Chelsea had more than enough room to grab the box.

Chelsea grumbled a thank you as she reached under the now lifted shelf, and let out a huff of relief as her hands held the peanut-flavored snacks - high in calories, and the same amount of protein as a pack of meat. Didn't get much better. She pinched the package between her fingers and just as she expected - straight crumbs.

"Peanut crumbs... my favorite," Chelsea remarked. God, how she wanted to down those crumbs in one gulp. She wanted to feast on the rare find, the holy grail of this stupid store, but her eyes wandered up towards the ceiling. She had a little human that she had to feed. Always.

"You aren't going to eat those?" the redhead asked." You seemed quite desperate for them earlier..."

"Long story..." Chelsea sighed as she pushed her hands through her hair. There was a point in time that she was getting hair treatments almost monthly. Constant haircuts and new colors, but now her scalp was oily all day every day. Her hair was matted to her head and she smelled pretty bad. Maybe before she left, she could get a look to see if there were any shampoos or conditioners. She knew it was a stretch, as she was already pushing it with the protein bars, but maybe she'd be surprised.

"You alone?" the redhead repeated her question from before.

This was the first time Chelsea was asked this question. How was she supposed to answer? Yes, she was technically alone, her boyfriend left her and no one was with her right now, but she had a child sitting in the ceiling.

"Hard to say," Chelsea replied with a huff. She knew that was a lackluster response, to say the least, and a confusing one at that.

It was then that the redhead removed her gas mask and slung the straps over her shoulders, more red hair tumbling out of their restraints. Chelsea wasn't sure what the point of a gas mask was, the disease wasn't airborne, but to each their own she supposed. With the gas mask off, Chelsea was able to get a good look at the stranger. Her eyes were a clear blue and her nose was hooked at the end. She had more freckles than clear skin, but the sun has brought a tan out of what Chelsea assumed to be paler skin. Her fingers moved to wipe the reddish-orange locks before they rested on her hips, the bones protruding from her skin. Everyone was unbelievably skinny these days - nothing like a zombie apocalypse to whip you into shape.

"What?" the woman with red hair asked, before being cut off by a jingle on the door's chains.

Both sets of eyes landed in the same place, the green-hued monster with long fingers coming towards them. It was obviously the body of a once young teenager or adult - long pointed acrylics extended from the rotting flesh. What used to be long blonde hair were now a few strands of clumped up knots that rested below the shoulder and on top of the head. She hobbled towards them, one foot still attached to a high heel, the other foot mangled and laying sideways as it dragged against the floor. The body that moved in next was another female which forced Chelsea to believe they were related. The same matted blonde hair, although this person was barefooted.

Chelsea began to back up, the bodies not in attack mode yet. It was the red-haired girl that tugged her gas mask back on, drawing back on her arrow. Chelsea felt the familiar panic set in, a feeling she's never adjusted or become accustomed to. It was her boyfriend that was the survivor. It was him that got some kind of high off survival. Chelsea knew she wasn't built for this. She used her small frame and quick feet to survive - never one for hand to hand combat like this. Her size merely came into play whenever it involved running or fitting it into areas that others couldn't. Other than those scenarios, Chelsea felt as if she was nothing more than an inconvenience. They made it work but now Chelsea was alone with a stranger, her daughter a silent secret in the ceiling. She hoped that the child was still counting or had found a new strand of dirt to play around with. Maybe she'd find a twig to bend and snap into a new toy to play with, but she ultimately hoped that her daughter wasn't listening to this. She looked over at the woman for guidance, the mask's eyes staring back at her.

"Can't you use the shotgun to blow them away?" the stranger asked, her head nodded towards the weapon on Chelsea's back. "Even if you're an awful shot, that thing will spread out pretty good. One fire could knock out two of 'em,"

"Been out of ammo for the past few days,"

Chelsea admitted, both ashamed and embarrassed to admit the shotgun was for show.

"Well," the stranger said as she looked at
Chelsea, "you better figure something out quick.
Because it's only a matter of time before these
bodies are right on top of us." The stranger
laughed as if now was a time for jokes and
humor.

Chelsea looked at the woman in disbelief. "You
have your bow," she pointed out, a head nudged
towards the large weapon. The stranger hardly
looked at Chelsea as she pulled back on the
strings and fired an arrow, the thin stick flying
forward and striking one of the bodies in the
face. She listened as the weapon lodged into skin
and through the makeshift skull, every sound in
the small store seeming as if it were magnified.

"You're right, I do," the woman said shortly
as the other body moved to instantly fall on top
of the shot down body, teeth biting into its flesh
and bone.

In all the video games she played, Chelsea
never expected to be in an apocalypse where
zombies would eat one another.

The sounds of chewing made her sick - the
gum-smacking was something she would never
get used to. It annoyed her enough before this all

started, but now she knew she couldn't escape it. Even the undead didn't know how to chew with their mouths closed.

"Let's go," the stranger said, "while they're distracted."

"I can't," Chelsea said as she shook her head. She approached the body, still eating, and stabbed it in the same spot. The screeches were higher than the last, this bodies death more dramatic. It stumbled over a shelf and fell before it really stopped breathing. Or whatever zombies do.

Chelsea poked her head under the door chain, making sure there weren't any more bodies coming their way. There were a lot down the street, but she assumed these two were rogue teenagers - sneaking out when they weren't supposed to. This little field trip cost them their lives. Or was it a second life? Chelsea wasn't sure of the logistics.

With a large huff, Chelsea leaned against what used to be the checkout counter. Everything shifted and creaked as she put her weight on it, her hand brushing through her hair. "Can you do me a favor?" She asked the stranger.

"Other than saving your ass and not shooting you in the back?" the redhead replied.

"Try to hide those... things," she gestured towards the bodies, all slumped up and as dead as ever. Even though their death was brutal, and their afterlife was even worse, a peacefulness washed over the room. Maybe the people were still left behind, and perhaps their death brought them the rest they needed.

She took a moment to collect herself before she walked over to the ceiling tile and pushed it up.

"How far did you make it this time, baby?" Chelsea asked as she lifted her arms up. She then helped the small child out of the ceiling and she heard the little feet land with a small thump.

"Hungee, mommy!" Jillian whined.

The redhead looked at the pair and shook her head, "I expected you to say you carried some bodies around on a leash. Not this,"

"Well, I feel like having a child in this time is scarier than having some of those things on a leash," Chelsea remarked as she held her daughter by the hand. Her daughter looked at her with large eyes before she looked at the stranger in front of them. She hid behind her mother's leg, not letting go of her hand. Chelsea didn't blame her, as she was scared, too. How couldn't she be? They were standing face to face with a stranger.

Who was to stop her from pulling out a gun and shooting them both? Chelsea knew it wasn't a farfetched idea, which prompted her to push Jillian further behind her.

It was then that the stranger removed her gas mask and crouched down, getting far too close to Chelsea's legs rather than the child behind them.

"I'm Spencer, what is your name?" the stranger, now having a name, asked Jillian.

"Spencer, dats a boy name," Jillian remarked.

Chelsea sighed at her child's innocence and inability to read the mood in the room. A comment like that could get them in a lot of trouble... but she had to trust the woman who knelt in front of her.

"There are some names, baby, that can be for both boys and girls," Chelsea explained as she took a breath and stepped beside Jillian. She kept her hand looped around the girl's waist and crouched down next to her. "Can you say hello and tell the nice lady your name?" she asked her.

Spencer looked at the child expectantly before she held out a hand and waited for a handshake.

The little girl reached forward, two dirty hands now connected, and shook the woman's hand a few times, "I'm Jillian," the little girl said.

"Well, hello Jillian, is it alright if I call you Jill?" Spencer asked as she released their hands and looked at the young child.

"Daddy used to call me dat," the little girl then remarked.

Spencer and Chelsea exchanged knowing looks, even though Chelsea could name at least six people who called Jillian "Jill." Of course, the child would remember the one singular person who called her Jill. No one spoke for that beat of silence before Spencer broke it and smiled over at the child,

"Jillian it is, then."

CHAPTER FIVE

Tatum knew that he had something going now. A young mother left to decide whether to take a stranger along for the ride with them. Tatum knew it was damn near perfect, and he typed until the tendons in his fingers ached. It wasn't a feeling he was used to, at least not anymore. He tried to push and pull on each finger, as he hoped to feel the relief of his tendons popping, but he didn't get any. His hands longed to feel again, and with each shake of the wrist, the sense of static dissipated. Even though his hands still felt numb, he stopped his tugging and pulling and stretched above his head. Once adequately stretched, he closed his screen and instead of pushing it under the couch, he set it on top of the trash on his coffee table. He listened to the crunch and crinkle of wrapping papers alike, and he watched as the small mountain adjusted to the laptop's weight

He stood to his unsteady feet, knees snapping at the pressure and popping as his toes tried to get their feeling back. He walked and stumbled, nearly falling onto the kitchen floor before he flicked on the all too orange light. The one above the sink flickered and the one near the fridge buzzed as he searched for any alcohol he could get his hands on. They grabbed at the bottle like it was their life jacket, and he lifted it to his lips.

He glugged down the bitter liquid - no part of the journey smooth or refreshing. He knew his diet was less than healthy - consisting of carbs, vodka, and black coffee. The weight loss would come next, as eating three meals a day and his helping of protein and water would be the least of his worries soon. There were always deadlines to be met and things to be written. The eagerness pulsed in his body and deep in his veins... God, how he missed this feeling. He finally had a purpose again.

He stood near the window and pushed vodka down his throat until the bottle was nearly empty and he had a slight buzz in his bloodstream. He tossed the glass container towards the trash, the damn thing clattering and spilling all over the floor. He cringed at the sudden sound and then he heard the commotion outside the window. He moved back to the glass, a mere pit of emptiness. All he could see was his own reflection staring back at him - nothing more and nothing less. He stared at the silhouette of a man - a soon to be bestseller. He grinned at the thought and for the first time in a long time, he went to bed hopeful. He went to bed with happiness in his blood and within his bones. He knew this was going to be everything. He knew this was going to be the best.

He didn't go to bed until the sun was coming up as, like most writers, some of the time that was supposed to be set aside for writing turned into mindless twitter scrolling and promoting. His twitter had been nearly dead for the past few months, and he hadn't realized how much his following suffered. He had the mixture of real fans and the mindless robots that only made him look more popular, but he fell asleep knowing that within the year, he'd be thriving again. Whenever he closed his eyes, he didn't wake up until the sun had already set - his body already thrown off. He stood at the kitchen window once more and he stared into his blackened reflection. He could no longer see the tree in the yard, he could hardly see his own features in the blackened blob, and he stared at nothing in particular. He listened to the low whirl of the wind outside and he listened as it hit the gutter he still hadn't fixed. It smashed and clicked against his house, a comfortable white noise of a sound. He listened for the rustle of the leaves and the groans of its old branches, the noises that came with the dead of night.

He had almost dozed off as he stood at the window, hands clenched on the sink until he heard a scream and then glass smashing. He looked up, almost like he magically gained the ability to see in the dark and looked for the source of the scream. It came from the house next door, the neighbors that he didn't know the names of. In those few seconds, Tatum tried to convince himself that this wasn't any of his business.

His neighbors were quiet, there were no block parties on holidays, trick or treating was more of a street of houses with bowls of candy that sat on the porch with one of those 'take one' signs hanging off of them. Both he and the people next door never had their lights on for Halloween, they never bothered him, so who was he to get into their business? He didn't commit himself to guaranteeing that the scream came from next door, or even if it was a scream. He wasn't a detective, it wasn't any of his business, and he sure as hell wasn't marching across the grass in the rain. At least that was his thought before he heard another scream

Okay, maybe it was some of his business. He was hungover and didn't feel like dealing with it, but his hazy mind pushed him forward. Another scream echoed, this one guttural, long and extended before it was simply cut off. His long legs stretched outward to gain more length and he moved as quickly as he could. As he moved across the lawn, their grass didn't tickle his ankles. As he moved up to the front door, his way was lightened with a bright light, another difference in the two households, as Tatum's had been burned out for months. He heard another scream, one that caused the hair on the back of his next to rise and his skin to become cold. He raised his fist, a shake in his hand, and knocked twice on the door.

"Hey, uh," Tatum began as he scratched his neck, "I hear screaming, and I uh… live right next door. I wanted to make sure things were okay, and I apologize if I'm interrupting anything." he called but got no response. That was when he raised his fist to grab the gold-painted door knocker, and just as his four fingers had clasped the pseudo gold, the door flew open. He was knocked off his feet, air leaving his lungs as he stumbled back against one of the columns outside. "What the hell?" he called out as he looked behind him, his neighbor taking off. What was his name again? He wasn't even sure if the guy had introduced himself. Was it a John? Brad? He wasn't sure, but what he did know was that technicalities didn't matter. Tatum straightened himself up and looked back at the neighbor who was now gone and running across the street.

Tatum felt a stickiness that coated his arms, and that was when he saw the blood that lined his limbs. It painted the front of his shirt now, too, and when he glanced up, he saw the blood that covered the walls. He felt the vodka boiling and burning his esophagus. For a few moments, he dedicated himself to the idea of throwing it up. He managed to swallow it down, burning twice as bad, as he fumbled for his phone and dialed feverishly. He wasn't some moron in a horror movie, but he also wasn't someone to sit around and let bad things happen. He was Tatum Hyland, bestselling author. He wasn't going to let anything bad happen to his neighbors, even if he has never met them.

"911 what is your emergency?" The woman's voice was laced in professionalism, but there was a slight hint of robotic-like functioning. How many times has she said those four words and those three numbers tonight? In her lifetime?

"My name is Tatum Hyland," he spoke as he looked at the blood that painted the walls, "I heard screaming next door, and when I went to investigate, my neighbor rushed out and left the door open... I'm inside now and the place is covered in blood." He couldn't help but hear the shake in his voice as he provided the address. The blood on the walls was fresh, still dripping like it did in the movies. This was the exact reason that he wrote romance novels... not horror novels. Real-life violence was horrifying enough, so why add fuel to that fire? His eyes watched as the fresh red blood painted the walls, dripping downwards. If this were a horror film, he was confident that the lights would flicker and the man in the mask would be standing somewhere in the distance - waiting for Tatum to stumble upon him. This wasn't a film, though. This was real life.

"How many injured persons are there?" the dispatcher asked.

"I know two people live in the house, and I only heard a woman screaming... I don't know if I want to find the body," Tatum replied, stuck near the staircase, carpeted but dark red liquid staining the surface. The house was eerily silent and all he could hear was the dispatcher typing on the other end of the phone. He held the phone so tightly that his fingers crunched awkwardly and the phone hurt his ear. He waited for what felt like years to get a response.

"Police are on the way... which direction did the

suspect go and could you give me a description?" She asked, "Did you see any weapons on his body or around the house?"

"Uhhh... he ran out the front door. Not sure where he went after that," Tatum replied, despite it being a lie. He saw his neighbor run across the street. Or did he? He couldn't be sure. "I didn't see any weapons on him and I don't see like, a gun, or anything in the house."

"Stay on the line... police should be there in three minutes," the dispatcher responded, and Tatum could still hear the ticks of a keyboard on the other side of the phone. He took in a deep breath as the smell of blood drifted into his nose.

If anything, he assumed, he would get good writing material out of this, right? Nothing like writing an apocalypse novel when your neighbor just went bat shit crazy. Did he know them enough to say it was out of character? They both seemed so normal, what in the hell was going on here? Who knows what goes on behind closed doors, he thought, but something swirled within him. He pulled the phone from his ear and placed it near his collarbone when he heard loud pounding and an animal-like sound coming from outside the house. A bang and then a gurgle. A bang and then a gurgle. A bang and then a scream. A bang and a scream.

"What the...?" Tatum asked as he moved outside. He spotted the neighbor across the street, hitting his hands on the front door. He could see the neighborhood kids as they poked their heads out from the curtains. His eyes dashed towards the man again, and he beat on the doors repeatedly. He saw the blood left behind and he pushed the phone back towards his ear.

"He's moved to the other house across the street," he announced to the operator, eyes wild as they watched the scene unfold. So what he had seen had been the truth - his neighbor moved on to terrorize someone else.

"Police are almost there, sir," the operator replied as he heard the *tick tick tick* of her keyboard.

"Should I try to stop him?" he asked, never one for heroism, but he thought back to Ellie. What if it was her child that lived in that house? Would it be a different story? One in which he'd be tackling that guy to the ground?

Tick tick tick tick tick.

"No, sir, police are almost there. Just stay put." she said

"I've been staying put," Tatum hissed into the phone. "There are kids in the houses across the street," Tatum said to the woman on the phone. It wasn't her fault that his neighbor went batshit crazy, but how could he not blame her? She was the middle-man to all this madness and Tatum felt the seconds tick by like hours and those hours quickly morphed into days. In reality, it had probably been five minutes since he walked next door, but he couldn't be sure.

It was then that he could see the red and blue stripes as they flew down the streets, but it wasn't anything like the movie. They didn't roll up on curbs, one officer jumping out of the car and shooting. No other cop cars pulled up immediately after, two tires lifting off the ground. No, they drove quickly, but safely, the action sequence was unnecessary.

He watched as the officer stepped out and then another one. They tried to give the guy, Tatum's neighbor, instructions. It didn't take long for him to lunge at the closest officer, and Tatum watched as his neighbor pulled out a knife and started swinging. He watched the blade's glisten disappear into skin, rise, and glisten again, until the shimmers were drowned out in blood from the officer.

Tatum gasped as he heard the slits and gashes of the knife cutting through skin. He listened to the screams of the cop and then the gunshots. Continuous gunshots that popped so loudly it echoed and hurt his ear. With each pop, he shrunk more and more into himself, hands touching the bloodied walls as he backed up.

"You... might wanna send backup," Tatum said as he found himself glancing over his shoulder. He didn't see a side door and he didn't dare move deeper into the house. No, he needed to get out of here. His hands were sticky with his neighbor's blood and silence fell through the streets. No more screams. He heard the feedback of the radio and then the shots across the street. God, he couldn't look. Were the cops dead? Was the neighbor some kind of terminator style robot? One that couldn't be taken down by the mere pierce of a bullet? Would he come here next?

"Fuck, fuck, fuck!" Tatum hissed as he moved out

into the open and across the lawn, feeling the tickle on his ankles. He moved into his house, bloodied hands dirtying the handles as he slammed it close, not caring who heard or who came for him right now. "Are you sending backup?"

Tick tick tick tick tick

"Officers will be there as soon as possible. Sir, I need you to calm down. Is there somewhere safe you can lock yourself in?" she asked the distressed male.

"I'm back in my house. I locked the door." Tatum said to her. The ticking on the line didn't stop and he could hear the distress in her voice.

"Okay, sir, just stay put," she encouraged. "You locked the door?"

What a stupid question, Tatum thought. He just told her that. What did she expect him to do? To leave the door open and invite his neighbors in for leftover alfredo? Fuck.

"Shit," Tatum said as he stumbled over a basket of clothes, the same basket that he's been meaning to put away for weeks. "Yes, the door is locked," he said as he moved to the back door next and locked that up, too. He moved to the kitchen, eager hands fumbling around in the cutlery drawer. He found himself a decent-sized blade, the only sound he could hear is the scraping of can openers and nutcrackers as they were pushed aside in his drawer. The knife was no bigger than his hand, but it would do. Tatum slid down the front of the counter in true movie fashion, hand on the phone with the other gripping his weapon. "Things aren't looking too good, are they?" Tatum asked the stranger on the phone.

"Help will be there soon," the woman replied.

"That's not what I asked," Tatum said to her.

"What's important right now is you're safe. The rest will be figured out later," the lady said.

"Okay," was all that Tatum could manage. He felt his heart thrash in its cage, eager to escape. Would it be so bad if he included this little snippet in his novel? Fuck, maybe Chelsea, or the redhead, could die of a heart attack and there's a moment where their heart jumps out and runs away. Who said an apocalypse story had to be completely serious? He sighed as he knew Jackie wouldn't be a fan. Not in the slightest. Comedic humor wasn't her thing. She'd say it's too cheesy. That it ruins a powerful scene.

He scoffed at the thought, his palm prickled with sweat and fear. He felt everything pound, from his heart, to his chest, to the arteries in his legs. Everything ached with fear, but his brain was equally hopped up on adrenaline. He felt a mixture of believing he could take on the world and the feeling that he could curl up and cry for a long, long time. He kept the phone pinched between his ear and between his shoulder until his ear felt cramped. He then placed the phone on the floor before he hit the speaker button, the ticking sound echoing into the room.

It wasn't long before more slices of red and blue shined through his windows. Damn it, did he leave the stupid things open? Nothing like a straight invitation for anyone to come barreling through the cheap glass. More police cars poured out of the vehicle, and he moved towards the blinds to force them closed. He put the phone back towards his ear, knowing he only wanted to hear one person's voice. "They're here now, I'm gonna go," Tatum said before he hung up on the operator - who he was sure wanted to take his report and some other information. Before she could call back, his fingers dialed the all too familiar number, and part of him expected it to go voicemail with the number of rings that echoed into his ear.

Whenever she answered, her voice was in a huff and the scratchiness of sleep lingered. "What?" she asked him.

"You'll never believe what just happened," Tatum said, voice breathy and chest heavy.

"Something worth waking me up for?" Ellie replied.

"You're usually awake for at least another three hours," Tatum checked the clock built into his oven.
8:37

"What's up, Tatum?" she asked and he could hear the ruffles of blankets on the other end of the phone.

"So, I just had to call the police because I'm pretty sure my fucking neighbor lost his mind and killed his girlfriend, or wife, or whatever the fuck she was." His voice couldn't catch up to the information his mind was taking in and the trauma was trying to process. Would this be remembered in vivid detail? Or would it be repressed behind layers of the brain and black stripes?

"You know that's like a big thing going on right now," her voice sounded more aware now, a slight hitch that followed her tone.

"Homicide? A crime of passion?" he asked her.

"No, no, no," Ellie said to him. "A bunch of people seem to be snapping and killing one another."

"Do you think this… thing… is here?" he asked as his hand found its way to his mouth. His fingers were already bitten raw, but he found a piece of skin to chew on anyway. "Fuck, Ellie." He said to her, "What happens now? I went into their house, did I get… it?" His eyes found his red-stained hands and he quickly ran to the sink, scrubbing the skin so hard that it hurt, and the blood circled the drain.

"I don't think there's anything to catch, Tate," Ellie replied, a small huff in her voice. Tatum closed into himself, had this been Ellie? His whole world would have had to been put on hold.

"Okay," Tatum replied to her, but the twist in his gut pushed his teeth into biting on his lip.

"I'm sorry you went through it, Tate," she said and he felt the fury build into his system.

"At least it gives me good writing material," Tatum said to her.

"Call me if you need me," Ellie said bluntly before she hung up.

Tatum pulled the phone away from his ear and stared at the screen that flashed his wallpaper now that the call was ended so abruptly. Part of him was so caught off guard that he sat, stunned. His actual best friend would've asked him a million questions. She would've stayed up for hours on end to get every detail, she would've made a stupid Facebook status about something so scary hitting too close to home. Ellie wouldn't have given this type of response, and he almost didn't know how to handle it. He didn't know how to take this, and he had to resist every urge to not call her back and demand to know what was wrong. Ellie didn't just hang up on him like that. Ellie never acted so rudely. The good part of him was drowned out though, and he fingers moved faster than he could process. He called her back and held the phone to his ear and he waited. Maybe she was just pissy, but the two of them were never like this with one another. God, the more he thought about it, the more they just seemed like a married couple. As he tried to pull himself together and calm down, he tried to convince himself that her actions were a result of her pregnancy.

In Tatum's mind, it shouldn't matter. The two were supposed best friends, so why was she treating him as if he had the plague? Was she afraid that he had gotten whatever this disease was? Did she think he was going to hurt her? No, Ellie couldn't be thinking that. He spent a few minutes more, pacing, trying to come down from his moment of anger. He needed to understand that Ellie was going through something that he would never understand. That had to be the reason she hung up on him. He pushed his fingers through his long brown hair and he felt the familiar tug on his hairline. Ellie always lectured him about it and always tried to break his habit. Back in *The Devils* era, when he did most of his writing in his college dorm, Ellie would watch as he tugged on his hair out of frustration. She would watch him, amused at what was the start of his self-destruction, before she'd walk up to him and pull on his hands.

"You're going to be bald by thirty," she would say as she took his hands. And here he was, thirty-four, and not yet bald.

He pulled his hands away, moved towards his bedroom and stepped over some of the mess that was still sprawled around, begging to be cleaned. He shrugged out of the bloody shirt and tossed it closer to the edge of the bed. A sane person would have probably tossed it in the trash, hidden it out of plain site, but Tatum didn't have time. He pulled on a shirt that was on the ground, this one somewhat clean and most importantly, not stained with blood. If the police would come over to interrogate him, he'd look suspicious as hell if he was still sporting a red stained shirt. He was sure they would be at his place by the end of the night, so he needed to get this out of the way before they bothered him.

The thought prompted his fingers to be brought up to his mouth and he bit down. It was a mixture of nerves - from witnessing a murder, and anger - from Ellie blowing him off. She was someone that breathed down his neck every five seconds and now he needed her and where was she? Missing, apparently. The thought caused him to rummage through the mess on his table and he eagerly pulled out his cigarettes, lighting one and holding it to his lips.

UNTITLED CHAPTER THREE

The store was ransacked from the rest of its goods and there wasn't much left. Spencer was able to find a small bag of chips, probably stale, in an employee locker she kicked open in the back. There was a jacket of sorts, one that had to be folded and tucked away for later use, and a pair of boots. The boots were three sizes too big, so they were left behind. Before Chelsea even knew it, they were on their way. Jillian demanded she walk this time, so the little girl's legs tried to keep up with the much longer legs. At first, no one spoke. The only sound that echoed was the sounds of Chelsea's boots crunching gravel and Jillian's little huffs of exhaustion.

"You ready to be lifted up yet?" Chelsea asked the little human.

"No!" Jillian nearly shrieked, which prompted her to walk more to the side instead of up against Chelsea's hand that hung low.

"You said your shotgun has been out of ammo for a few days?" Spencer finally asked as she pulled her long red hair out of her face.

"Sure has," Chelsea replied. "He who shall not be named sucked up most of our ammunition trying to shoot at bodies that were far away. He'd alert them in attempts to kill them from a distance, which drew them closer to us. Resulting in more ammo usage," Chelsea said. "It was quite stupid, but when he left us, he took most of our supplies with him. Basically, anything that wasn't under my head and being used as a pillow was gone when I woke up."

"You talkin 'bout daddy, mommy?" Jillian asked as she tried to jump over a small puddle, but her short legs landed right in the middle of it.

"No, baby," Chelsea lied with a smile.

"My uncle owns a gun shop that's a few miles from here. We could head there if you want, see what he has. I have wanted to try to locate family anyways... see who is left," Spencer mentioned.

"Gun shop, huh?" Chelsea smirked, "That's convenient."

"We don't have to go if you don't want to," Spencer replied defensively.

"I never said that. I just know she's not gonna make it a few miles in one day. So, finding a place to rest will be mandatory by nightfall," Chelsea replied, trying to soothe the woman's anger. "Trust me, I've tried to go all night. Things are a lot more complicated when you're lugging a little girl around,"

"Hey!" Jillian shrieked, "I'm no little!"

"You're the strongest girl I know, Jilly." Chelsea smiled as she looked at the little girl. "Do you wanna tell Spencer what the plan is when a body gets too close?" she asked as she looked down at the girl.

"I run super far away and until I can't hear no grumbles. Then once I get away, I hide and count as high as I can cuz 'momma always comes and finds me." Jillian said as she toddled along and moved closer to Chelsea, little legs already starting to give out.

"That sounds like a great plan," Spencer grinned down at the little girl. "Did you come up with that?" Spencer asked as she ruffled the girl's hair.

"Momma did," Jillian replied. "I helped." She said as she reached her arms upwards, hands opening and closing.

Chelsea smiled weakly and picked her up, the child going onto her hip. Jillian rested her head on her mother's chest, and it didn't take long for the little girl's light breathing to turn into quiet snores and her grip to become loose. It no longer clutched the shirt that used to be green but was now stained in black and brown, it rested at her sides and her back curved like a C.

Her child wouldn't sleep in a princess bed again. Jillian wouldn't get to experience life on a jungle gym, and she wouldn't experience the pain of a scraped knee. Most nights, as opposed to sleeping, Chelsea laid awake. It was out of fear of something happening, her child becoming infected, her father making his inevitable return, and everything that came with this world. Whenever she became a mother, she expected the nights to become more restless and for sleep to avoid her, but she expected it to be for other reasons. She smoothed out Jillian's hair as they walked and Chelsea let out a sad sigh as they moved, boots crunching against the gravel under their feet.

"So, your husband left you guys?" Spencer finally broke the silence and looked over at Chelsea.

"Boyfriend," Chelsea corrected. "And yes, he left us. Like I said, took most of our things. Left us a lovely note saying our daughter was holding us back." She said as she looked over at Spencer with a smile. "It's alright though, he was a douche."

Spencer used her imagination to fill in the blanks and she looked over at Chelsea for a moment before she looked up at the summer sky. The heat was sweltering, the kind that prompted sweat in every place on the body. The kind that was so hot that her skin created cold chills. The sun was too bright, and Spencer only managed to lift her eyes just slightly before she had to drop them. She watched the squiggles of heat as they danced ahead of her, conversation coming to a halt.

"What about you, though?" Chelsea asked as she used her free hand to shield her eyes from the sun. She would kill for a singular pair of sunglasses right now. Even if they were the cheap ones that do nothing but add a pink tint to the world around you. "Parents? Siblings?" Chelsea asked her.

"Anyone I cared about is the same as everyone else's right now. Either dead or missing." Spencer replied, "I was supposed to meet my brother at one of the safe houses, but he wasn't there. I was gonna stick around but it got swarmed by rebel groups. I had no choice but to leave."

"Oh God," Chelsea huffed, "Are rebel groups already a thing? I thought that was the kind of shit that took place in the movies and video games." Chelsea said as she looked over at the woman with red hair. Jillian shifted in her position once more, flipping over onto her right cheek. The child's cheeks were bright pink and sweat covered her face as they walked. The child would be whiny in an hour (if they were lucky), so they needed to find shelter sooner rather than later.

"Of course." Spencer replied shortly, "That being said, I'll give you a pass because you're probably concerned with the well-being of your child and not the world that's going on around you."

Chelsea wasn't sure what this woman's intentions were, as she couldn't finger what was going on. Chelsea knew that Spencer had every opportunity to kill both her and Jillian, but she hadn't done so. Maybe they were part of something much bigger, but right now, Spencer seemed to hang around. Chelsea wouldn't complain as it was nice to have the company there with her. It was nice to have someone that didn't blame her for everything, but then again, they hadn't known each other or more than an hour. That didn't seem to stop Chelsea, though, as here she was... blindly following a stranger into their supposed uncle's gun shop.

"So, no family," Chelsea repeated as she brought her arm down and continued to walk ahead. "Do you think they will be at the gun shop? Or do you think that maybe they wiped it clean?" she asked as she adjusted Jillian on her hip.

"Couldn't give you a legitimate answer there." Spencer pushed a hand through her hair as she glanced over at Chelsea. "It won't hurt to give it a check. If it hasn't been wiped clean, I imagine my family is long gone."

"Why aren't you with them?" Chelsea asked after a moment, which prompted a look from Spencer.

"Why aren't you with yours?" she asked, an edge in her tone.

"I moved in with my boyfriend shortly after I got pregnant with Jillian. He was dead set on moving away... getting a new start and what-not. My parents weren't crazy about the whole premarital sex thing." Chelsea shifted her child once more and then wiped the sweat from her hairline.

"Ah, so I'm befriending a sinner." Spencer nudged Chelsea with her elbow, a smirk dancing on her lips as she did so.

"Suppose so," Chelsea let out a laugh before seeing a small stretch of houses coming up. Some sort of gated community, one that looked untouched by the apocalypse. "We need to find a place for her to get some sleep and get her out of the sunlight." Could Chelsea keep walking? Without a child on her shoulders, maybe.

"What's wrong with that place up there?" Spencer pointed at the exact same gated community that Chelsea had noticed moments prior.

"It's gated as all hell...I'll bet that they're all still there... sitting with snipers," Chelsea said as she threw her head to the side to get a lock of blonde hair out of her face. The humidity caused everything to stick to her face, which prompted a huff of frustration.

"So?" Spencer asked. "And to be fair... once all of this broke out, everyone panicked and left. I doubt anyone is on guard. Let's just scope it out and hope that we don't die." Spencer picked up her pace and didn't leave a single moment for discussion.

Chelsea struggled to keep up, Jillian's cheek bouncing off her shoulder blade harder with each increased step. "We're just gonna walk in?" she asked, tone breathy and strangled.

"Not walk in... sneak in," Spencer replied as

she looked back at Chelsea. "Keep up. I'm not gonna be slowed down," she said, despite the blatant slowdown in her movements. Chelsea managed to stay a few steps behind the woman in green before they were at the back of the gated area. The black bars reached upwards of several inches taller than both females, and a fussy Jillian was starting to make an appearance.

"We should walk and find somewhere else. No way we are making it in there." Chelsea tried to tug on Spencer's arm, but the woman pulled it away.

"Hang on," she said as she gained enough footing to pull herself upwards, foot wedged into the slot and began to climb. She moved quickly and efficiently, moving over and hopping onto the other side of the fence. "I know you can't do that with your kid, but I'm gonna scope it out... see if there's an easier way for you to get in," Spencer said. "Try not to get shot," she said as she slid on her mask again and drew a bow into its spot.

CHAPTER SIX

He wasn't sure how long he had spent writing, as he was lost in his own little world. This was his creation, something he was able to pull from his mind and put on paper. As he wrote, he remembered precisely why he did it. He had forgotten the feeling of the flutter in his chest when he thought about his art. He had forgotten the excitement he felt whenever he thought about seeing his books on shelves. It had been so long since someone told him that his book was their favorite. So long since he thought about his legacy that would be left behind when he inevitably died. This was his footprint on the world, this was his baby, his child. He was going to make history; this he knew and manifested. This is where he belonged. He didn't belong behind a desk working a nine to five. He belonged here, in the safety of his home, making his own worlds and creating the rules within them. This is where he found his happiness.

He typed furiously, back hunched and the tips of

his fingers numb. He knew if he stopped his hands would be in far too much pain to pick it back up, so he typed in fear of losing his gusto. It wasn't until he heard a knock at the door that he was forced to stop. His pupils burned as they were pulled away from the screen, and he focused on the windows. No strips of red and blue lined the streets, everything was silent, his tapping no longer creating white noise. He moved and then realized that he hadn't stood up in a very long time, and the alcohol and cigarettes he mindlessly burned through didn't help the disorientation. He stumbled momentarily and nearly walked into the wall before he recovered and made his way to the door. When he pulled the door open he was greeted by two men in uniform.

"Tatum Hyland?" Two cops stood at the door, the one speaking having a tag on his shoulder that read the last name Bettman. Or it was something like that, Tatum's vision was slightly blurred, the letters more exaggerated and stretched out. Tatum rubbed his eyes in attempts to snap out of his digital haze before he stepped aside and waited for them to cross the threshold.

"That would be me." Tatum let out a hiccup, unable to tell if he looked drunk or traumatized. He yawned for a long moment before he shut the door and locked it behind them. "Sorry about the mess," he fumbled around like an idiot, nearly hitting the same wall that's been there since he moved in. They were certainly going to think he was drunk out of his mind, but he could shrug this off with his way of coping with the trauma. "Can I get you something to drink?" Tatum then found himself checking his skin for any evidence of the night's events. Did he miss a spot of blood? Whenever he saw the blank canvas of paleness, he looked over at the officers and waited for their answer.

"No, we're afraid we have a lot of police reports to take as your call wasn't the only one to come in," Deputy Whatever replied to him as they both took a seat on the couch.

"Right," Tatum huffed as he moved to sit on the coffee table in front of them, crisscrossing his legs before he tucked them under his body. "It's kind of late, so ignore my manners and my sleepiness... it's been uh..." His eyes spotted the bottle of whiskey at their feet. It hardly had been sipped from, but the police wouldn't know that. They probably already assumed he was drunk. "Long night, to say the least." He gave them a smile that didn't shine his teeth.

"I'm sure it has been, Mr. Hyland. We just have a few questions for the report. Just a few reminders... this doesn't mean you're under arrest or that we're going to be harassing you or anything. We have a lot of witnesses and we just need to get your side of the story. So, start from the beginning and that's all we need you to do."

"Right." Tatum scratched the back of his neck. There was a shake to his fingers, but that was merely the aftershock of the things he had experienced within the past couple of hours. He felt the fuzz behind his eyes and the beat of a headache in his head.

Only then did he feel the exhaustion that crept up on him and hit him like a truck. How was he supposed to sleep after being first on the scene after his neighbor killed his girlfriend? How does one ever recover? He waited for the police to prompt him, and he felt the pin prick of nerves as they started to form. He had nothing to hide. Why would he? There were no elaborations of the truth needed and there was nothing that he needed to change or alter. He just needed to tell his truth. The officers were staring at him and he felt himself slouch over. His shoulders nearly reached his ears and he felt everything collapse inward. "Am I good to start?"

"Whenever you are ready," Deputy Whatever prompted as his partner pulled out a notepad and the pen from his front shoulder pocket and got himself ready.

"Alright, so," Tatum started as his feet began to fall asleep, his right foot tingling more than the left one. "I was at home... working." Did they need that detail? Probably not, "I was standing over by that window and I heard some arguing... or what sounded like arguing." He cleared his throat as he scratched the back of his neck. His fingers cut up into his skin, which reminded him he needed to cut his fingernails.

"I don't stick my nose where it doesn't belong, so I wasn't too concerned. Not until I heard some... actual screaming." His voice was slurred and panicky now, he could hear it. "Like not drunk girl squealing kinda scream. Like, I'm in pain and need help kinda scream." He expected them to ask him more ques-

119

tions or to prompt him, but they remained quiet. "So... I went outside and knocked on the door, just to make sure everything was okay. I've never spoken to them before, so I introduced myself... through the door... of course." His voice was slurring more now, and the more he tried to articulate, the worse it got. "And I went to knock, but the guy burst through the door, nearly knocked me on my as-" he struggled and cleared his throat, shrinking down like a childish teen, "butt." He said to them as the blush rose to his cheeks. "Then I called the cops and... yeah," he said to them.

"I- I knew you guys would be coming to talk to me, so once things calmed, I just went... home... here, and I just went back to work. Figured you wouldn't bother me till tomorrow," he announced and hoped they felt bad for disturbing his work.

He almost felt their eyes as they instantly moved to the bottle, to which Tatum grabbed it with his hands and looked over at them. "That's my truth," he said to him. "I called my friend right after that if you'd want to check my phone records. Shit, she even blew me off if you wanna hear that, too," he tested as he stood up on his feet and started to sway. He really needed to stop standing up so quickly.

"That won't be necessary, Mr. Hyland," the younger cop replied as they both tucked their notepads into their breast pocket. Tatum stared at the guns on their waistband, large and bulky. Pepper spray lined the belt on the other side, along with what Tatum assumed to be a taser. The objects that were their line of defense brought discomfort to his bones. It was three deadly weapons all at the ready, but they weren't there to save his neighbor. Maybe it was a freak thing and an unfortunate timing to murder a girlfriend, but something in his body didn't feel right. This was all a part of something bigger - the stuff that he saw on the news. He shook his head and looked at the cops, fingers threaded together with a small sigh.

Tatum had nothing to hide, but he felt the secrets being pulled out of him with a fishhook. The truth always burned, and the truth always hurt coming out, even though no lies pushed through his lips. What Tatum said was true - he didn't know his neighbors or their names, and he didn't know what transpired between the two humans. He did his neighborly duties and stepped in whenever needed, but that wasn't good enough. He called the police, which is why they were sitting in his living room right now.

"I know I already asked, er, at least I thought I did, can I get you something for the road?" Tatum asked as he wiped his sweaty palms on his pants. What if they said yes? What would he give them when he didn't even have enough food in his fridge to feed himself?

"That won't be necessary, Mr. Hyland. We don't want to disturb your work any longer. Unless we find something, we will have no real reason to keep pestering you. If you think of anything else or if you see anything suspicious," the one deputy pulled his card out and set it on the table, "You give us a call." They both smirked in Tatum's direction and gave one last look around the house before they left. Tatum watched out the window as the blue and red lights flashed, but no sounds came from their car. They rolled out just as casually as they came in, but a deadly silence fell over the once lively neighborhood. Most people were unbothered by tonight's events. Others were right next door. A police department will be changed forever. Tatum knew he'd never be able to look at the kids from across the street and not hear their screams.

It was a sound that was etched into his memory. The blood-smeared doors, the screams that echoed into the night. The ticks of a keyboard in his ears. The cops with large bulky seatbelts of protection. Tatum met them all face-to-face, but the woman that lives down the street probably slept through it. Ellie would never know what it was like to nearly be knocked on her ass by a psychotic neighbor. The only people that would understand what happened would be him and the neighbors across the street. He didn't stick around long enough to see if the other neighbors were terrorized by the same man, no. He chose to escape. To create in a way most others would never understand. He made the characters and relationships - set them up for arcs and problems. He created a new world and situations - those that were bigger than his own.

He wasn't safe. His neighbor could have very well killed him, and with how cold Ellie was, how long until she found him? Would it be the neighbors that found him or the police? Would they know to call Ellie? Would the neighbors call the police and report the crime? Tatum thought of the horrors that probably still existed next door. Had they cleaned up the body yet? Tatum tried to think about how many slices through bones it would take to murder him? How many times would the knife skip an artery? How would it feel for a knife to scrape bone? He couldn't keep thinking like this. Not whenever he needed to stay sober to write his book, to become more than the Tatum Hyland that existed ten years ago. But how was he supposed to drown out these intrusive thoughts? Okay, a few sips of his whiskey wouldn't hurt. He'd use it as a way to take the edge off, and then he'd stay sober. Just like he promised Ellie. With this thought in mind he took down a few gulps of the strong liquid. It wet his throat and flushed down the ideas of the bullets piercing that man. He wet the feelings of tasers striking skin. He washed down the thoughts of screaming children. He just needed to get to sleep and he would be fine. Everything was going to be fine.

He collapsed onto his bed, but nightmares proceeded. He felt the dirt that rested on his skin, the blood that still stained his chest. He felt the wetness of the blood that stuck to his shoes. He heard the scratches of children's fingernails against glass windows as they begged for help, and Tatum stood around and did nothing. His grasp was loose on the bottle, even though he knew the alcohol would be the only thing that got him through this demanding time. Writing a book was always hard, but writing a book during what was sounding like the start of an apocalypse? He'd be crazy to try to do it sober. He'd hold out for as long as possible but deep down Tatum knew that rougher times were in his future.

Tatum didn't remember when his body chose to go to sleep. He didn't remember the lost grip on his bottle that caused the liquid to seep into the floorboards and the papers that covered it. He went to sleep with the intentions of his body working its magic. He could only hope that his brain would build up over the memories of the evening, that it would repress and block out the trauma. He couldn't get held back by events that would only prompt breakdowns and therapy. The sooner he forgot the images the better.

Whenever he woke up, he rolled around a few times in attempts to get comfortable. He yanked the blankets over his head so hard that his feet popped out, and then he kicked his feet so hard that the blanket pulled off his torso. He tried to hide from the sunlight that beamed through the blinds like a spotlight, and he grew irritated – despite the fact he had been awake for all of thirty seconds.

He tossed his legs over the bed and stepped directly into the puddle of alcohol. As he side stepped to avoid the liquid, he jammed his hip into the bedside table. He heard the marble-like bottle as it spun around and hit something under the bed, and his hands fell at his sides. He glanced up at the ceiling, as if asking whomever or whatever was up there why his morning had to start so terribly. He didn't want to start his morning off hating the world and his life, but at the rate he was going, he knew this was likely. He moved to dry off his feet with the small pile of dirty shirts that were by the door and knew that he'd later be annoyed with the sticky floorboards. That was a problem he'd deal with later.

He zombie-walked out into the kitchen and found himself yet again at the sink where he stared down into it. Yes, it was still filthy, something that would annoy him later. Dishes still lined its surface, caked with stains that would later result in him having to throw the whole plate away. His vision was sparkled with bright yellow dots, blurred slightly in the edges. He could hear this brain's heartbeat in his ears, and the wavering of his body made him nauseous. He swayed back and forth for a minute as the vomit tingled in the back of his throat. His limbs were numb, a tenderness still pounding in his shoulders. He groaned as he tried to swallow back the bitter vomit that tried to force its way upwards. He rolled his head around, skull too heavy for his shoulders. He really hadn't drank that much last night, so he wasn't comprehending why the pain resided in his head and neck. He wasn't getting any younger, this he knew, but a few gulps of whiskey shouldn't have him so sore the next morning. Did trauma really effect people this badly?

"Get it together," he said aloud, "You won't be able to get any writing done if you keep this shit up." Tatum knew he needed to eat. He needed to put nutrients into his body and he needed to get writing done today that wasn't alcohol-induced or driven by a need to escape his trauma. Whenever he wrote *The Devil's Bride*, he hardly had any alcohol and he certainly didn't smoke. His parents were still alive then, and that was back in the day when he'd send them each chapter of his work. Of course, back then he still lived in his college dorm, still had to answer to the university policies, and lived in a room that didn't have any central air. It wasn't until the sequel that he could move into a real apartment. During *The Devil's Bride,* he couldn't smoke himself into oblivion or drink until he was blacked out even if he wanted to. He merely couldn't afford it until the sequels. So, if he could write a best seller stone cold sober, he could do it now, right? Besides, who bought the stupid tortured author story anymore? Straight edge is what's in, not alcohol and drug abuse. If Chelsea could survive an apocalypse with zero booze, no cigarettes, and a child, he could write her story sober. But when he wrote his best sellers, he didn't just live through a potential murder. He didn't witness the police shoot his neighbors, and he certainly wasn't shut down by his best friend when he reached out for help. Back then, Ellie was in his room every step of the way, stationed on his roommates (who was never in the dorm) bed, watching never ending reruns of some unidentifiable reality TV show. This was back before Netflix and YouTube, which forced Ellie to channel surf for minutes before finally settling on something. If he could do it all over, he probably would. He'd say to hell with *The Devil's* saga, he'd write something with substance, hell, maybe he'd even propose to

Ellie.

Those were simpler times, but much like all of his previous hardships, he'd get through this, one layer of trauma at a time. He just needed to eat and get back on his feet.

He rummaged through his fridge until he found what he was looking for - a few eggs and a carton of orange juice. He would've gone for milk first, but it was five days past the expiration date and the white clumps gave it away that the shit was spoiled. He dumped it down the drain and crunched the carton of milk, having to jam the overflowing trash with his hands to close the drawer. He scrambled himself some eggs, which in general didn't seem appetizing to him, and sat at the table. Orange juice in his hand, he tried to swallow down the unnaturally fizzy beverage and he chewed on some overcooked eggs. As he chewed, the eggs lacked any source of flavor, and he felt as if he were ripping cardboard off a box and chewing that instead. He ground the pieces with his teeth and swallowed it down with orange juice. Could orange juice expire? Tatum wasn't too sure.

The silence was usually what Tatum preferred. There was a reason he lived in a house and there was a reason he lived alone. The thought of needing to work around a roommate's schedule, having to share a bathroom, having to shorten his usual thirty-minute showers to fifteen, and having to socialize already annoyed him. After all, he was Tatum Hyland. Famous writer, one that could afford to live alone and support himself. So why the fuck did he have spoiled milk and orange juice in his fridge? In his prime, the guy could be seen in his designer suits, now four sizes too big on him, and expensive watches on his wrist. The times between books two and three were the best in terms of his popularity and finances, it was a shame that he had to sizzle out into a big pile of nothing.

He moved to the medicine cabinet and fisted a handful of ibuprofen and Tylenol and washed it down with the tap water from his sink. He tried to open his mouth enough so that the water only fell into the gaping hole in his face, but water dribbled out the sides of his mouth and onto his chest. When did he even take off his shirt? Better yet, what would he do with the bloody one that was still on the floor? He shook his head as he felt the pills push down his throat like globs of cement before his phone went off. The sober feelings were starting to move into his system now and coherence pulsed in his bones. He picked up the phone and looked at the screen, a text from Ellie. How was he supposed to forgive her for what she did? Was he supposed to pretend like it never happened? That she treated his experience so flippantly?

Feeling much better today. Breakfast?

Three emojis this time. A smile, a face with sprawled out fingers near the face, and a smile surrounded by tiny red hearts. Yep, Ellie was back. Tatum looked back over to the plate of cardboard tasting eggs and then down at his phone. Could he really forgive Ellie so easily? Was he going to base this decision off his need for food? As his fingers moved, he got his answer.

Sure. Normal place?

You bet.

He started to get a move on. He put on a new-ish shirt, pulled on some pants, and slid his feet into some shoes. His curled hair was starting to knot at the ends, but he just ruffled it some more and grabbed his bag. As he left his house, he noticed that there were cops outside, but not the ones from last night. Police tape rounded the perimeter of his neighbor's yard, stopping just short at Tatum's. He moved out to his car and avoided eye contact, and moved on with his life. As he drove to the breakfast place, his breaths were quickened and his left leg bounced repeatedly. He needed to get it together. He needed to act un-bothered by Ellie's antics, he needed to get some food in him, and then he'd be good as new.

CHAPTER SEVEN

The breakfast spot was a small cafe that barely extended past the size of a master bedroom. It wouldn't take much to have people wall to wall, shoulder to shoulder, but the thick brown curtains that concealed the windows created a layer of secrecy. Everything felt closed off and hidden away and it was their own little safe place. The pair ordered their usual: Ellie, a French vanilla cappuccino with extra whipped cream, and Tatum his black iced coffee. Ellie ordered a bagel with cream cheese and Tatum the same. They slid into their usual spot - three booths back and as close to the back corner as they could get. Ellie faced the door and Tatum kept his back to it, a certain system they worked out a long time ago. Ellie preferred to watch the patrons that came and went, chose to see an attack coming, and Tatum wanted the opposite. It put his nerves to rest when he didn't know how many people entered when the bell rang. He didn't want to see what sketchy creature was about to wander into the cafe next. An unspoken wave of understanding was the way the pair worked. As they slid in, Ellie folded her fingers together and crossed one leg over the other, kicking both Tatum's shin and table in the process.

"Sorry about last night. I just… wasn't feeling well," Ellie explained. Did she forget about his call or about the fact he tried to call back and she ignored him? Did she just not care or not believe him? Did he ask her about it? He shifted a few times in his seat at the thought of it all.

"Yeah, you were a bit…cold." Tatum had other words and adjectives that he would prefer to use, but the past was the past now. He felt malicious in it that he could forever use this, hold it over her head, but she didn't deserve that. At least not right now. "I know you're going through things that I couldn't put my finger on or even begin to understand." Tatum knew next to nothing about the female struggles, no less what one goes through when she's pregnant, but at least he was honest about it. He could feel the way his brain started to repress the previous nights events, making him feel as if it was just all some extravagant nightmare. While he had been sleeping somewhat decently, there was that part of him that worried he may have lost his mind. If this was some kind of nightmare, he only hoped that the unconscious Tatum would wake up, write it down, and make it into a decent book. Right now, though, it all felt too real.

Ellie lifted the beverage to her lips, and he watched

as the white cream touched the pink tones of her mouth. "Going through something is putting it lightly," she remarked as she leaned forward to rest her elbows on the surface of the table. He studied the rounded, yet pointed, body part, knowing they were probably resting in a pool of sticky syrup right now.

"Well, as I said last night... I'm here now. I'll be here with you for as long as you want me to be. I'll admit I was a bit of an ass previously and only concerned with this book. But you're ultimately my ride or die and it's time for me to show some support to you." He knew he had to be better for her. He knew that he needed to support her in any way that he could, and he owed this to her.

Ellie smiled at that and slowly nodded her head at the words that Tatum spoke. "Alright, all emotional stuff aside," she said as she sat back for a moment. "Let me read your stuff. No excuses this time!" She pointed a thin finger at him. "I promise I won't rip you to shreds... yet." He watched as her right eye winked at him, leaving him with only a sliver of her left green eye.

"Alright, alright. It's just the first snippet of a first draft if I could even call it that... still lots of things to work out, change, edit..." Tatum bit on his lip as he dug around in his bag, fingers finding his laptop. He quickly signed on with his information and pulled up the document that was just opened six hours previously. He slid it over to her and he watched as she immediately started to read the words that flowed from his brain and onto the same screen just hours before. He watched with anxiety that welled in his chest, a feeling he would never get rid of, despite his thirty-four years of life on this earth. Ultimately, the only opinion he cared about was his own. That didn't stop him from trying to read her face - waiting to see anything on her face. He waited for disgust or a smile of pleasure. He waited until she finally looked up at him, sliding the device back over.

"How did you come up with Jillian?" she asked him.

It wasn't the question he expected. In fact, he didn't expect a problem at all. Was a name choice a problem? Was he being too dramatic? He expected adjectives and words of support to roll off her tongue like they always did. He expected smiles and praise. Instead, he got a question. Tatum took a drink of his coffee before he spoke to her, clearing his throat.

"Uh... she's been on my name list for a while. I guess that I chose it because her name means things like determined, powerful, intelligent..." he trailed off, never really having to explain why he chose the names for his characters. She's never asked him a question like this before, but maybe there was a reason.

"So, what do you plan to do for the story? I mean, is the dad gonna show up?" Ellie took another sip of her coffee. Tatum's beverage was bitter as he couldn't remember if he added his sugar or not.

"You know I'm not going to tell you, right?" Tatum popped the lid off his plastic cup and dumped in two sugar packets. He used the red straw to spin the sugar around in attempts to stop it from settling at the bottom before he took another long sip.

"Leaving me on the outs, huh? I'll bet baby daddy shows up and messes things up," Ellie conspired. "You better let me read the ending before you give it to anyone else, though," she said as she sipped her coffee again.

"Of course, my number one supporter would get to read it before Jackie," he let out a chuckle. "I need someone to hype my ego up before Jackie rips it to shreds." Jackie tended to be all too hard on her clients, but that was what made her as successful as she was, Tatum supposed. He wasn't sure how she chose him, of all people, to take under her wing, but he was glad he managed to sneak in.

"Tate," Ellie finally spoke up and he watched as her white teeth made an appearance in order to bite down on her lip, "Did you... want to talk about last night?" she asked him finally.

"Last night?" Tatum felt his muscles tense and his shoulders grow rigid as he looked at her and brought his coffee up to his lips. He took a long sip and watched the way Ellie's hand reached outward to take his.

"What happened is all over the news. It's terrible," she said to him.

"Police were still at their house when I left," Tatum nodded, but why hadn't he thought to check the news? He wondered what they were speculating, if they thought the same thing he did. What if the thing that was spreading all over was in their small town now? What if his neighbor was about to be the first case of many?

"Did you, like, see it?" she asked as she rubbed her thumb against his skin.

"My dead neighbor?" he asked bluntly, to which Ellie nodded, "No, I didn't *see* her. I saw all the blood, though. And I saw the guy," he said as he shifted in his seat.

"What guy?" she asked stupidly.

"My neighbor... the guy that killed her?" he asked as he raised his eyebrow slightly but crossed his arms in front of his chest. He pushed the cup of coffee off to the side, not having a desire for it any longer.

"Oh," Ellie started before suddenly she was hunched over, her hands grabbing at her stomach. She moved to cough into a napkin, every person in the café stopping to look at her, their faces a mixture of confusion and concern. Some of their faces twisted in disgust as Ellie's coughs became more intense, the kind that nearly cause her to vomit. Tatum looked at those that seemed to be kicked back and ready to watch a show as he stood up and rushed to Ellie's side. "The show's over, guys," Tatum said as he looped his arm around Ellie's waist and lifted her up to her feet. "Come on," Tatum said as he fished his keys out of his pant pocket. "I'm gonna drive you home and get you laid down," he said as he pushed out of the door, the ring of the bell alerting everyone to their exit. Ellie was uncooperative to say the least, her feet stumbling and her body resisting as he got her into the passenger seat and managed to get the seatbelt across her body.

"How are we gonna get my car?" Ellie prompted as she turned on her side, hands gripping her stomach. Tatum assumed it was pregnancy pain. Was that a thing? Tatum never in his life wanted kids, so his research on every aspect of pregnancy or childbirth was inexistent. He was the type of guy to be completely oblivious to things he didn't want or didn't determine as useful, and now it was coming back to bite him hard in the ass. Maybe there was a reason he didn't have Chelsea lugging around her sweet little bundle of joy. At least Jillian could piss and shit on her own. At least the girl could walk and knew how to communicate and eat and drink. He didn't know anything outside of his basic knowledge, and now he knew why. He watched as Ellie kept her eyes closed and stomach gripped, the woman hardly able to lay still.

"Hopefully you'll feel better later and we could come by and get it," Tatum said as he started to drive on the streets of their small town and found his hand in Ellie's as they drove. She squeezed it so tight that his hands were pale and numb by the time that they got in front of her house. Almost as soon as he was parked, she was out on her feet, hunched over and vomiting into the shrubs that lined the front of her house.

Tatum immediately was at her side, hands tugging back her long brown hair despite it already being pulled back by a hair tie. The hand that was still numb moved to rub her back until she was finished making sickening vomiting and gagging sounds. He couldn't handle looking at what the woman was vomiting up, as he merely didn't want to. He had to convince himself that this was a pregnancy symptom. Ellie was carrying around another human in her stomach, Tatum needed to remind himself of that as he held her hair back. She made a few more coughs, to which he heard splats of vomit hit the ground. Almost as quickly as she was sick, she seemed to have a pep in her step again. It was morning sickness, he assumed, as it was the only part of pregnancy struggles he knew of. Swollen feet, that was a thing too, right?

"Let's go back and get my car." Ellie rolled out her shoulders and wiped the vomit from the corners of her mouth. She pretended as if it didn't happen, and she was already walking back towards his car. She pulled harshly on the door handle - clicking and releasing echoing into the streets as further evidence of her impatience. He wasn't her baby daddy and he wasn't her servant or boyfriend, but he did whatever he could to keep her happy - to keep their conflict little and their lives happy. He was a smart man, one that knew better. Happy wife, happy life, isn't that what the douchebags say?

Ellie pretended like that whole episode never happened as she sat passenger in his car. He watched as she messed around with the car radio that was once more all static.

"Where's the aux?" Ellie huffed as she opened the center console and rummaged and then she lifted the passenger glove box.

"Oooh, scandalous," Ellie remarked, and Tatum paled instantly as he watched her pull a box of condoms. She flipped around the box as if she had never seen a condom before and let out a giggle, "These things have an expiration date, you know." She teased before she tucked the box back into its rightful position.

"Aux is somewhere in the back, Elle," Tatum said. "By the time you get it, we're gonna be there." He clicked his teeth together to avoid the irritation that lingered on his breath and he clenched the steering wheel. There was an embarrassment that came from her finding his stash, despite the condoms being nowhere near hidden. His cheeks were a tinted pink color, his pale flushing out of his face. Sex wasn't a topic of conversation that came up in his day to day, especially not between him and Ellie. He was shocked that the woman was so willing to tell him the nitty-gritty details as to how she got pregnant. Maybe she should've used one of his condoms. He kept his teeth biting down on his tongue to prevent from digging himself a grave, but the smirk still danced on his lips.

As Ellie reached back, he could smell the coffee and the sweetness that followed her. As she hit the back of his head on accident, he felt the anger boil over his body. As he moved to look back at her, he realized too late the red taillights ahead of him. He slammed on the brakes so hard that his car stuttered and skidded loudly, tires screeching, and brakes screaming. The collision's sound was the worst -

metal crunching on metal, even though it was a small tap to someone else's ass-end.

"Easy!" Ellie used her hand in attempts to stop her from flying out the window. Once the car was at an official stop, Ellie leaned back to look over at Tatum as a hand moved to rub her neck. "What the hell?"

"Some asshole just stopped in the middle of the fucking road," Tatum hissed as he tried to look at the damage, but he couldn't see the front end. He climbed out of his car and slammed the door, not waiting for insurance cards, papers, or a license. His knuckles clenched as he moved towards the vehicle that still had its brake lights on. He relaxed his hands for a moment in order to twirl his keys around his finger as he continued to approach the vehicle that was much bigger than his.

"Hey!" he yelled as he hit the side of the guy's truck a few times before he approached the window. A man sat in the driver's seat still, with a face that made Tatum feel as if the guy had forgotten his own name. He seemed to be dumbfounded which prompted Tatum to move around the truck and look at the accident that took place just beyond Tatum's car and the truck he had rammed into. From what Tatum could see and comprehend, he had rear-ended the truck, which had also rear-ended the car in front of him. There was a car that resembled an accordion, and that car had been hit from the side. It was a carnage of vehicles, bent in bumpers, broken windshields, and everything alike.

"Tate!" Ellie yelled as her body hung out of the

passenger side window. "Let's get out of here," she begged him as her eyes focused on something in front of her. He wasn't sure how he didn't see it before, but that was when his eyes landed on the scene that took place next to the vehicle that turned into a large tin can.

A woman was on top of a body, and her hands came down time and time again. Blood splashed upwards and onto her face as another person approached and tried to pull the woman off the victim. It was then that the screaming started as the woman moved onto the person who was merely there to help the situation, and now there was more blood that started to appear.

"Tatum!" Ellie hissed from a distance. "We have to get out of here." Panic was setting in now. A pile-up of cars was starting, even though everyone and their mother was out of their vehicle, watching the scene unfold. The faces of everyone in the streets were paled and there was an eerie silence. No cellphones were held to ears, no one tried to intervene. They watched the sight unfold, most from the beginning, and watched as the woman took down two people in a matter of minutes, it seemed. The woman whipped around, on the lookout for her next victim, and now Ellie was at Tatum's side. She yanked him towards the car as more people started to awaken from their slumber. Chaos started to erupt, and people started to move. It was every man for themself, people moving from their frozen haze.

"Tatum!" Ellie hissed again as she tugged him back.

He then realized she held a phone to her ear, which made Tatum snap back to reality. He played with the keys in his hands and slowly moved back to the car. His movements mimicked that of the others. He moved in slow motion, one step backward and then the other. Eventually, he reached his car, forgetting his keys were in his left hand as he tried to plug something into the ignition. Once the key was in its rightful place, and his phone was in the cup holder, he started up the car.

"An accident it looks like," Ellie said as she held onto his arm and Tatum tried to escape. Everyone had the same damn idea. The crunches of bumpers and the crackle of tires rolling over glass. The push and pull of bumper on bumper action and the screech and screams of more people. Tatum laid on the horn as the person behind him refused to move, probably still stuck in their dreamlike state.

"There's quite a jam over here," Ellie breathed into the phone. "But there are at least three people involved. One is dead, I think." She turned over her shoulder to look at the scene and then relaxed in her seat. "My name is Ellie Moore," she said into the phone. "The driver is my friend, Tatum Hyland."

Tatum glanced over at her, knowing damn well that the officers from last night would come to investigate and ask more questions. Now he is a face that has been involved in two of the same essential crimes - people going apeshit and killing everyone in their path. He knew that he looked more suspicious and Ellie calling them while leaving didn't help the situation. He looked over at her as he finally broke free from the traffic pile up and began to drive back to her house. Forget the car at the breakfast place, they needed to be thankful that they still had their lives, right? The moment he pulled up in his parking spot, he stepped out of the car and killed the engine. Whenever he got out, he moved to look at the front of his car. The front was bent inwards and cracked, leaving him to wonder why his airbags didn't deploy. He knew if that were to happen, they would have been stuck there, but they could break away from it all.

"I don't know," Ellie huffed, "Tatum, how many cars do you think were involved?" She held the phone to her chest before she lifted it to her ear again. "You're meaning to tell me that you haven't received any calls of an accident?" Ellie had her 'can I speak to the manager' voice on now as she slammed the door closed. Tatum didn't get to respond to her question as she spoke into the phone once more. "At the very least, there were five cars involved, ma'am." Ellie let out a huff through her nostrils and her hands moved to pull her hair out of the hair tie. Tatum extended a hand towards her and took her keys as she ruffled a hand through her hair, the brown locks falling in tendrils.

He pushed the door open and looked at her house, it being in just as bad condition as his. It made him feel better seeing that Ellie was also a hot mess, and he closed the door behind her as they walked in. His on-edge feeling prompted him to lock up the door behind their two bodies and he slumped on the couch.

Drinking Ellie's alcohol just didn't feel right at all, mostly since she was pregnant and could no longer taste the alcohol until a child was no longer inside her.

He pressed his palms into his forehead and then squeezed them back until they pushed through his hair. Ellie promptly moved to stop his hand once it reached the crown of his head and lifted it out. The hand stayed tangled in some of the knots before he placed it in his lap and then chewed on his cheek. He listened as Ellie gave an address and then she moved to sit down next to him. As soon as she sat down, she hung up the phone and turned to face him on the couch. Both of her hands fumbled to grip his own and Tatum brought his brown eyes to look up at her. The cracks and broken features of her face showed in an instant. Her face was no longer hardened with the need to be the hero. She was small again, her skin pale and lips blue. She avoided his gaze for a long moment before she looked at their hands, threaded together. Both of their hands were cold, nearly frozen at the tips and Ellie's were white as a sheet. Tatum took in the image of his broken friend - one haunted by the sights that fell before them. Her blinks were spread out, so much so that Tatum thought her eyes would dry out.

She pulled her green eyes upward to meet his and her mouth was gaped open slightly. "Do you want coffee?" she asked, voice no higher than a whisper. She spoke as if she were telling him all her secrets and spoke as if she would receive a whipping for her words. There was a shock that spread over her body, her hands like a vacuum on his own. She gripped him like a life-vest, as if his hands were saving her from her nightmares, saving her from the pit of nightmares she dangled over. What was once his strong friend - one that called him back into the safety of his car - was now a broken figure. A shell. And he didn't know what to say to her.

"Uhhh," he struggled. Once again, as the writer, he should have all the words. He should be eloquent in telling her they'd be fine, that their world wasn't being flipped upside down. His words of comfort should roll right off the tongue, despite knowing he had witnessed a total of three deaths in the past twenty-four hours. "No," he said in reference to the coffee. He wanted to ask her what was going on in that head of hers, but she could build up walls and shut out trauma better than he ever could. For the first time, since they've been friends, she built a distance between the two. At the same time, she couldn't let him go. He was stuck, the several episodes of murder and crime playing in his head, but his face remained blank. He didn't utter a word as he continued to sit there with Ellie, neither of them speaking for a long moment.

Ellie stood to her feet and looked down at him. "Is our world ending, Tatum?" Her voice was monotone, asunder. She was so close to him that she may as well be sitting in his lap, but she still felt so far. Neither of them spoke, both of their breaths light and small gasps. Her eyes stared down at him, but at the same time they didn't. They looked past him and didn't touch him. They treated Tatum as if he were a window or a see-through door, his body seemingly transparent.

Cessation wasn't an option. Not when he had so much work to do. So much brilliance to empty into the world. He was ready to do it - he was prepared to commit to the process. The world still had so much to see from him. They needed to read his art. They still needed time to consume, write about it in school, and discuss what they thought his words meant. He had to have his words dissected, ripped apart by critics but loved by many. People had yet to hold his creations in his hands - to ask him to sign it at book fairs and on the streets. He couldn't watch it come to an end before him - he couldn't have the world end before his eyes, the story still held within him. Cessation wasn't an option. The world had yet to see him, praise him, welcome his new craft, and to receive his new form.

"No," Tatum's voice was quiet because he was unsure. Promises of survival couldn't escape his lips, not when he was so uncertain. How could he promise to be her safe house when he didn't have one himself? How could they brave the storm when so many hands were trying to throw them into the eye of it? Death had come near him twice now in the forms of brutal, bloody deaths. Humans ripping apart other humans for the sake of it. There was no personal gain to be found, no fetish behind it. Just blood lust. A need to murder. All of it swirling in the worlds around them.

"No," he repeated. A refusal for cessation is what needed to happen. They couldn't have the venomous words roll off their tongues. They couldn't be spoken into the universe. Isn't that how manifestation worked? Isn't that how it breathed? His mother was into that shit - daily affirmations and manifesting good vibes. She had the little plaques all over the walls, little things taped to the walls in the bathrooms near the mirrors. She had a good life, and maybe that was the secret. Would his mother be disappointed if she knew that this is what her son has become? Depending on manifestation to prevent his slip into insanity?

"My brilliance has yet to be seen." That word was foreign to his tongue, and yet, well known. He never knew brilliance in the form of mathematics or sciences. Hell, he even struggled to understand Shakespeare in his English classes. He was never Ivy League material, and maybe that was why he never went to college. But Tatum Hyland was brilliant, shadowed by those more attractive and those with better political footing. Sure, he was a bestseller all those years ago. But that title came off the backs of cliches, romance stories, and hybrids of other famous books and movies.

"Tatum," Ellie called as she pushed a hand through her hair, brown locks still tangled at her fingertips. Tatum wanted to tell her more, but again, was speechless. His words didn't come off as slurs in a drunken haze. They didn't stutter or come out clearly. He was silent, elbows rested on his knees. He stared at everything and nothing - the thousand-yard glance in his deep brown eyes.

Ellie sighed as she sat down on the couch next to him and her fingers found themselves intertwined with his. He was certain he could feel the thud of her heart beat in her hands and he looked at her for a long moment. Her eyes darted back and forth, unable to find a place to focus on. Like his own, the orbs of life were both on him and beyond him, her lips parted slightly and lightly as she spoke again.

"I've always seen your brilliance," was all she needed to say to him. There was a pull towards one another, something that swirled deep within their cores. Both felt it, but Tatum was the one to pull away from her. He was the one to stand up on his feet and move towards the shelves of alcohol. They had built it in their freshman year of college and it hasn't been touched (nor cleaned) since. He grabbed a dusted over bottle, this one fresher than the rest, and spun the cap off. It swiveled down to the ground as Tatum tossed back the awful and most likely expired beverage with a twist in his face. It kicked him in the ass - that bitter taste. He could feel the acidic liquid break down his teeth on impact, little worms moving to creature holes and decay in his teeth. He swished the beverage around, almost wanting to speed up the inevitable process before he swallowed harshly.

"There's a part of me that doesn't want to leave you alone, Ellie." Tatum clutched the bottle in his palm and moved towards the window, a hand pushing the blinds to the side. His eyes scanned the streets three times over. He memorized the colors of the cars parked on the streets and the colors of the mailboxes in front of the houses. These details weren't essential, but it helped take his mind off the impending doom. He pulled away to look at Ellie, still stationed in her same spot. The distance was growing, her hands still cupped in their form, holding an imaginary hand. Her face hadn't moved and her eyes never dashed. She was a frozen shell as Tatum moved to gently nudge her leg, but even then, she remained stiff and still.

"I'll be fine," was what came out of her mouth as she moved to lean back, eyes staying where they've been this whole time.

Everything was far from fine. It was a burning pit of a dumpster fire, nothing but more fuel being added. Their world was going up, and no one seemed to notice, nor did they care. The thought made his stomach swirl, and despite not believing the few words spoken to him, he stood up and gave Ellie a nod of his head.

CHAPTER EIGHT

There Tatum sat, a brand-new bottle of beer in his hand, despite not remembering stopping at the local liquor store to get a new case. He was sure he stopped at the one that was just outside of his neighborhood and on the right, the one with a sketchy Latino owner, and the one where he left his debit card in the machine when he had a late-night binge of alcohol. He was informed that after it was left there for twenty-four hours, the owners just destroyed the card to protect from theft and identity being stolen, and Tatum remembered the blind rage that followed. He said some fucked up things to the teen he assumed was only working part-time, and was only doing her job, but he hadn't seen her since. Things at that point had caused some tension between him and the owner, despite the many strings of apologies, and Tatum couldn't remember the last time he got to walk out with a case of beer for free. That had to be where he stopped to get his booze, but what scared him was the fact that he didn't remember. He didn't remember unlocking his doors, climbing into his vehicle, he didn't remember driving, and he didn't remember paying. It was a miracle that he somehow managed to live through this, and the bitter taste of his red apple flavored beverage reminded him of that.

He stared at the madness on the screen, but it wasn't a movie. He didn't get to control a character on the screen, didn't get to decide whether they sprinted, or they stood and fought. The people on the screen weren't standing in the middle of an apocalyptic panic. They weren't filming as bottles filled with cloths and fire were thrown at them. No explosions or people running and trampling over one another. What he did see was the continuous names and faces coming across the screen. More people dying, death tolls rising, and now the jails are overcrowded. People aren't being given their constitutional rights due to the lack of lawyers and judges - a lack of resources, and a lack of time in the day. There are riots and protests, but even those are being shut down in fear of more random murders - which only enrages the extremists. Tatum's thumbs pulled down on his twitter news feed continuously, watching more tweets and hashtags as they trended.

He needed to remind himself this was just another blip, just like another Ebola or swine flu, mass hysteria at its finest. He wasn't sure what a murdering pandemic meant, or even if it was real, but he refused to believe that his world was ending. This couldn't be the end. Cessation wasn't an option.

There was a sadness that lingered as Tatum realized there was so much left to do. He hated relationships, but he was never turned off by the thoughts of soul mates and marriage. He merely just never took the time to find them. He never took the time to look for a relationship out of drunken hookups and one-night stands. Would he ever get to experience that again? Would things be different now? Were kids in his future? Probably not, but he wasn't sure if he would even have that choice now. He never got the chance to find the perfect friends with benefits, the kind that they could truly fuck like crazy with no emotions attached. He never got to travel the world and discover its treasures. Instead, he's always been so focused on extravagant clubs with their purple-hued lights and top-shelf booze. He was too focused on red carpets and landmarks like the Empire State Building and Hollywood boulevard. And now he watched as the world started to go up in flames. How it began to shift, change, and he wasn't sure if that was for the better.

He tuned back into his form of reality whenever he heard the clunk of the bottle that was once gripped in his weak hands. He felt the liquid seep and spread from his big toes and into the other four digits, despite how fast he pulled his toes up, knees to his chest. He stepped on his couch as if the beer was hot lava or some flesh-eating virus and he quickly ran through the house to get paper towels. When he couldn't find anything, his hands rummaged until they found a washcloth, one with mysterious brown stains in it.

He ran back into the living room and tossed the cloth onto the pool of liquid. He watched as the towel sucked up the liquid, the white napkin turning into a blank, wet canvas. He stepped on the cloth as opposed to wiping it with his hands. He moved his feet like a windshield wiper - back and forth a few times over. Eventually, the liquid was streaked instead of being a puddle, and Tatum tossed the cloth near his makeshift hamper. He picked the beer bottle up, the glass still on its side. He sighed as he pushed his hands through his hair and tossed the bottle into the sink, flies sweeping out from the sides.

Drinking more booze, drowning out the reality of this world, they were all options. They were the simple things in life that took away the complexities of the pain that lingered under the skin. With the drowning came the inevitable relapse of air in the lungs, and Tatum knew he'd just be more depressed, angrier, and more prone to refusal of the world as it shifted around him. Of course, he didn't want to admit that the world was ending - not whenever he had been born again. Sleep was the best bet, as it left the potential to awaken from this nightmare. He knew that if he laid his head down, slept for twelve hours, that when he woke up, the world could be back to normal. He thought back to after Jackie's meeting. Did he call his dealer? Was he on some kind of long acid trip? He wasn't sure, but the sooner he slept, the sooner he could wake up from his nightmares. Sleep meant the pain would be subdued and the potential would arise for more ideas, more fuel. He knew binge drinking and smoking would only lead to self-destruction, but he found his water bottle was replaced with more beer, and he chugged down the bitter liquid with an unknown number of circular sleeping pills. They were chalky and white, and the weird residue coated his throat as it went down. He wasn't sure the brand or the type of medication he was taking - whether it was herbal or cold and sinus shit. He wasn't even sure if the pills were potent - as he couldn't remember the last time he bought himself any kind of medication. He tried to convince himself that he potentially bought sleeping pills the one time he had gone three days without sleep, but a rational part of him tuned back into Ellie. He could see her now, moving into his house with a white plastic bag rattling. He could see a phantom image of Ellie, hunched over and showing him her purchases as if he sent her on a shopping spree. She'd pull out familiar objects - one filled with blue liquid, the other with orange. She'd pull out Gatorade bottles and pull out ginger ale and popsicles.

He laid back on his bed and let the blankets welcome him and let the mattress form around his body. He wrapped himself and held himself close, one arm draped around his shoulder and the other around his smaller frame. His body was both hot and cold - all at the same time. He shook with cold sweats and everything beaded at his hairline.

The sleep wasn't long, it was restless and the tossing and turning was relentless. This was the first time in a long time that he longed to feel a body pressed up against his own, to have a body to curl into. The blankets over his shoulders were too hot, then draped around his legs were too cold. The rings in his head were relentless and it took him a long while to realize the ringing phone was his reality - none of it fiction. His phone rang under his head, but he didn't remember whether he placed it under his pillow or not. He tossed and he turned to find it, the vibrancy of the cell phone blinding him momentarily. He fumbled for the blue light protection of his glasses, and the way they creaked and cracked when he opened them caused him to try to place the last time he wore them.

"Ellie?" he grumbled, a rasp under his voice as he held the phone to his ear.

"Can you come to me, please?" Her voice was panicked and higher in pitch. He listened to the rustling of things in the back - papers, bottles, he heard it as she moved. He heard the objects as they brushed past the microphone on the phone, whipping and hushing. "I just... need to talk about what we saw today," she sounded as if she was crying, and that was all he needed to hear. He threw the blankets off of his legs, and he got moving.

He stumbled through his room for any semblance of clothes, a random article getting plucked off the floor. He didn't care if he matched or looked insane. He pulled on sweatpants with all too many stains and a shirt that was too tight around his arms. He moved quickly and hopped into some sandals and pushed around the all too dark house to find his keys. He kept

his glasses on and moved out to the car, hands fumbling and rushing to plug them into the ignition. The
roads were empty and yellow lines moved in quickened dashes - blurs that came and went all the same.
The whooshes of each object flooded the sounds of
the vehicle - as the speakers ebbed and flowed with
vacancy. There was no crackle of the fuzzy and in-
complete stations. There was no smooth man on the
radio signing off for the night. It was merely a glow
of the radio console - a vibrant speck in the sea of
darkness.

Ellie's house was a few minutes away and he
parked sideways on the street, the ass of his car hanging outwards. One wrong miscalculation would wind
up in his back end getting scrunched even further,
but right now, he didn't care. Ellie needed him. This
wasn't like Ellie. She didn't call him and beg him to
come over unless something was wrong. He couldn't
think of the last time she had done this - because
she had never called him in a panic before. This was
something different, and his best friend needed him.

His mind went through hundreds of different scenarios as he walked up to the front door, phone in his
hand and held to his ear, and he heard her stupid ringtone echoing inside. He pushed down on the handle
and gained entry instantly. The house was as silent as
the car, the only sounds being that of her phone and
the squeaks of floorboards under his feet - shielded
with cheap rubbery flip flops. He didn't need to call
out her name as he listened to the all too familiar
sound from the kitchen. The spoon hitting the side

of her favorite mug, the drag of the metal against the undissolved sugar on the bottom. He moved into the kitchen, and there Ellie sat.

Her arms were folded at the elbows and they rested on the table. The thousand-yard stare was back, her eyes rested as if they were looking at something far in the distance. They didn't dart and they didn't blink. They didn't lift to greet him or to stare at him. They focused forward - they looked past him. Tatum was merely a ghost before her - transparent and floating. He looked for a long moment, uncertain as he took a step forward.

"Ellie?" Tatum's voice was a hushed tone, one of which moved with hesitation. His right hand was flat as if to keep her calm and to not scare her off. There was a shake in his voice despite the need to be the strong authoritative figure in this story, and he slowly pulled one of the wooden chairs out from under the table. He flipped it around so that he could straddle it, arms rested over the back of the chair and his chin in his hand. Ellie didn't move. He hurdled through more scenarios as he looked at her. Was it the baby? The father of the baby? Did someone die? Was she going crazy? Did she have some kind of illness?

"What's going on, Ellie?" he asked her with a cautious tilt of his head. He stared at her for a long moment and he kept his head cocked and cautious before her eyes finally pulled up to meet his. She looked straight through him; it seemed, and her gaze was anywhere but on his face. She cocked her head again and offered a small smile before she spoke, no panic tracing in the pitches of her voice.

"Nothing is wrong," she replied, and a smile nearly tugged at her lips. A submissive flutter of her eyelashes was next, and he watched as she stood to her feet and carefully tucked the chair into its rightful place. Her movements seemed robotic and planned ahead of time, her body quiet as she moved. He couldn't even hear the whistle of her throat or chest, and she no longer violently coughed or tossed or turned. She merely existed.

Her coffee mug rested between the two of them, no steam fluttering over the surface, but the way she handled it made him believe that it was a fresh pot. His eyes dashed to the pot in the sink, filled with water and bubbles resting in the clear case. She had been sitting for a while, maybe before she had even called him, so why was she stirring her coffee like it was a new cup?

"You sounded distressed," Tatum said, not moving even though Ellie stood to her feet and was once more a moving human.

"Hmmm?" she asked and now she had a second cup of coffee in her hand, held with both fingers as her eyes stared out the window. Where in the hell was that cup? "I didn't call you, Tate." She whirled around and rested against the sink and her eyes showed mere traces of confusion. She was in there somewhere and a new scenario popped into his head.

"You're concerning me." He wasn't sure where the word concern came from, but it seemed to fit the situation. It seemed to peg the emotion he felt for his female counterpart and he needed to find a way to express it - he knew that was a shitty word. It wasn't his vernacular. It was his way of avoiding repeating, "you're scaring me," or, "you didn't sound okay when you called."

"Did you fall and hit your head?" he asked as his eyes scanned over her body. Not predatory in nature, but to view and look over every surface he could manage. He looked for blood, cuts, bruises. He looked for anything in between - willing to settle for some paranormal force doing damage to her. As long as he had his answer.

"I'm good," she said as she brought the mug to her pink lips, but once more, no steam rose to the surface and she didn't retract from the bitter liquid.

"Should I go home, then?" Tatum didn't want to leave, of course he didn't. He knew Ellie was more than in distress, and that her behavior was past concerning. No, his friend was downright losing it and he felt like he was the conductor of a train wreck. "You have two separate cups of coffee, neither of which are hot." He pointed out, but he wasn't sure why.

"I don't want coffee," Ellie snapped as her head whirled to look at him. Her eyes met his now, a deep annoyance shooting from her body.

"Then why are you drinking it?" Tatum nudged towards the cup that in her firm grasp and he watched just as quickly as it dropped to the floor and splintered at their feet.

"Fuck, Ellie!" he hissed, "What has gotten into you?" He stepped back from the shattered glass like it was hot lava and watched as the brown liquid spread out. Ellie looked at him, a smirk on her face as she stepped on the shards of glass. She paid no mind to the shattering pieces and didn't flinch at the blood that seemed to slick her heels. The real Ellie would've damn near fainted at the blood, and she would pass it off as the pain being too much for her. But this form of Ellie didn't care as she moved towards the cabinet. Tatum was too focused on the blood to notice what Ellie's small and fragile hands had reached for - a bottle of Captain Morgan. She hadn't drank that shit in years, not since she threw it up on the fourth of July block party two years ago. It was the kind of vomit that made you promise that you'd never drink again, and Ellie stood true to her word.

"Ellie, knock it off," His tone was a hiss now as he attempted to pull the bottle away from her.

"Relax, Tate." She smirked as she lifted the more than likely expired beverage to her lips. She took a few glugs before she pulled it away and used the back of her hand to wipe her mouth. "The world is ending, may as well enjoy the ride, huh?" She sneered as she went to take another sip.

"You're pregnant." There was a struggle to remove the bottle from her grip. The pair struggled, Tatum's firm hand wrapped around her slender wrist. Once the bottle was pried from her hand, Tatum pushed her out of the way. There he stood and Ellie stepped away as he poured the deadly drink down the drain. Would he have to take her to the hospital? How would he get her there whenever she was having a mental breakdown of sorts?

Then came the immense pressure that hit the back of his head. As he hit the ground, he heard the gong-like echo of the pot as his knees crashed into the tile flooring. He groaned as his hands moved to grip at the back of his head and felt the relief wash over him as he discovered his fingers weren't coated in blood. He fell face-first whenever Ellie pounced on him, her hands grabbing a fistful of his brown hair and smashing it into the shards of glass. Now he could feel the prickle of blood as he flipped himself over, Ellie still on top of him. He struggled against her, the pair nothing more than a set of limbs, hitting and pulling at each other. Her hands clawed at his tender skin as animal-like grunts escaped her throat.

"Ellie!" he pleaded; his voice strangled as he struggled against her. "God damn it, Ellie!" he yelled as she brought a closed fist down to his face. "Drink all the fucking booze you want!" He tried to fight her off, never feeling right with hitting a girl, no less a pregnant woman.

He managed to throw her off and he tried to scramble to his feet, still feeling the aftershock of a good hit to the head. Ellie stood up quicker and his eyes focused on the knife that was in her hand. She looked at him now, her eyes crazy and intense. This wasn't Ellie. It couldn't be.

She advanced towards him and he heard the knife as it glided through the air. Anything in front of them would've been sliced in half, even if it was just the room's tension. He reached forward in attempts to grab her or the knife, the blade cutting against his forearm. "Fuck!" He yelled as he held his arm with his left hand. "Ellie, stop!" He took a step back. He didn't want to remove his attention from her for too long, in fear that she would lunge at him. He knew that his attempts to fight her were failed, and he had two other options left: to run or to die. He couldn't fight his best friend anymore. He edged himself towards the stove, trying to move quickly so that he wasn't cornered. He heard the glass crack and scratch under his flip flop and he watched as Ellie tried to swipe at him again. He jumped back and sucked his stomach in and avoided the blade. He stood against the stove now and he knew he only had a few inches to go until he was at the kitchen's threshold. Ellie was fast, but he was faster.

"Can we talk about this?" he prompted, but he wasn't sure why. He fumbled for his keys as the blood oozed down his arm.

"I'm fine!" Ellie swiped at him again and nearly hit his hips.

"Okay," he said as he sidestepped and broke free from the kitchen's hold. He took off as fast as his legs could carry him. He knew now was the point of the movie where he'd drop the keys or come across a locked door, but he was smarter than those in the movies. His vision was blurred, tunnel vision working its way into his eyesight. He just needed to reach his vehicle before Ellie could grab him or slash his tires. He reached the door and fumbled, blood smeared across the handles as he tugged it open and climbed in. He hit the little button that locked all of the doors and he scrambled with his keys. He just needed to get out of here, hoping that Ellie found someone else to chew on. Tatum wasn't going to be a number in this pandemic. By the time the car was on, Ellie's body was smashed up against his window, her fists smacking the glass repeatedly. He was reminded then of the similar sounds of his crazed neighbor trying to gain access into the house across the street. He remembered the fists hitting repeatedly, trying to break through whatever barricade held them back. Ellie tried to do the same and he watched the blood that smeared on the window.

He tore out of there now, not caring if he ran over Ellie, or hit her mailbox, or ran over anything. He wanted to live and would do whatever it took to do that. He wasn't going to die at Ellie's hands. He wanted to live. He watched in his mirrors as Ellie sprinted after the vehicle, her body moving faster than it ever has. He could hear her screams and he watched as a once moving human became nothing more than a black blob in the background, before she disappeared entirely from his view.

Did he call the cops? Fuck, what was he supposed to do? What would they say whenever those two officers got word that Tatum Hyland was once again the victim? When would they stop believing the never-ending stream of coincidences? When would they realize that people were dying at the hundreds and Tatum had managed to survive three different incidents?

No, the distance was what they needed. He was just being dramatic, right? His best friend wasn't out to kill him. No, she was merely having an episode. She wasn't going to be lost to the world's madness, because there wasn't a virus to be caught. His Ellie didn't go crazy. Fuck, did he take some kind of drug to get himself to this point?

His brown eyes located the stinging sensation in his arm and he found the long red streak that was from Ellie. The blood dripped onto his legs and bloody fingerprints stained the steering wheel as he drove. He looked at it for a moment until he heard the rumble of the strips, a prompt that caused the wheel to jerk hard to the left. He moved into the other lane and hit the strips over there before the car was finally steady and he could focus again. He wiped his eyes of their tears and tried to work up some kind of story. The world was homicidal, sure, but why would it have gotten to Ellie over him? Ellie was a better person, a sweeter one. She was pregnant, something that he thought gave women a little 'get out of jail free 'card. In all the movies, pregnant women were safe until they had the child. After that they were fair game.

"This isn't a movie, Tatum." he said as he batted his tears away once more. "Ellie just tried to kill you," he stated, but there was the little piece of positivity and hopefulness that stuck out. Maybe Ellie didn't try to kill him. Maybe it was a mental breakdown – something he could get her help for. Ellie wasn't a violent person, so what had come over him?

"Look at your arm, you idiot," he grumbled as he looked down at the blood that continued to drip. He didn't get that from some kind of accident. Even if it was a mental break down, she had still tried to take his life, something that couldn't be forgiven.

Ellie had whatever this disease was, and he needed to put as much distance between her and him as possible.

CHAPTER NINE

It wasn't some kind of fucked up pregnancy symptom. No, his best friend had tried to kill him. She seemingly had gotten the disease that was taking over all of them, and he wondered how long it would be until she came knocking on his door. This was the part, Tatum assumed, where he was supposed to arm himself with some kind of gun. This is where he was supposed to lock himself into a room, board the doors and windows shut, and hope that the threats would disappear. That was what they did in the movies, so that was how it worked in real life, right?

Tatum was scared shitless of his friend, of course. He was afraid that she was going to kill him or kill someone else. He was scared that she was going to cause more harm to her or to the baby. God, would the few sips of alcohol she had kill it? He knew he needed to be worried about his own survival, and he knew he needed to think of himself. There was a part of him that knew damn well he needed to protect himself. He couldn't die like this.

He moved into his house and locked the door behind him. Instead of rummaging through drawers in attempts to find weapons, and instead of going to his attic to find some mysterious gun his father left behind, his hands found his storage of booze. He took a long drink from a beer bottle - the liquid piss warm and flat. He chugged it down as he paced back and forth and tried to make it make sense. His best friend tried to kill him. How was he supposed to handle that? He assumed he could sit down in front of his computer, write, and relate these events to the writing. He could have Spencer kill Chelsea, raise Jillian on her own. It would be too fucked up to have Spencer kill both Chelsea and Jillian, Tatum knew this. No, the people needed a light. They needed happiness and they needed something to look forward to. If he were to put his real-life happenings in his book, he'd take away his readers' chance of having an escape. He knew that Chelsea and Jillian, if anything, had to survive. He wasn't writing a story in which he killed everyone and anyone that had their name on a page. No, he had to be the light in everyone's life. He wanted parents to name their children after his characters. That was why he loved to write and create. He gave people the characters they didn't even know they needed. He needed to be in line with his desires, with his wants and his aspirations. Anything less gave him lackluster work - the kind of work that he's been trying to pass off for the past ten years. He was going to come back the right way - bigger, better, more successful, and more famous. What else could anyone else ask for?

He set his beer down and moved to the bathroom to tend to his wounds. He couldn't see the back of his head, but as his fingers reached around the back of his skull, his fingers were slick with blood. He could tell that it still seeped the red-hued liquid, but he didn't feel the dizziness of blood loss, so he deemed himself as fine. His arm wasn't bleeding as bad as the night sky had made it seem. Ultimately, if things were normal and people weren't trying to kill him, Ellie would force him to go to the hospital to get it stitched up. Then again, if things were normal, Ellie wouldn't have cut his arm and he wouldn't be in this situation to begin with. His sink was covered now in fingerprints that were red and splotchy, and that sight alone started to mess with his head. He quickly ripped the bottom of his shirt and wrapped it around the gash a few times. He held the material with his teeth in order to hold it in place, feeling like he was the star of his own survival movie or something. He tied the material and started to erase the evidence of his bleeding body.

He shoved his hands under the lukewarm water and tried to scrub the blood off of them. He then moved to his arm, hoping that the bandage he used would help stop the bleeding, but until then, he tried to clean the wound up. He felt the fire like sting that pushed up into his shoulders as old blood was replaced with the new, and he watched the red circle the drain. He turned off the water and searched for a new towel, and once he found one, he wrapped it around his arm. He held it there until he heard a knock and that was when the panic pulsed in his body. Did he call the police and not remember? Was another neighbor here to kill him? Surely Ellie couldn't have gotten to his place so fast.

"Hello?" he called out. Was he a mad man? Would his neighbors hear him calling out into the night?

"Tate?" Ellie called out. She wasn't at the front door though, she was at the kitchen window. He could see her silhouette as it popped out from the edges, her eyes staring straight into him. There was no ducking and hiding, and there was no pretending to be out of the house. Her dead eyes caught him, stared into him. She didn't move and her head didn't cock to the side. He could hardly see her moving.

"Tate, let me in." Her mouth moved, but nothing else did. They stared at one another for a long moment and he watched as she lifted her hand to knock on the glass. "Tate, I'm sorry." She pleaded with him as her ghostlike white hand had tapped on the glass. Who was this person?

"Ellie, you need to go home." There were the tears again that threatened his eyes. This wasn't his best friend, he needed to remind himself of that. This was a psychotic killer that had already tried to take his life. He needed to locate his phone and call the police.

"I just wanted to talk," He could hear her whimpers, the rasp in her voice. Was Ellie back? Did she hurt anyone else, or was he the only victim of her madness?

"You need to go home." Tatum locked his jaw. What did she expect him to do? To say, *"Hey, Ellie, you called me to your house and tried to kill me. Pregnancy hormones, am I right? Come on in! Have a beer and kick your feet up, you crazy bitch!"*

"I don't want to go home." Ellie's voice thickened and he could see the slightest features in her face now. She didn't drip anger - she showed nothing.

"Ellie, please don't make me call the police." Tatum's voice shook and he looked to the right and then to the left. He needed a weapon, but he couldn't find one. He needed to get to the kitchen and he needed to arm himself. This wasn't going to end until he got help... actual help. He wasn't sure if he could take this version of Ellie on more than once.

"No!" Ellie shrieked and she took a step back and grabbed her head. He watched as she started to shake and whip her body around, hands gripped at her ears. "No!" She yelled as she hit the window with her hand, mouth pulled up in a snarl. For a moment, he was sure that the cheap window pane would shatter at the impact, but it still stood firm in its ways.

"Okay, okay." Tatum held his hands up. "No police!" But how was he going to get her out of here?.

"You're lying!" Ellie hit the window again. "And I'm gonna kill you!" she yelled and without warning, a hard object came barreling through the window, glass shattering everywhere.

Tatum took a few steps back and began to frantically search for his phone.

Ellie screamed and lunged for him, which

prompted Tatum to step to the left. Ellie's careless body once again moved like she was in a cartoon, and she slammed into the wall. He listened as her fingernails scratched at everything in their path and it didn't take her long to get back on her feet. "Come here!" she yelled at him.

Tatum stood in the kitchen now, a knife with a blade as big as his forearm in his hand. "Ellie, stop!" he yelled as his hand trembled.

Ellie lunged and once again, Tatum stepped to the side. She ran into the countertop, and for once, Tatum was glad that Ellie was always a klutzy bitch. Again she rushed him, and this time she made contact with him, scratching his arm before he was able to pull from her deadly grasp.

"Ellie, please," Tatum begged her, eyes filling to their edge with tears, "Don't make me do this,"

Ellie didn't respond anymore, she was just a lunging, clumsily, and screaming idiot in front of him. This wasn't Ellie, this wasn't his best friend. This was some mindless and brainless zombie. This was a madwoman in her body. He watched as she lunged at him and knocked him on his ass, her hands moving to grab his throat. From her throat were escaped grunts and groans of struggle, spit and slobber coming from the corners of her mouth and dripped onto his face. Would he go mad now, too?

"Ellie!" He coughed as he fought against her, the thing on top of him not having the strength to overpower him. He clawed at her face, amazed at how easily his fingernails cut through her skin, and with a hard hit to the side of her head, her body was off his. He climbed on top of her and it was his turn now - his arms wrapped around her throat, occasionally lifting her head up just to smash it back down.

He didn't realize the tears that fell off his face and onto hers. He tried to ignore the sounds of her screams. He looked away from her batting hands and he shrugged away from the scratches of her finger-nails. This wasn't his Ellie.

He could feel her getting weaker underneath him and for a moment in time, he heard the whimpers that escaped her. Was that the real Ellie shining through? He felt the exhaustion kicking in, uncertain as to how people use strangulation as part of their MO. His muscles burned and his skin was on fire as his grip loosened just slightly, still thrown off by the cries that had escaped the body underneath him.

That was the only moment of hesitation that Ellie required to hit him on the side of the head, hard enough that he too fell off her. It was a wrestling match now, trash and bottles crashing under their bodies. They were a blender of limbs and grunts of anger and frustration, her fingers grabbing his hair and his grabbing hers. If they weren't in the middle of an apocalypse, all of this would feel and look very different. Tatum reached for the knife that he didn't remember dropping, and he felt the blade between his fingers. The two bodies moved against one an-other, resistance and violence alike. Tatum felt the fist that got brought down to his face and he groaned at the impact. How could a girl be so strong and so weak at the same time? He would never understand, this he knew, and he wasn't about to give Ellie the opportunity to explain it to him.

She punched him again as he found the knife and jerked it upward, no exact plan as to where it was going.

It was then that Ellie stopped grumbling, groaning, and fighting. Her body went limp on top of him, her mouth went silent. Her blood oozed onto his hand and her new accessory was that of a knife that was jammed under her jaw. Her eyes laid open, but Ellie was dead.

And Tatum had just killed her.

CHAPTER TEN

Tatum laid under Ellie's body for longer than he was comfortable with. The blood still pooled from her chin and onto his hand that was white knuckled around the knife. Once he released the deadly blade, he pushed her limp body off of his, and he scrambled to his feet, slipping and sliding amongst broken glass and blood. His head throbbed, as his red stained fingers fumbled for his phone. He punched in the three numbers he dreaded most, knowing they'd surely suspect him now. He paced as the phone rang for what felt like minutes before he got through to someone, and once he did, he was placed on hold. "Is anyone in immediate danger, sir?" A voice asked him. "Not in immediate danger, no." Tatum sat down in his chair as his body seemed to move in slow motion. He wasn't sure how long he waited or if they asked him any questions, he wasn't even sure if he gave his address before he hung up, the technician telling him she had other calls to attend to. Their whole world was going up in flames, wasn't it?

He wasn't sure how much time had passed between her death and the police showing up, but he
watched the unfamiliar faces as they came and went.
He sat until a paramedic found him in the kitchen and
pulled him to his feet, wrapped a blanket around his
shoulders, and lead him to the front steps. There was
a morbid curiosity that came with wanting to stick
around to see what they did with Ellie. Maybe there
was a part of him that didn't believe the fact that he
had just killed his best friend. He wanted to see their
process, wanted to ensure they treated her body with
respect, but he was basically forced into a sitting
position outside. He sat and let the cool air settle
around him, his body still reeling from what had just
happened. They did what happened in the movies – a
flashlight shined in his eyes that he was asked to follow. On two separate occasions, they tried to ask him
to talk about what had just happened, but he never
elaborated.

He watched as the coroner arrived - disgruntled
and angry looking. The coroner was gone for a while
before they reemerged with a stretcher that clanged
around like a shopping cart against the pavement.
He watched the flat board as it carried Ellie out, the
stretcher getting caught a few times on the cracks in
the sidewalk before they reached the ambulance. The
coroner got the help of two other officers and Tatum
watched as the trio lifted the stretcher and loaded
it into the back like it was another piece of cargo. As
the vehicle left as quickly as it came, Tatum's dark

eyes stared at the blocky white letters that read **CORONER** that was painted on the back. He half expected the other window to have a grotesque image of a cartoon man holding a shovel and whistling. He wondered how many dead bodies this guy had seen in the past few days. Wasn't he worried about getting whatever was spreading? Part of Tatum wondered if the delay was due to the influx of dying people around him. What was happening to Ellie now that she was one out of thousands? Part of him was left to wonder if everybody was being picked up and dumped, as they already seemed to be wrapping up the scene at his house.

"Follow this light." Tatum sat, a white blanket thrown over his shoulders and a few bandages taped on to stop the bleeding on his arms. He did what he was asked and let his eyes follow the blinding light. He was uncertain if they were testing for concussions or loss of sanity, but he obliged. He watched as the paramedic scribbled some things down, and he watched as she started to close everything up.

"What are they going to do with her body?" Tatum asked quietly, "What are they doing with any of the bodies?"

It was then that the paramedic forced a smile, "They're being taken care of." She didn't catch his eyes and looked away quickly as two officers walked up to them. They forced him to his feet and while one cop held his shoulders, the other wrapped handcuffs around his wrists.

"What the hell?" Tatum asked. He struggled

against their grip, two sets of hands easily over-powering Tatum's smaller frame. He flailed against the stronger cop; his body not prepared for the sudden loss of freedom. The wounds that were still left unattended on Tatum's head started to ooze blood at the sudden movement, his body in no condition to be thrashed around.

"This is for your personal safety, Mr. Hyland," the younger one spoke with more uncertainty, and a lack of confidence lingered. Were they scared of him? Were they afraid he'd snap next? His hands were three incidents deep - and he didn't blame them for thinking he was another one of them.

"I'm not sick if that's what you're getting at," Tatum said lowly as he felt his freedom dissipate with each click of the handcuff. Was sick even the right word? Were these people sick? Was that an offensive word to even use? What in the fuck was going on?

"You're not under arrest," the other spoke as they started to walk. Even he, Tatum noticed, seemed on edge - uncertain. How many others were there? "This is for both of our protection. So, I need you to listen to my instructions so that I can keep both me and you safe, Mr. Hyland."

"Then why are you pressing on my head and pushing me into the back of a police car?" Tatum wiggled in his seat and tried to stop his shoulders as they twisted at odd angles. Due to the negligence of his limbs, he felt the handcuffs tighten one more click. He shifted again to gain comfort, but nothing gave him it. No position hit the scratch that needed itch-ing and he felt the abrupt closure of the door.

"We're just taking you to the hospital, Mr. Hyland. You should be able to get some rest there," the younger cop turned in the passenger seat to look at him. Tatum stared at the younger male's shadow of a beard that had started to stubble over and then he looked at the bald head of the man next to him.

"I don't need sleep," a bold-faced lie, as Tatum was spiraling without his sleep. It was only a matter of time before his walls were talking and his vision was blurred - sights he was all too familiar with.

"You've been through a lot in these past few days, Mr. Hyland." Tatum hadn't even realized that the car was moving once more and that they were once again headed down a road that Tatum figured had no true destination in mind. He watched as the night faded away into the distance and he watched once more as the dashes in the roads blurred into one. He watched as the red glowing plus sign slowly and surely got closer. What was a distant symbol of life was now above his head like some kind of all-knowing God, and he could feel his sins coming to the surface. Tatum Hyland went from only seeing death in the movies to seeing people murdering one another in cold blood. He went from being a mere passerby to being the witness. He went from being annoyed by his best friend's presence to having to stab his best friend through the chin to save himself.

"Can you get these things off of me?" Tatum shook his body as he was pulled from the car. They lead him down some side hallways and into the general waiting room, one where the people were spread out in some kind of formation he didn't understand. From there, they were called up one by one, hospital security watching the room from behind a layer of glass. Once they reached the front and got checked in, it was another set of hoops to jump through, it seemed. Tatum didn't know what it meant for those that needed help urgently - for those with their arms taken off or a gunshot wound. He wondered how many of these people were victims of the disease, how many would get it next. The police officers seemed to have gotten him ahead of the waitlist, as he was led to the front of line and taken back into room number six.

They swiped his temperature and then they checked his heart rate. They stuck another thermometer under his tongue and then swiped it another across his forehead. They looked in his ears and they listened to his heart rate. They took a few different pressures - the cuff around his small bicep and then the small clip around his finger. One nurse administered the tests, another reported his results, and one stood in front of the door, arms crossed, and eyebrows threaded inward. The jingle of yet another set of handcuffs hung from a belt loop and the handle of a gun was its neighbor. A hospital was bad enough, that went without saying, but being treated like a prisoner? That was a different layer of stress. He was innocent, Tatum knew this, but the looks and the treatment made him question the traces of his own sanity. Was there any left, or was his world and image tainted by murder? How many things could he be witness to before the cops start fingering him for some kind of similarity in circumstance?

"Your vitals look great and you seem to be quite healthy, Mr. Hyland," the nurse claimed as she sat back in her chair but typed away on the computer. Tatum found her comment to be laughable - as chain-smoking a pack of cigarettes and chasing the bitter taste down with alcohol was far from healthy.

"...thanks." What was Tatum supposed to say to that kind of comment? Where did the cops that were so up his ass five minutes ago go? The handcuffs were the permanent reminder that he was, in fact, under arrest. Their words echoed over and over: he was seen as a danger to himself and to others. They put the cuffs on his wrists to prove it.

"Birthdate?"

"February 15th 1986." He struggled for a moment, feeling as if the past two days has aged him twenty years.

"Smoke or use any drugs or alcohol?"

"No." Tatum was already headed to hell, may as well keep his lying game up.

"Work a high-stress job?"

"Nope." Tatum wasn't on the front lines, fighting for his country. He didn't carry a gun on his belt, a flashlight in his hands. He didn't run into burning buildings. He kept himself away from humans and in front of a computer. He had the anxiety that came with deadlines being pushed back and then forward.

He had stress over editing and meetings. He wouldn't sleep for days and weeks, and he'd push himself to the point of breakdowns time and time again. His work life was filled with stress, but it was the kind that was in no way conventional.

"Have you suffered from any headaches, migraines, nausea, vomiting?"

"Nope."

"Diarrhea?"

"Gross. And no."

"Have you experienced a persistent cough over the past few days?"

Ellie. Ellie coughed up lungs and mucus. Was she sick? There couldn't be any other reason. He knew something was wrong, but Ellie being another statistic? God damn it.

"Nope."

"Have you been feeling a disconnect from other coworkers or family? Depression? Lack of interest?"

"Nope." Tatum didn't have friends. His family was dead and have been for a long time. He didn't work in an office with other people, and he didn't run his own company to have workers under his name. There was no one to disconnect from, his only friend now being dead.

"Thanks for answering those questions, Mr. Hyland. We're gonna get you settled in the back and send someone to stitch up that arm and make sure you don't have any injuries to the head." She pushed the suspended monitor back against the wall as she stood up and nudged a head towards the door. The stand-in bodyguard moved into action - he stood Tatum to his feet and, once again, he was held by the thick chain that separated his two cuffs. Down another hallway and into another room.

"We're sorry things have to be this way," the nurse's voice was monotone as they moved into the room and both bodies moved to press Tatum downward and into the hospital bed. He pressed against them and tried to resist their forceful pushes. The man held him down and uncuffed his hands but kept his shoulders pinned as they pulled his arms out to the side.

"We don't think you're sick, but the onset of the illness can be quick, and we're trying to figure out the signs. Until then, you're more of a risk to yourself and others and we're trying to keep this thing under lock and key," Tatum watched as the nurse snapped the rails around the bed into an upward position - a set at the foot of the bed and then at the sides.

"I didn't agree to this," Tatum near growled as he was pushed back and his wrists were grabbed.

"It's just... the way things have to be done here," the younger woman replied as fabric restraints were placed around his wrists. They looked comically soft in comparison to the freedom holders he had on earlier. These had small paddings around the string that kept him tied to the bed, but with each extension, he felt the cord pull his wrists back.

"These are soft restraints, Mr. Hyland. Enough to give you mobility, but it will keep you in place and safe for now. Once this is over, and you're cleared, they won't bother you anymore."

"Of course, they won't bother me, once I'm cleared, I'm going the hell home. Or are you telling me there's gonna be some obscure quarantine wing I'll have to be committed to?" The irritability rolled off his tongue in a very, *"don't you know who I am?"* demeanor. A card he rarely played, if at all, but mainly because he knew his place in the world. He wasn't an A-list celebrity... he was no King and he was no Dickens. He was merely a one-hit-wonder, a title he earned two years back by some Reddit user named bigdaddy66. Tatum could only assume that 69 was taken, and possibly 96, so big daddy chose 66. Ellie has told him that maybe that was the guy's age, or perhaps the user didn't even read his books, but the words still stung the same. No writer takes criticism well, every negative comment was a hit to the ego, just as every compliment boosted it. Some writers were better at concealing it, though. Some could take a bad review and laugh at it, others burned and crumpled, swore away writing for the rest of their life. Tatum tried to not be that guy. But, to live in a world where everyone loved him and his writing? That would be ideal.

"We're going to get you in and out as soon as possible," was all the nurse could reply to Tatum before leaving, the security officer following and shutting the door behind him. Tatum could only assume that the man stood outside, waiting for the moment that Tatum broke free and tried to get past him. Was a lot of that going on these days? How many security officers did they have stationed outside the doors and in the halls?

"So much for security," Tatum huffed as he started to sit up in his bed. The gates at his right and at his left wobbled as he adjusted, the ability to move somewhat freely residing in his bones. He pulled his right arm up until he was met with resistance, and even then, he proceeded to reach outwards until the restraints tugged irritably at his arm and wrist. His left arm moved next and that beginning was met with the same end, an unnecessary tug of his joints and a tug of his skin. He went to pull upwards again until he heard the door kick open, two nurses moving into the room. He saw the security guard who loitered in the hall, arms crossed and veins popping out from his bald head and thick neck.

"Can we just get this over with?" Tatum grunted as he relaxed his body as much as he could - a challenging feat when you're locked up like a crazy person. Neither nurse uttered a response and neither even seemed to look at him. He looked at one nurse, her eyes sullen with dark grey circles under her eyes. Whenever he was admitted (was that the right word?), he noticed the small nurses' station had both a coffee pot and a Keurig machine. Has she even had her first cup yet? Was she about to go home and say to hell with the coffee? He watched as she dropped her clipboard on the ground and how the other nurse scooped up the papers that flew in all kinds of different directions.

"Oh, shit!" the sleepy one cussed, "Sorry. It's been

a… long shift." But as quick as the emotion was there, the quicker it left and seemed to taper off. The woman took back her clipboard, but Tatum was sure that the stupid thing was merely a decoration, as she set it down on the table to his left and didn't bother picking it up again. Tatum sucked in a long breath as the the tired one reached over him. He got a whiff of the sanitizer that all nurses seemed to bathe in and he let the pungent smell bring him some comfort. She messed with a few of his wires before she pulled away and then the other nurse was at his right.

"Care if I ask you some questions?" she asked, much more aware than the other one.

"I don't think I get to say yes or no," Tatum huffed. "I just want to get out of here and go home to my own bed, please."

The statement made the nurse uncomfortable, but she smiled through it. He could tell it was part of the job description and her pen in her hand only stood still for a moment before it started to push towards movement once more. "I'm sorry to inconvenience you, Mr. Hyland." She clicked her pen closed and then crossed her arms.

"What did you just write? Patient is showing signs of losing his sanity? Patient is being difficult?" Tatum felt like he was being an ass, but he truly just wanted to get home and sleep in his own bed.

"Neither of those things, Mr. Hyland, Sharon here will be asking you some questions while I go find the doctor so he can look at you." She said before she left the room and left him with the woman he assumed to be Sharon.

Sharon looked about as good as Ellie - gaunt and exhausted in more ways than one. He watched as the happier of the two left and then he watched as Sharon reached over him once more. Sanitization flooded his nostrils and he tried to pull away as her breasts hung down into his face. He felt as the pillows behind his head were removed and rearranged and he felt the back of his head as it slammed down against the bed.

"What the-"

Suffocation. Lack of oxygen. At first, Tatum couldn't grasp what was taking place. He felt the impact of his head caving into the all too stiff hospital bed. The air couldn't push out of his nose in a frustrated huff - the air couldn't come out at all. His arms flailed as much as they could, but the restraints pinned him down - the pillow over his face cutting off his air. He tried to resist and tried to pull at an SOS call of sorts, anything to draw attention to him. He struggled, and for a moment, his air was gained back. The fluorescent hospital lights beat into his sensitive eyes that felt as if they were going to bulge out of his head. If he had his limbs free, he'd grab at his throat - but each pull was unsuccessful, and each tug was met with more resistance. He went to grab his throat and he should've tried to scream - but the nurse was now wrapping clean and sanitized hands around his throat. She was stronger than he would have expected - her hands creating a vice grip on his windpipe. He tried to pull at her hands and any attempts for a scream were raspy and strangled. He kicked his legs - waiting for someone - anyone - to come to his rescue. Her eyes were vacant as they stared into him - she was hardly looking at him at all. The circles under her eyes grew into nothing but an empty ring of a life that was once there, and the nurse that was supposed to be saving his life was now taking it.

The edges of his vision had started to turn black, speckles, and spots of light dancing in the spot that belonged to his pupils. He blinked back the tears as lack of oxygen began to pulse in his head. The brain that once thrived for knowledge and stimulation was now being starved, and there was nothing that he could do to get it to stop. He knew he had about thirty seconds before he lost consciousness. He knew that he could have anywhere from thirty seconds more or less - unless the nurses or doctors were about to come in to save him. Where was the buff security officer? Was he flirting with the nurses? Talking to them? Being as useless as he was just five minutes previously? His feet, involuntarily, were kicking now. He heard the slap of his feet. He felt his Achilles as it smacked against the gates. Where was everyone else? Where was his help? They were supposed to be saving him, not hurting him. His eyes opened, feeling as if they were about to pop out from their sockets. He gasped against her and his right arm grabbed the stethoscope that hung around her neck and down in front of his face. He joined the two ends together and yanked downwards, bringing her far enough down to swing on her, his right arm hardly hitting her. Even though his punch was near inexistent, the scream she released was guttural. He hit her again, doctors starting to come into the room now. Her grip on him was still firm, and he thrashed against her, legs slapping, throat gasping, and eyes popping wildly. This was his last hope.

The security officer moved in, pushing her off his body. The nurses moved to him, unfastening his restraints and once he was free, his hands moved to grab at his throat. Much like Ellie, he coughed so hard that his eyes nearly bulged out of his head and vomit tickled the back of his throat. Wasn't coughing a side effect? He noted a nurse that wrapped her arms around his shoulders in attempts to hold him up, a stream of apologizes escaping her mouth as she helped him up. It was then that Tatum looked at the nurse he had thrown to the ground, who was now up and on her feet. "He tried to attack me! I didn't know what else to do!"

None of her story would hold up, as Tatum was restrained and did what was required for survival. He didn't attack her, it was quite the opposite and they all had to know this, didn't they? They all went to college and were educated, and this meant they had to see right through the liar of a nurse. However, all eyes were back on him and the security officer released the crazy nurse long enough to start fumbling for the same pair of handcuffs. No, Tatum couldn't go down like this. Not in the face of a liar. This was all the distraction she needed, though, because as soon as their eyes fell on him, she sprung up and wrapped her arms around the neck of the officer. More mad-

ness ensued as they all tried to fit through the same
door, tried to reach safety as fast as possible. It was
every man for himself as they poured into the pris-
tine white halls. People fell over one another, others
scrambled. Others poked their heads out of their
rooms, confused. The screaming, much like it always
did, started to pick up. People started to get tackled,
people started to get punched. He watched as one of
them ripped apart one of the stands that moved the
monitors from room to room. He managed to look
away as the monitor was brought down in attempts
to crush a head like a grape. It was at that moment
that a pair of deadly eyes locked onto him, and then
another person joined in the homicidal rage.

He picked up speed and started to run before he
reached the elevator and pressed the down button
furiously. In the movies the elevator never came
in time, but maybe he'd get lucky. He jammed his
thumb into the same spot, the light glowing, but the
doors never opening. They were getting too close
now, and Tatum needed to get out of there. He turned
over his shoulder and towards the glowing exit sign.
He was going to have to rely on adrenaline to get him
out of this hospital – whatever it took.

Tatum moved towards the glowing sign - a sign
of hope and freedom. He moved faster than them -
despite his condition. He pushed through the door
hard enough that it hit the wall and his fingers moved
to grab at the railing to his left. He skipped steps on
the way down, nearly stumbling and falling into the
walls between the landings. The feet behind him

advanced quicker and quicker, skipping steps no longer keeping him far ahead of the two on his tail. He reached the next floor down, only for a man's body to fall at his feet, blood pooling onto the floor. He kept moving and looked over his shoulder, disappointed to see that it wasn't like the bodies in his novel. Homicidal idiots didn't eat other homicidal idiots or their victims. These sick assholes were out only for blood – nothing more. He pushed open the next available door - groans and grumbles escaping the mouths of the women behind him. They stumbled along with him - he listened as they swatted their arms, nearly hitting him each time.

More madness and carnage. Bodies everywhere, blood on the walls, and the screams never let up. Codes were coming across the intercoms now and Tatum needed to do what was necessary to get the hell out of here. Of course, he didn't need to be concerned with the safety and wellbeing of everyone in this hospital - Tatum Hyland didn't care about anyone. But his hands found the nearest red alarm and pulled it down - a loud screeching echoing into the halls with a white flashing light. He moved, the nurses seeming to get distracted by either the noise or another piece of meat, and he continued to push. Down another hallway, down some more stairs, and then he found his source of freedom. He saw the darkness that awaited him on the other side of another closed door, and he felt the cold air as it hit him hard in the face.

Tatum fell to his knees - gravel wedging under his

skin and onto the palms of his hands as he fell forward. He then felt the pain that pulsed in his body - he hissed at the feeling of the woman's hands around his throat. He gripped there, the imprint seeming to last forever. His head pounded with pain and his vision was still blurred around the edges. Rain popcorned against his back and the cool pavement tried to relax his body. His fist moved to grab a small handful of pebbles - jagged and brutal to touch. Blood dripped down his forearm as he chucked the stones as hard as he could. He watched as they scattered like roaches and killed themselves via the small puddles on the blackened pavement.

He knew he needed to get out of there, despite having no ride. By the time it would take an Uber to get there, he would be a wanted man if they already hadn't found him. He would have to get home on his own, and he would have to support himself like he always has. He wondered where he could go. Was Ellie's place too obvious? Would they expect him to go there? Was he even a wanted man? No, he couldn't be. He was innocent, despite being in the middle of crime and murder. He was always in the worst place at the wrong time, but they knew he killed his friend in self-defense. That had to know that, right?

There was a pang in his chest when his mind drifted back to his once best friend. Ellie was the kind of girl that was scared to be alone and now her body was sitting in a body bag in some examination room. Ellie waited now to have her blood drained from her body and her organs scooped out. Was she an organ donor? Were they still donating organs in a time like this? He took a few steps back to look at the hospital building that sat behind him. It was unmoving, but at the same time, looked as if it was on the brink - ready to collapse. The red plus sign - one that once signified hope - was flickering. The screams of the world losing its mind echoed from the inside. What was once known was now uncertain. Brother was turning on brother and nurses were trying to strangle their patients. Cessation wasn't an option - the world couldn't crumble before his eyes. Not whenever he had so much to prove - so much to work for. The flickering of a positive light was something that haunted him - with each pulse, he felt his hope dry out like the back of his throat.

He turned on his heels and started to run - unscathed and uncertain. His neighbors were dead, Ellie was dead. He had no one to call for help. He couldn't call Ellie - she was in a body bag. His parents were dead, and his stepparents wanted nothing to do with him. He had no siblings. He had no girlfriend. What was he supposed to do? He pulled out his phone when he was five minutes away from being at his house. He held it to his ear as he thought about the one person who has saved his life before. It only ran twice before there was an answer and he felt his heart lurch at her voice.

"Jackie," he breathed out as he looked around the vacant streets. Did they know what was taking place in the world around them? How long until a murderer was knocking on their door, ready to murder them with whatever object got into their hands first?

"Tatum! How are you doing out there?" she asked, for once, not seeming inconvenienced by his call. She didn't seem worried and Tatum wondered how long it had been since she got out of the house, since she experienced what the world now had to offer. Was she in her safe little bubble, oblivious to the world around her?

"I'm keeping on." Tatum knew his response was stupid and it was a lie – plain and simple. "Listen, I know that the world, right now, is a crazy place. I think it's only gonna get crazier. But I want to bring over some work. I did what you asked of me - I re-wrote my story and I would love to hear what you think… are things okay over on your end?" God, if he found out they were shutting down, he'd simply lose his shit. Was it insensitive to call his publisher just mere hours after his friend was murdered? Was murdered the right word? He couldn't be sure, as his mind was scrambled and uncertain. Were these the onsets that nurse was talking about? Was he going crazy? He knew Jackie would be uncertain and he needed to convince the older woman. Ultimately, she held his fate in her hands, and he needed to get her on board with the ideas that started to pump into his head.

Yes, this was the inspiration he had hoped for all those days ago. His next bestseller was right within his grasp.

"I just… think in a time like right now… people need something to look forward to. They need some sense of normalcy and a world to get lost in." That wasn't a lie. If he wasn't going to be the next best-seller, he needed to be a beacon of hope. When all of this was over, they needed to be saying that Tatum Hyland got them through the apocalypse. They needed to say that whenever their world was ending, they channeled their inner Spencer or Chelsea to get through. He'd stop at nothing to see this to its end. He'd even go door to door, city to city, safe house to safe house, to deliver his book if it got his name out there. He would do whatever it took. The world needed to know him again " –this" him, the real him. They didn't need to know the fact that he drove a knife through his best friend's chin. They didn't need to know that everyone they loved would probably be dead within the month. No, they needed to know Spencer and Chelsea. They needed to know Tatum's story.

"Things are a bit uncertain right now and changing every day," she replied and he heard the rustle of something in the back and then the chomp of her teeth down on something crunchy. Jackie was all he had right now, but the sound made him hold back his temptation to hang up on her. The sounds of her teeth grinding only edged his mood towards the threshold of losing his mind. He needed to stop this; he knew.

"But, then again, I am the boss." Jackie had the audacity to laugh in the back. Tatum knew then that her world had probably gone untouched and without any malfunction. He guessed that she was going to figure it out sooner or later, and Tatum didn't know how she would handle it. For now, though, he'd take advantage of her oblivion. "Right now, we are trying to keep things as normal as possible. At least until we are forced to shut down. I would love to see what you have. Can you email me something and we can talk tomorrow?"

Those were the words he needed to hear. He didn't need to hear anything else as his nimble fingers moved to send the PDF over to her before he hung up. He took the long walk home, just waiting for the squad car to roll up and take him away. He didn't immediately go to his neighborhood, as he was paranoid that it'd be put on lockdown - them searching for him.

Whenever he walked up to his house, though, there wasn't a soul to be seen. Police cars weren't lined up on his street or in the front of his house. While the police tape was removed from his neighbor's house, they plastered it all over his. He wondered if they just took the tape from his neighbors and put it onto his, and he wondered if he was going to get in trouble for ripping the stupid shit down. He killed his best friend in self-defense, so why did they feel the need to beat him over the head with it? Would they even be worried about him whenever their entire world was being turned on its head? He didn't want to think about the bloodbath that was taking place at the hospital, or the number of people that would be infected. He didn't want to think about the defenseless, the people who couldn't protect themselves. He didn't want to think about those that were under anesthesia. Would they wake up to an empty operating room? With their chests still carved open? Would any of them live to see these grizzly sights?

Right now, he couldn't think about it. He needed to be normal. He needed to keep his ruse going. He was an innocent man with nothing to hide. He was living his truth. The police couldn't do anything to him, he knew this. If they wanted to arrest him, they would have been here already.

Still, he paced and he waited. In the sixth pass, he stepped incorrectly on the pieces of glass still,eft behind, and the pieces crunched under his heel. What was a few more spots of blood on the floor, anyway? The air that cam through the window was cold and created the kind of draft that made doors slam when you meant to close them. He didn't bother with touching the thermostat to flick on the heat, as he figured he didn't want to use up the resources. He wondered if the police even remembered his name, no less if they were coming. How many bodies needed that same coroner that came and took Ellie away? Would he call for reinforcements soon? Tatum assumed that the police could call for backup, use their numbers, and come for him. So Tatum waited for them, but he just sat in silence. It wasn't until the sun was rising that he relaxed, knowing damn well that if they wanted him, they would have come and gotten him by now. He was a victim in this situation, he wasn't a perpetrator. He knew this. He needed to be normal, and he needed to have something more to give to Jackie in the few hours it would take until he saw her.

He tried to forget about his near-death experience. He tried to forget about the fact Ellie was dead. His art - it didn't wait around for anyone. It didn't take breaks. Especially not whenever it meant that he was going to get signed for book deals and movies. Okay, maybe that was a bit much. But wasn't that what manifestation was about? With this thought in mind, his fingers moved to the document that was still pulled up, and Tatum started to type.

UNTITLED CHAPTER FOUR

"The place is empty," Spencer called from the other side of the fence.

"What do you mean it's empty?" Chelsea called back as she looked at the woman with red hair. Her fingers still grasped the gun in her hand and the mask was just now being pulled from her face.

"There are a few signs, a bit on the nose about trespassers, but there isn't anyone around," the woman called as she nudged her head towards the small road. "I'll let you in the front. The gate is unguarded and unlocked."

Those words didn't sit right with Chelsea, something seeming off about a gated community just getting left behind. The place seemed nice enough, some would even say ideal, so why did they leave? She tried to fight these feelings by reminding herself that it would only be for a few hours at most. Chelsea assumed that they would work in shifts- she would let Spencer sleep while she kept watch. Then, she would sleep for a few hours, and they'd be on their way again by sunrise. If they made sure the place was se-cure, what was the harm? They would be smart about it - as Chelsea figured someone like Spencer wasn't about to make some stupid mistake.

It was a short walk to the front gate and the metal groaned and creaked as it was pushed into an open position. It was just enough so that Chelsea could squeeze her and Jillian through without the child stirring. It was then that Chelsea looked around at the neighborhood that they had gained such easy access to. Silence surrounded and pushed onto their shoulders as Chelsea's eyes darted around, taking in everything. Her eyes moved upwards to the rooftops, almost as if she was waiting for someone to gun them down, but nothing was heard. There were no gunshots, no explosions, no conversations to be heard. What made these people leave? What stopped anyone else from getting in?

"Most of these places are boarded up... but if we see one we like, I'm sure it'll be easy to get in." Spencer walked ahead of Chelsea, boots pressing into the gravel sidewalks.

"On the nose was right, Jesus Christ," Chelsea breathed as she held Jill a little closer and she looked at the messages spray-painted in red.

You Loot, I Shoot
TRESPASSERS WILL BE SHOT ON SIGHT.
DONT THINK WE DONT SEE YOU!

A few of the houses showed spray paintings of eyes, and Chelsea wondered if that was supposed to simulate the all-seeing eye. Discomfort pushed under her bones and made her blood run thick. She held Jillian a little closer as she tried to avoid the warnings - tried to avoid the thought of snipers stationed up on buildings.

"And you are sure this place is secure?" Chelsea asked as she moved a sweaty piece of hair out of Jillian's face, the young child's grip still on Chelsea's tank top straps.

"I mean, we aren't looting. Besides, they had ample opportunity to shoot me... Twice as much as the opportunity to shoot you, you know," Spencer pointed out as they reached a house that seemed to have less boarding than the others. It was a large white house with too many windows, but Spencer walked right up to the front door.

"You don't think a place with huge windows is too... open?" Chelsea asked cautiously as they walked up the front steps - the entire house croaking over at the pressure.

"You gonna question every judgment call I make?" Spencer snapped back at her. "If it were up to you, we'd still be walking, yeah?"

Chelsea didn't feel the need to respond to the other woman's meaner tone. Chelsea bit her tongue and took a few steps back, letting Spencer do all the work. It seems that's what the female wanted, at least. She watched as she bent over and scooped up a brick in her hand, using it to bash open one of the windows. Before Chelsea knew it, Spencer was through the window and the front door jingled as it opened.

"Must've set up some kind of alarm system," Spencer said as she looked up at the bell attached to a thick rope that ran over their heads. "I wonder if it wound up working for them... the house seems clear," she informed Chelsea as she shut the door behind them.

The house was ransacked. Furniture overturned and what was once a coffee table was a collapsed pile of wood on the floor. Glass caked the floor and crunched under their boots. The television appeared to be ripped open and broken beyond recognition, most of the place in shambles. As Spencer tucked into one of the spare rooms downstairs, Chelsea moved to the second floor. Everything seemed as though it was in the same condition - looted and wiped of its memories. Chelsea set Jillian down on the bed, feeling no need to cover the child in the dirty blankets, especially not in this heat. Once Jillian was settled, Chelsea rummaged through drawers - finding papers with now useless meanings. Hotline numbers and business cards, a menu to the Chinese takeout place she assumed to be near this place. She searched through what she assumed to be a teenager's box of mementos - pressed flowers that fell apart like glass, ticket stubs from a Red Hot Chili Peppers concert and a ticket to 'A Night Under the Stars, Howard High School Senior and Junior Prom. 'Chelsea wondered how long the kid made it, what kind of dress she wore to her high school prom. She liked to hope that the teen was out there some-where, thriving in her own way. That had to be what happened, right? The world couldn't take high schoolers, just like it shouldn't take chil-dren or babies. This place was at one point, she assumed, well off and thriving. They probably had the best of the best - survival instincts in-cluded. That was the mindset that was required in a time like this one. The world was cruel, but perhaps those who were better off had better chances of survival. The cruel world wouldn't kill kids and teens.

"Find anything?" Spencer called out, which caused Chelsea to jump. She turned to look at Spencer who hung in the doorway, and Chelsea shrugged her shoulders.

"Want some old concert and prom tickets?" Chelsea replied as she finally let a load off, her bag falling to the ground with a solid thud. She took a moment to sit at the edge of the bed her daughter laid in and watched the dust as it lifted itself off the blankets. There was a part of her that could only hope that Jillian would die from something like illness or run of the mill old age, despite the rarities of that happening these days. That was a fucked up thought, she knew, but she didn't want her child murdered or taken by the disease. Nobody wanted that, Chelsea assumed.

"I found some food in the kitchen. This place isn't totally useless," Spencer announced as she pushed off the wall and joined Chelsea in the bedroom. Her green eyes scanned the surface of the boxes contents and plucked the ticket off the nightstand.

"God, I miss things like live music and bars," Spencer lamented before she put the ticket down. Her hands moved to stroke the medals that lined the head of the bed, "I wasn't much of a sports girl… a prom one, for that matter," Spencer said before she moved out of the room and Chelsea heard her boots squeak down the hallway. Chelsea rose to her feet and pressed on the wood that boarded the windows closed. She pulled open the closet door to ensure nobody was in it before she closed it again. Once she was sure Jillian was asleep and somewhat content, she shut the bedroom door behind her. She once again stopped as she found the pictures that lined the hallways. The photos of the family on the beach, all wearing matching blue-hued t-shirts. Her fingers touched the photos of children posed with Mickey Mouse, ears on their heads with bows and glitter. The smiles were ear to ear, the family having no way of knowing what the future held for them.

John, whenever they were together, always wanted to take a vacation to Disney. Chelsea assumed it came from the fact that his parents never took him - something about wanting to prove they were better off than his parents ever were. They always said that they would go to Disney once Jillian was five years old - as that would be the perfect age for the child to still ride rides but appreciate the magic that Disney brought.

"I wonder what that place looks like now," Spencer said, suddenly next to Chelsea.

"What place?" Chelsea jumped for the second time as the woman appeared and disappeared like a ghost.

"Disney." Spencer pointed a dirty finger at the mouse. "You know all those rumors about underground tunnels and having Walt Disney's body frozen somewhere in the haunted mansion. I wonder what all those secrets are doing now and if anyone has tried to ride like, Thunder Mountain or something."

Chelsea laughed at the thought of some teenagers climbing onto the abandoned tracks, trying to jumpstart a rollercoaster that people would wait hours for.

"I'm sure they were raided of all their super

expensive goods and food. And I'm sure the billionaires that run the place are safe and secure in some of those underground bunkers," Chelsea replied as she pulled away from the hall of memories and down into the kitchen. What waited for her was a can of baked beans. Not her favorite, but there was no pickiness in an apocalypse. She would save the cans of chicken noodle soup for Jillian and maybe the child would eat for once.

"God, I could kill for an expensive Mickey Mouse sweatshirt right now," Spencer lamented as she dug a dirty spoon into the contents of the baked beans.

"Sweaters in this heat?" Chelsea twisted her face and shook her head. "One of those fans that spray water, maybe," she said as her hands hesitated towards the can of soup.

"Eat it, momma." Spencer rolled her eyes. "There are two more cans in the cupboard. You can't keep going like this and just not eat any food. Trust me, dying of starvation is probably a lot more miserable than dying at the hands of one of those things," Spencer said with a small smile.

"I really do miss the times where I could eat three plates full of food and everyone would judge me because I didn't take four plates," Chelsea sighed as she rummaged through the drawers in attempts to find a piece of silverware. Her options were a knife or a fork, so she settled for the fork and bummed a few spoonsful of beans out of the can. She shoveled the food in, uncertain as to how her stomach would handle the food.

"Thanksgiving was always my favorite." Spencer smiled as she took another spoonful and looked over at Chelsea. "My family was huge, so we'd always have so many leftovers." She smiled at the thought and shook her head - different times.

"My family was also very large and so was John's. We usually just tried to drop in and then leave as soon as possible from my parent's place... avoid as many arguments as possible," Chelsea admitted as she took another forkful of the beans. They weren't fresh, not that she ever liked beans anyway, but she forced the lobs of food down with a twisted face of disgust. "Black Friday, though." She smiled, "John would always watch Jill and I could go out with my friends. I'd kill for some coffee and shopping." She smiled and let out another dry laugh at the thought. "I put a whole new meaning to shopping till I dropped."

"I could see that," Spencer replied, and Chelsea wasn't sure whether that was supposed to be a dig of hurtful words or if it was supposed to be a genuine statement. Maybe it was rude to judge, but something about Spencer told Chelsea that the woman didn't really do that much shopping. Her rough around the edges look was truly intimidating, and she wondered what the woman was truly like before the apocalypse brought out the survival of the fittest. Either way, Chelsea smiled back over at the woman and closed her eyes, trying to remember a time before this one. She thought of Jillian sleeping in a room filled with reminders of a life that once was: concerts, prom, and musicals. Everything Chelsea had experienced but had trouble remembering. What color carpets did the big event hall in town have? Did they have a chandelier in each room or not? She couldn't remember those fine details, a statement that hurt and tugged deep in her chest. She could remember a time of high heels and little black dresses, a time with a rum and coke in her hands as she bummed a cigar off John. Better times, happier ones.

"Black Friday I would always sit at home and watch a movie with whoever I was seeing at the time. My record was six movies in one sitting," she said to Chelsea. "Thrillers were my favorite, but I could always adjust my genre to whatever the other person was feeling. I couldn't stand whenever they whined about my movie choices." She rolled her eyes and leaned against the countertop, kicking one heel over the other one.

"I used to love going to the movies," Chelsea said as she opened her eyes. "Especially in the summertime. Sitting in a cool, air-conditioned, dark theatre? Nothing better," she replied with a sad sigh, fork smashing up some of the remaining beans at the bottom of the can.

"I'd kill for an extra-large popcorn with extra butter and salt. I'm talking salty to the point you're dehydrated and certain your hearts gonna give out in any second," Spencer laughed and shook her head, tossing the now empty can into the sink with all the other trash. The place had been looted and looted well, but Chelsea wondered why so much food was left behind. Did it come down to the question of preference? Room in a backpack? "I also loved those good n plenty's. My mom thought they were disgusting," Spencer added.

Chelsea was about to bring up her candy of choice - the melty and savory chocolate that were snow caps. She would always buy them at the theatres, as John was always running too late for them to be able to stop at the Dollar Store, and they were still worth the four extra dollars. But they were disrupted by laughter in the streets - the first sound they've heard since the convenience store. Both females sat up, Spencer unwinding her legs.

Spencer automatically grabbed her bow, an arrow slid right into place. Chelsea wanted to ask if she could fire that thing quickly if needed, but there was no time. Spencer crouch walked over to the now busted open window and she looked out onto the streets. A party of six were walking around - all with guns slung over their shoulders. They looked like they would be victims to an ambush, especially if Chelsea had her shotgun. Chelsea immediately began to wonder if they could get Spencer to the roof so she could pick them off one at a time from a secret location, but Spencer didn't seem as determined to go for blood.

"Well, that's probably why we weren't shot on sight. They might've been on a food run or doing rounds somewhere." Spencer's voice was low as she spoke, fingers clutched onto the ledge around the window. They watched as the group rounded the corner, officially skipping over their safe house.

"What do we do?" Chelsea asked. "Why don't they know that we're here?"

"We wait it out. They haven't found us yet," Spencer replied. "We can work in shifts... watching the streets from those big windows upstairs. Once the sun goes down, they shouldn't be able to see us. We can't risk leaving now as you can't get Jillian over that fence, and we aren't going to be able to waltz out of here," she announced. "One watches the windows while the other sleeps. We do that until the morning."

"Okay... I'll take the first shift." Chelsea offered. "Unless you want me to sleep, and once Jillian wakes up, I will take over babysitting duty and watch guard," Chelsea said. There was the smallest part of her that understood why John left. Life and survival would be a lot easier if they could just take off, hop a fence, and make it out of here. But with Jillian, that wasn't possible.

"You can take first shift. I love kids," Spencer said as they watched the group of people round the corner. They dispersed into smaller parties, all talking and laughing without a care in the world. Once they didn't seem to be coming for them, both girls slowly sat back on their heels, Chelsea wiping her hands over her face.

"Come on, sun is setting soon, and we need to be on it before they start moving around too much," Spencer hit Chelsea in the back, and again they were on their feet, setting up shop. The stairs creaked under their feet, in no way a quiet house to be stuck in, and they started to set up their makeshift watchtower. Jillian stayed fast asleep in one of the bedrooms, and Spencer quickly claimed her place of rest.

Watch duty was never fun, and Chelsea couldn't remember the last time she had an actual safe house to stand watch at. With her back to the wall and an open window ahead of her, she watched as the group of six slowly separated and went into their separate houses. A small cluster moved into the house with red window shutters, and the other small group moved into a white house with black shutters. Chelsea watched the flicker of fire in one of the windows - wondering how long it would take before a house fire would take place. She watched the small movements on the insides of the house and couldn't help but wonder what they were talking about. She couldn't help but wonder what life these people lived, why they didn't have someone watching over the gate for people like her and Spencer.

This place was too nice to get into and they should have known it was all too easy - all too perfect. A place like this doesn't go unlived in, unnoticed. Places like this thrive and it was now that Chelsea realized they had thrown themselves right into enemy territory. If she didn't have her child with her, she would consider scoping out this group, see if they were worth joining, but people don't want children around. They are an inconvenience - someone they have to carry around - literally.

As she sat, and as she thought, she watched as the flicker of the lights bounced back and forth in her eyes. She felt her chin as it nearly touched her chest, she felt her eyes feel as though they were held down by bricks, held down with massive sheets. Her blinks were slow and deliberate - like Jillian's blinks an hour or so prior. Her head sunk and grew heavy, her neck bending forward and backward as it tried to hold up the heavy head.

"Just stay awake," she whispered as her head rested on her hand. She felt the weight of the world as it pulled onto her shoulders, and she watched as the fire keeping her awake started to burn out. The bright red edges were starting to go orange, the flicks weren't as harsh and weren't as high. It was a wave from one fireplace to the other in the house across the sidewalk. The shadows of humans stopped moving, but Chelsea knew she couldn't sleep. She had to take her turn. She had to hang tough for just a little while longer.

She thought back to her conversation with Spencer - what she wouldn't do for a big cup of coffee right now. The kind that burned the tip of the tongue and the roof of the mouth. The kind that had the bold aftertaste and made you wake up on contact. She would even settle for the watered-down, wimpy Starbucks beverages - anything to give her the boost of energy she needed. After she had Jillian and John went back to working doubles and triples, energy drinks ran through her veins. So much so that she had to lay off them - as they were causing heart problems. That was when you knew you had a problem. The lack of energy and the lack of movement did her in, though, as next thing she knew, her head was starting to slouch down lower and her wrist had been released, letting her head collapse and her eyes shut down.

Whenever she woke up, the sunlight was in her eyes. Jillian must've needed the sleep more than she realized, as she couldn't remember the last time her child slept through the night. She adjusted herself slowly but surely and rolled out her neck and then her shoulders. She sat up straighter as she looked at the houses across the street - both with open doors. She sat up quicker now and quickly turned around. How was she supposed to explain this to Spencer? If they still moved undetected, it didn't matter, right?

"Hey there." Chelsea heard - her feet frozen in their spot. This prompted a swivel on her heels as, once again, she stood face to face with a stranger. This time? Two of them - both men. Both three times her size and both with more facial hair than blank skin.

"We're not gonna hurt ya." The front man said with a smile on his face.

CHAPTER ELEVEN

With all the death and destruction happening in his life, maybe Tatum ought to stop while he was ahead. Kill Chelsea and Spencer, have the group take Jillian, raise her, and live somewhat happily ever after. In a world of despair, why not make his fictional world that way, too? He shook his head as he sat up straight and closed his eyes for a moment. He took in a deep breath in attempts to calm himself down, to think about what was going on. Death and destruction plagued his mind - but that wasn't Tatum. Killing off main characters for the sake of shock value and to make everyone sad was the kind of shit that got you canceled. That was the kind of move that would turn off your hardcore followers and that was the kind of shit that people created YouTube videos about you over. He could see the YouTube titles now.

"THE FALL OF TATUM HYLAND?!"

He could see the stupid person's face now. He

could imagine the thumbnail, a photo of Tatum on the red carpet, the same photo his mother hated so much, with big block letters close to his face. To the right of the picture of Tatum would be the Youtuber, their face twisted and their mouth in the shape of an 'O'. He knew their tricks all too well. Ten years ago, a bad review was usually written either on a blog or in a magazine. These days you were more likely to become popular if someone thrived off of your failure first. All it *really* took to make it anymore was a video on YouTube made by someone with a prevalent following. A has-been will suddenly fall into the spotlight again, their work inspected, torn apart from the inside, digested, and made into memes. The true talent would shine through, Tatum knew this, but was YouTube going to be a thing anymore? Would vloggers hold their cameras up and film until they too met a likely fate?

No, he needed to stop it. Tatum Hyland wasn't going to fall. Not again. He was going to rise from the ashes and everyone would know his name. They'd praise him. It was his phone that pulled him out of his thoughts and he scrambled to reach it on time.

"Hello?" He pinched the phone between his ear and between his shoulder and he looked towards the computer screen in front of him.

"You did get some great work done, Tatum. I hope I didn't wake you." Jackie sounded happier - sounded more like herself. She sounded more like the woman he met all those years ago - eager to start a company and to pick up a young writer like himself. Back then, there was a whole lot of unknown. Back then, they were both so young and unaware. Now they could do this thing - the timing was there now. The experience was something they held in the palms of their hand. Now they just needed to get everything into motion.

"I actually just finished up another chapter." Was writing something his stupid mind should be focused on? He moved to the bathroom and looked at himself in the mirror. His eyes were sunken, exhausted. He had a few scratches along his face - uncertain about which near-death experience those came from. His neck was the worst - dark purple and red bruises in the shapes of fingers. They danced around different parts of his neck and his hands traced the imprints. He could see her face now - so unaware and yet so dead set on killing him. Those deadly eyes seemed to know so much and seemed to be so unafraid of the world around her. Or did she know she was going to die? Did she accept it and just try to take Tatum down with her? He would never understand. He tilted his head as he stared at the markings - if asked, he'd just say he was involved with some kinky bedroom stuff. Or maybe he should just wear a scarf - ignore every ounce of attention possible.

"Tatum?" Jackie hummed out.

"Yes?" Tatum asked as he turned to lean against the bathroom sink. The damn thing wobbled and shook against his smaller frame and he heard the clatter and clang of his toothbrush as it fell into the small bowl.

"I said," an edge in her tone lingered, "that I hope I didn't interrupt anything or break your focus."

There's the old Jackie.

"Never," Tatum lied. "It's late, I was just calling it quits and I was gonna head to bed. See you in the morning?"

"See you in the morning."

He took in a long breath as he looked at the call ended button before the brightness of his empty phone screen remained. He took in a long breath as he slid his fingers to unlock the screen. First, he moved towards the text messages and he stared at the nearly empty screen - texts only from Ellie, Jackie (that were over two months old), and then texts from the pizza delivery man. It was the most depressing thing he's seen in the past few hours, and he sighed as he swiped left next to Ellie's contact name. He needed to forget her - as she was only holding him back. She held him back and he needed to remind himself of that. She was his best friend, the woman he had just spent some time crying over, but those tears were now wasted on a girl that was never coming back. She would be everywhere now. He still felt her blood on his hands and he heard her screams in his head. These were the reminders that would distract him for whatever time he had left on this earth, and the sooner he erased the memories of her, the better. He watched the red button as it appeared and he never hesitated when it came time to delete their history. To delete their years and months of texts, frustra-tions. He deleted the times she flirted with him and the times he drunkenly responded back. He deleted the unreplied texts - sometimes days at a time. It was time to wash his hands of Ellie - the world was ending anyway, right? He couldn't get so hung up on the loss of his friend when everyone was dying. Ellie was in heaven if that place even existed, and Tatum was left behind in his own personal hell. The world would end soon, but before it did, the world needed to go out with Tatum in their mind. They needed to see his smiling face on the 'about the author' page. They needed to read his books, travel to see him. Whenever they were living in their post-apocalyptic world, he wanted there to be rumors of his where-abouts. He wanted people to come find him, to come pick his brain. He couldn't make this dream a reality if he stayed at home crying over the loss of his friend. He needed to move on. He would be better than this within the week.

At the thought, he moved into his bedroom and stripped out of his clothes and laid out in his bed. As he lay there, his eyes were closed, and he turned onto his side - but he could hear the chaos of the world. Whether it was real or imaginary, he wasn't sure. He wanted to believe that this would come to an end. He wanted to think that this was a fluke - Ellie would call it a glitch in the matrix.

"Goddamnit, you need to stop thinking about her," he grumbled to himself, turning on his opposite side with a huff. He pulled the blankets so tightly around himself that the heat automatically came with it. It was suffocating - much like his run-in with the nurse. He felt the warmth that radiated in his body and he felt his skin grow hot and prickly. His eyes were

squeezed so tightly shut that he felt the instant headache work its way into his body. He fought against the
warmth and he fought against the sadness and tried
his best to fall asleep.

Whenever he woke up, he found a bottle of alcohol
on the floor. He didn't remember resorting to alcohol
in order to fall asleep, but as he threw his legs over
the bed, he bumped it like the other bottle. He heard
it roll around and crash into the other one, now lost
in the world under his bed. He reached for his phone,
usually left on his table, but he didn't find it.

"Fuck," he said as he witnessed the white cord -
unplugged and hanging by his mattress. His phone,
found on the right side of the bed, was on 20%. Did
he need to worry about that anymore when he had
no one to text? How long until they lost power? This
thought in mind, he put the phone on the charger and
started to move. The only thing getting him through
this was knowing, and hoping, that Jackie had only
good news for him. The thought pushed the jeans
over his legs and pulled the shirt over his head. He put
on a scarf and adjusted it so that the handprints - now
black, were hidden and concealed. He moved his head
left to right, dropped his head to his shoulders, all to
ensure that the material covered everything well and
without any major problems. He sighed as he sent a
quick text to Jackie - the first in weeks, and he moved
out to his car.

There was a silence that lingered in the streets and
he watched as the yellow police tape waved in the
wind. Another crime scene neglected, he assumed.

Tatum knew that the police never came for him
because of the number of murders he saw last night.
There had to of been over five in the hall he was in,
not to mention the madness that was taking place
on the lower levels. That was just in one building and
he was scared to think about what was happening
in colleges, hotels, and apartments. There was no
way they'd be able to say he was responsible for this.
Not whenever the entire world has lost their mind.
No one is safe – clearly, and this illness is just taking
anyone. He was still thinking rationally, or at least
as far as he was concerned he was, but there was that
part of him that waited for the police lights to show
up behind him. He waited for the police to take him
away in handcuffs, for the world to end while he
awaited trial. He expected that they'd forget about
him, leave him in a cell, and he'd rot and die in there.
There was that part of him that wondered if that was
the better option. Sure, starving to death would suck,
but wouldn't that be better than being murdered?
No, he couldn't think about that. He needed to keep
true to the words he told Ellie - the world wasn't ending. They'd figure this out and he'd be saved.

He flicked through the radio stations as he drove,
he listened to the voices as they covered the cases -
the death numbers were rising. Jails were overcrowd-
ing. People weren't getting put in front of a judge.
Prison riots. Rioting in the streets. More spreading of
whatever... this was. It had the official title of a virus
now, and it was now being labeled as an epidemic.
They weren't sure if it was pandemic level yet, as no

reports of random murder was being reported anywhere else. There was that same sick part of Tatum
that wondered if that's because all reporters are
being murdered before they got the chance to warn
everyone.

"When do you think military involvement will
take place? Do we think it is going to get to that
point?" a male's voice asked, his voice smooth and
his voice eerily calm despite all of this.

"If the military isn't moving in already, I would expect that to happen sooner rather than later. People
are being murdered at random by the hundreds...
most experts expect it to keep happening unless
some action is taken," a woman's voice replied.

"But what kind of action can be taken against
people murdering one another in seemingly point-
less or unprompted ways?" the male asked. "Who's to
say this isn't just some outbreak of anger that could
be related to the heat, or something else, for that
matter?"

"Thank you!" Tatum celebrated at the break-
through this man just had via the radio. This is what
he's been saying all along. This was just a misunder-
standing - it had to be. People murdered, yes. Some
people did it for entertainment and fun. But this was
their world filled with billions of people. For so many
to turn into random murderers? Is that something
that could be heat related? Even the most hopeful
part in Tatum's mind struggled to convince himself
of that idea.

"Everything is so uncertain right now." Yeah, no

shit. "It is going to be a trial and error process, but right now officials are begging people to stay away from overpopulated areas, to keep their distance, even from loved ones. At least until all of this is figured out."

Tatum hadn't realized that his fingers had found their way into his mouth, chewing at pieces of flesh until blood poked out from his cuticles. The blood's taste was bitter in his mouth as he pulled the hand away and placed it on the steering wheel in front of him. He took in a long breath and exhaled, his other hand turning the radio down and leaving himself with his own thoughts. Being distant and away from others would be easy enough for him - he didn't have anyone left. Sure, he had Jackie, but that was a work-oriented relationship. He couldn't turn to her for anything unless it was something to do with writing. He had no family, no girlfriend to turn to. He could just hold up in his house, drink his booze, smoke his cigarettes, and write. Shit, he may be able to finish this thing in two weeks if required to stay home. That sounded like heaven...if that kind of thing existed.

Whenever he arrived at Jackie's building, he put the car in park and didn't bother locking the doors as he walked inside. He rode the rickety elevator up to floor four and then he walked to suite four-thirty-seven. He moved into the office and waited to be greeted by the woman that worked the front desk. She was too young for him, too innocent even, and all too annoying. Her voice was too high pitched, and her smile was all too wide - something he was never able to get over. But the desk was empty - along with the waiting room. Usually, the place was busy with clients in suits - bouncing knees, hands brushing through hair, briefcase with their manuscripts eagerly waiting. Some would have the damn thing in their hand - rolled up, sweated on, bent, and unprofessional. Jackie ripped him a new one on their first meeting. Told him that she should set the thing on fire and send him on his way. He never turned up with a manuscript in less than ideal condition ever again. At least he learned something, right?

But the room was empty, the halls ghost-like. There wasn't a soul that populated the building, the only sound coming from his feet as they scuffed up against the carpeting. There was a buzz of light above reception, the tinking of a fly trying to kill itself in one of the lights. Or maybe it was trying to escape, Tatum would never know. He listened for something to happen, a buzz of a phone, a slam of a door, the rustle of paper, but he heard nothing. No welcoming committee awaited him. Loneliness. This was about to be their new normal, and no part of Tatum resented that thought.

Despite no watchful eyes, he hesitated at the edge of reception. He knew where Jackie's office was, but why couldn't he find the nerve to keep walking? Maybe he should call first? As he weighed his options, the door kicked open.

"Tatum!" she exhaled. "How long have you been waiting?" she asked as she moved to wrap her arms around him. He shrunk against her frame as he felt the electric shocks of her touch. He felt the handprints around his neck pulse, his hands gripping at the thin material. He adjusted it around his neck and he pulled away as quickly as he could to get a look at her.

"Not long, I just got here. Was kind of shocked at how quiet it is," he admitted as he followed her back into the stuffy office. He watched as she moved to sit down, his manuscript sitting on her desk. He could see the red pen scribbles and he watched as her hands threaded together. Her manicure had grown in and her hands appeared to be drier than normal. This apocalypse was affecting everyone, he supposed.

"So, most publishing houses are shutting down, as you may know by now," Jackie admitted, a small smile on her lips. "We're going to be up and running, even if it means working remotely, wherever that may be. Now, the problem lies in getting books out there," Jackie said to him, "We can only do so much here. The rest of the things are reliant on other companies, warehouses, and the like. Think about your manufacturers, the book cover, the production company, the list goes on." Jackie moved to flick through the pages she had printed out.

"So, what does this mean for me and you? For Chelsea and Spencer's story?" Tatum asked as he leaned back in the stiff chair, his ankle crossed over his knee.

"You're going to go home, and you are going to write this book. I have a list of edits and other things, suggestions, even. You will keep me updated, but we will try to meet as little as possible...government standards or whatever." Jackie waved her hand dismissively. "I just want you to be aware that the world is very... iffy right now. We're going to stay open for as long as possible and we are going to push whatever content we can," she said to him.

"So, what was the point of this meeting, then?" Tatum asked as he felt his fingers clench.

"I just want you to know where we are all standing in all of this," Jackie replied as Tatum immediately stood to his feet. "I also figured it would be good to see another person that wasn't my husband." Wasn't that what the people on the news just told everyone to avoid?

"Just write the rest of the book, Tatum, send it my way, and we will see where the world is. I just can't promise anything right now, but I don't want you to waste this gift. Right now, you have me hooked, and I think that once all of this is over, we could sell it to the right people and get a deal of some sort. We're talking movies, TV shows, isn't that what you want?" She asked him, "I know it is. So let's work together and get this done."

Even through the pleasantries, Tatum could feel the sizzle of stress and anger in his body. What a crock of shit. His gift being wasted? He found that laughable as Tatum stormed out of the office, his face burning and his stomach churning. He knew that Jackie wasn't to blame for all of this. Not an ounce of it was her fault, and yet, that was where all of his anger felt directed. He knew he needed to blame it on the end of the fucking world, and he knew his ego yet again boosted him a bit too high. Why did he expect to go into this meeting and for her to give him everything he wanted to hear? He knew just days prior all he wanted was for her to love the story, and now that she did, he wanted more? His anger pulsed, and he knew he was starting to decline mentally, but he couldn't stop himself. He moved out to his car and got into the driver seat - not caring if murderers or the next infected person was hiding away in his back seat. As far as he was concerned, no one was going to mess with him right now. He drove, fingers white-knuckled and arms on fire. As he drove, the music was down, the thought of listening to someone else's voice being unbearable, and he stared at the open world in front of him. He could end it all - what was with the 'don't waste this gift 'bullshit that Jackie was trying to feed him? Something to make him feel like she didn't just waste his and her time? All it would take was an acceleration of the gas, pedal to the ground, and a jerk of the wheel. Whether that be off a cliff, into a ditch, into a tree, he didn't care right now.

Somehow, though, he made it home. He wasn't sure if it was the blind rage, if it were his anger that pushed him, or the need to get home, he just knew that one minute he was considering driving his car off somewhere, and the next he was back at his place.

He clenched and unclenched his fingers, his fists balled up and then relaxed. He shook out his hands in attempts to calm down and he tried to push through the feelings in his body. What was he feeling? Dread? Pain? Hurt? Remorse? Anger? He wasn't sure as his hands moved to sweep the entirety of his table's contents onto the ground. Everything was everywhere and the sound of plates crashing, papers flying, all echoed a hundred times over in the house. He picked up an empty bottle of vodka and chucked it at the wall. All his work, all these gifts, all about to be wasted. For what? Some virus? Some temporary blip? He yelled out as he threw the next bottle and watched the liquid spray outward and watched the glass splinter outwards and onto the ground.

What was the point of it all? Why did he sit around for so long doing nothing? Sure, the end of the world would still be inevitable, but at least then he'd have something for the survivors to find. He'd have books, movies, he'd have interviews. He'd have it all, and his words would be left for the survivors to put in their backpacks as they traveled on foot - trying to survive this crazy world. Right now, though? All they have is a stupid series of books about a devil falling in love with a mortal. The book series is tasteless. It isn't the man he is now.

"Why couldn't Ellie get pregnant sooner?" he asked as his hand drove through the wall. At least then he would've gotten the idea sooner, maybe he would've come up with something better, even. The story he has right now is good. Everything is making sense. The beginning, the middle, and the ending - it's all there. Would anyone get to see it? Or would he die as a pile of wasted potential? The thought made him sick - vomit flying out of his mouth and onto the floor with a sickening splatter. As he shook out his fingers, blood from his now probably broken hand showered the floor, creating a concoction of blood and stomach contents. He hissed out as he tasted the vomited chunks that rested in his throat, uncertain as to whether they wanted to come up with the rest of their friends. He wiped his mouth, blood smearing from his knuckles to his face.

His laptop was in his hand next. The rose gold colored shell getting coated in bloody fingerprints. He should write - the only thing that has managed to save him all these years. The only escape he's ever truly had. He could write whatever he wanted - it didn't even have to be Chelsea's story. He could write his heart out - write a story about blood and violence. Write a story about kinky underground sex clubs. He could write a fucking vampire love story. Or that damn last book in *The Devils* series Jackie keeps begging him for. No one was going to see it anyway, right? What was the point? What was the point?

"What's the point?" he asked as he lifted the heavy object above his head and there it went - splintering against the ground. The damn thing didn't even break into pieces like he expected it to. No, it just clattered and clanged to the ground as he brought his foot up to kick the stupid thing. It did him more damage than it gave him relief, his body starting to grow with more and more fury. His fingers found another bottle of booze, but he didn't chuck this one. He pulled it open and chugged down its contents within a few minutes. As he wiped the blood from his skin, the vomit and alcohol too, he moved into his fridge. There really

was nothing in the stupid piece of shit - the light bulb
was broken and the inside contents weren't that cold.
He pulled out a bottle of beer - probably expired
and flat as hell, but he chugged it down as his fingers
fumbled for cigarettes. He brought the cancer stick
to his lips and inhaled as blood dripped from his fist
and he unwound the scarf from around his neck and
he wrapped it a few times over. He wound the thing
so tightly around his knuckles that he felt it as the
material stuck to his wounds, mopping up any wet
blood that tried to spill out.

He dug through the contacts on his phone and
the ideas started to come at him slowly. What if he
didn't need Jackie to find the things he needed for
him? He could edit the book himself. No, he didn't
go to school for it or anything, but it didn't matter.
The only people that really got upset over grammar
were the people that had too much time on their
hands. Who really cares if a stupid comma is out of
place or if there's a run-on sentence? If you could
read what the author was saying, who cared about it
being grammatically correct? Tatum surely didn't.
Okay, that was a start. He'd edit the damn book himself if Jackie didn't want to help him, fine. He knew
of a few graphic designers, they all didn't need to be
huddled into one studio to work, right? That's what
computers and programs were for - easy to transfer,
easy to work from home. But what if the graphic designers were dead? Fuck, he didn't think about that.
Okay, so he'd have a basic cover. People, for the most
part, already knew his name. He didn't need an eye-

drawing cover to bring attention to his books. He'd do fine in sales based on his name alone. Okay, now he was getting somewhere. His fingers flew eagerly, blowing up Jackie's phone with his manic ideas and thought processes. The entire screen was purely little blue bubbles, but Tatum kept going. Now he wished that he didn't slam his laptop into the ground and shit, now he'd have to type the damn thing on the documents app on his phone. That was fine. He'd do it old school if he had to. Things would be more complicated, sure, but that was probably going to be his life now. He'd have to slum it.

He chugged more beer than his throat had time to take down, resulting in the sputtering of alcohol. It burned just as bad coming up, and he moved his feet to step over the pile of vomit in the kitchen. It's something he'd clean up later - he had no time right now. He moved to plop his body on his bed and laid on his back. The quicker he wrote the book, the faster he got Jackie on board, and the quicker he could get his book out there. He wanted to get it out pre-apocalypse. How cool would it be for his book to be known as the last book written and published before the world ended? Yes, he was writing his legacy. This is the stuff they'd find in abandoned bookstores. He wanted this more than anything, so he pulled out his phone, and started to write.

UNTITLED CHAPTER FIVE

The two men stared at her - both with yellowing teeth and the signs of poor hygiene. They smiled at her and the one tilted his head. "We saw you guys come in, and you never left, so we decided that we may as well introduce ourselves," the man, who was presumably the leader, spoke.

"My name is Oliver, this here is my buddy, Ethan," he gestured to the man with the all too deadly scowl painted on his face. "What's your name?" he asked.

"Her name is none of your goddamn business," Spencer's voice called from behind the two bodies, arrow drawn and ready to fire. That was the motive Chelsea needed as she pulled the knife from her pocket and pointed it towards the man. She knew her little knife didn't stand a chance, but for a few moments of empowerment, it was worth it.

"You move, I shoot you in the leg, my friend slits your buddies throat. Understand?" Spencer asked as she looked over at Chelsea. Chelsea was unable to read whether if the woman was upset or disappointed in her - she had one job. Chelsea also wondered if Spencer really counted on her to slit anyone's throat, but Chelsea hoped she wouldn't have to find out.

"Easy," the man named Oliver said as he held his hands up. "We just wanted to welcome you aboard. What do you need? We have food, clothes," he offered as he took a step closer to Chelsea.

"Don't. Move." Spencer pulled back tighter on the bow as she watched the man intensely, green eyes focused on both men. "We don't need anything from you."

"But you broke into our neighborhood? Staying in one of our houses?" Ethan spoke up.

"We just needed a place to stay, and we will be out of your hair," Chelsea replied quietly. "We didn't want any trouble."

"We didn't break into anything. You left your neighborhood unguarded. Unprotected. We were just taking what was open to us," Spencer replied.

"Just tell us what you want," Oliver replied, mainly speaking to Spencer now.

"You're going to walk your creepy ass out of here, and you aren't going to bother us. Come nightfall, we will be out of your hair, and no one will bother us or follow," Spencer replied as she stepped closer, the tip of her arrow nearly touching the center of the man's stomach. "Sound fair?" she asked, an overgrown eyebrow raised.

Chelsea watched as the man shifted on his feet and she watched as his throat swallowed down a huge glob of spit. She stood ready, and before she knew it, Ethan was swinging, and Chelsea watched as her blade hit the floor with a solid thud. She yelled out as Ethan got her to the floor, a fistful of her blonde hair wrapped around his dirty fingers, a hand at the back of her skull. Her head met contact with the wood as she heard the scream of Ryan. It was the distraction she needed as she lifted her knife up to Ethan, and a simple lift upwards sent the blade into the side of his cheek. Chelsea watched as the man gripped the knife and screamed, trying to pull the blade out from his skin.

Spencer moved into action next, her arrow piercing the back of his head. No words were spoken as Chelsea looked at the two bodies, arrows lodged in their skulls, and as Spencer reached a hand forward. A simple tug brought Chelsea up to her feet and she took in a small breath as the sickening sound of the knife being pulled from Ethan's cheek was brought to her attention. Her blade was handed back to her, covered in bright blood, and she watched as Spencer placed her boot on Oliver's chest. She pulled up, releasing the arrow from its position, and tucked it away.

"We need to get out of here. The others will come looking for them when they don't return," Spencer said as she tugged the mask over her face. "Get Jillian, I'm going to take whatever supplies I can find." Before Chelsea could reply, the sound of boots echoing down the hall could be heard.

Chelsea took in a deep breath, her fingers finding her way to the back of her head. The fingers, slick with blood, were wiped on her shorts as she moved down the hall and made her way into Jillian's room. She gently shook the small girl - still in a deep sleep. For that, Chelsea was thankful, as explaining death to children never got any easier - even in the world in which they lived. The child had slept through it all, another blessing in this world filled with horror and destruction. Now to get out of here - unscathed and alive.

"Momma, your head," the girl reached her fingers up, but Chelsea caught her hand. Jillian's eyes were heavy with both sleep and confusion, blinks slow and drawn out. Chelsea kissed the girl's hand with a gentle smile and a squeeze.

"Just keep your head down, baby," Chelsea said as she grabbed a blanket and wrapped it around the child. "Don't look no matter what, 'kay?" she asked as she brushed the matter hair out of her face. "Just go back to sleep,"

"Is Spencer okay?"

"Me and Spencer are great, baby, we just need to get out of here," Chelsea kept her voice firm as she scooped up what she could - a blanket for the cold summer nights and a ratty elephant stuffed animal that Jillian seemed to cuddle up to. As she moved down the stairs, she found Spencer tossing stuff into a bag, a dirty bottle of water, some crackers, and another can of beans. She rummaged through the drawer and threw a pair of scissors at Chelsea before she brushed past her and towards the black door.

"We're not going to be able to get out the way we came. And we can forget them not being on high alert," Chelsea mentioned.

"That's why you're going to fall behind me. I take out whoever I can with my bow, and we do what is needed so that we survive. I don't think I need to remind you to stab someone if their survival odds seem higher, right?"

"I'm not an idiot, and I've made it this far," Chelsea replied as she hooked her fingers into the scissors 'loops. Jillian had seemed to fall back asleep, but she didn't count on the young child staying that way.

"On the count of three. One. Two..." Spencer's fingers found the door handle, pressing down on the gold-painted object. It opened with ease, the door creaking and groaning with age. The floor to ceiling blinds waved back and forth, dust falling from each line. There was a deadly silence that settled between the three of them and the neighborhood. They didn't know how many were out there and if they were on their way. They may have had no idea that Ryan and Ethan were heading to them to confront the intruders. Maybe they hadn't even noticed their absence.

"I don't see anybody," Spencer whispered as she looked back and forth, hand moving to shut the door behind them.

"I don't hear anyone, either," Chelsea re-marked as she looked over her shoulder, in the direction of where she saw the fires last night. She could still smell the smoke, but she could no longer see the movement. The place was just as quiet as it had been when they arrived, but they'd surely notice that two of their own were

missing. Chelsea scanned the empty streets -
decaying houses and playsets. Jillian would've
loved the red slide and would've gone down fifty
times had they not been in the middle of an
apocalypse. Jillian would've eventually jumped
from the top of it, fallen and scraped her knee.
Chelsea would've listened to John yell at her for
being so reckless- and Chelsea would've gotten
yelled at for not stopping her sooner. Chelsea
wouldn't have replied as she wiped the small
droplets of blood from her knee and cleaned the
dirt from her hands. Jillian would've whined if
she got the hello kitty band-aid as opposed to the
Spider-Man one, and Chelsea would've had to
either peel off the Band-Aid or listen to Jill whine
and complain all night long."

"Just give er 'the damn sticker for Cry's sake!"
John would lecture.

Different times. This wasn't how they were
two years ago. John was gone, either in a rebel
group of his own or dead. They were trying
to escape an enclosed neighborhood. Chelsea
would be lying if she said she didn't understand
John's frustration. Had Jill not been here, a run
and jump over a fence would've been completed
thirty seconds ago. Hell, they would've been able
to walk further last night. At the thought, she

brushed down Jillian's hair and made sure the child's eyes were still closed.

"How are we getting out of here?" Chelsea asked lowly, staying on Spencer's heels. The grass was yellowing and every dad's worst nightmare - weeds brushed past their slender hips and was harsh against tender skin. Chelsea watched as Spencer crouched down, the grass nearly going past her head as she did so. Chelsea followed and mirrored the female's movements, the grassy and summer-like scent flooding her nostrils. Jillian rubbed her nose into her mother's strap, stirring just slightly as the grass hit their body.

"We're gonna get as close to that gate as possible. Throw Jill over if we have to. They're not gonna let us walk out of here," Spencer replied as they looked around once more, but then they heard a loud whistle.

"We know yer 'out there!" a female yelled out, voice all too thick for a state that isn't in the south. She must be an outsider, Chelsea assumed. It led her to question what happened to the people that once resided in this neighborhood. Where did those people go?

"We were gonna be nice, but we found what ya did to our friends. But we'll give you a chance.

Expose yourselves now and we won't send the dogs out. Stay hidden, we send them out. Your choice,"

Chelsea wasn't even sure if Jillian had pet a dog, no less had one chase after her. Chelsea looked at Spencer, "There's no way they can know. They aren't even at the house," Chelsea tried to say to Spencer, who was already up on her feet.

"Okay," she said shortly. "You caught me," Spencer said to the group.

"Where's yer little friend? And that little girl?"

"She left this morning. Before you guys woke up."

All Chelsea could do is look up at the woman, shocked and uncertain on how long she'd be living in the grass.

CHAPTER TWELVE

If Tatum wanted to kill the trio off, now would be the time to do so. Or maybe he could see it off as some kind of short story - give the world a little ray of hope in this world filled with hatred and despair. Whenever he was a kid, he loved cliffhangers as it gave him something to look forward to and gave him something to work towards reading. His heart panged at the thought of Ellie never getting to finish her shows. She died uncertain as to whether her favorite characters on that stupid mystery show would live. She wouldn't force him to sit through another rose ceremony on both *The Bachelor* and *The Bachelorette*. He'd live his life without her - even though she was more eager to live her life than he'd ever been. Some would call him ungrateful and some would probably trade his life for hers. He shook his head again - no, he just needed to focus on getting this book out. He needed to write, finish their story, but get it out as quickly as possible. People loved coming up with their own theories and endings, right? He could put this short story out, re-engage his old audience, and build up a new one. This wasn't a love story - this was an apocalypse story. People would relate to it, he knew this. He knew this! Whenever their world was turning to shit, people weren't going to relate to a sappy love story, no. They were going to relate and fall in love with fighters and survivors.

He sat back and pressed on the pressure point between his thumb and pointer finger. He pressed until the pain was unbearable, and nothing gave him the relief he looked for. He examined his hand and squeezed again, part of him wishing he could pull the tension out of the muscles and unknown vessels. The tingles flooded through his fingers and he shook them out in attempts to gain feeling back. As he tried to stretch and pull at his hands to bring awareness to them, he stood up and moved towards the window. It was hard to look at it the same without thinking of Ellie staring at him - staring through him. It was hard to imagine the last time he looked out this window - both Ellie and the girl next door were alive and breathing. They were both taken from the world now, cruelly, and too soon. But he was writing to bring justice to their deaths. He was going to avenge them through Spencer and Chelsea, part of him tempted to change their names. He could dedicate Ellie to Chelsea - the small, mousy, and agile type. He didn't even know the characteristics of his neighbor, but he could make something up he was sure. It was the thought that counted. He'd dedicate the books to them - to the people that were lost in this time. Yes, that all sounded right in his nearly scrambled mind.

He pulled the curtains over the window that stared into the starless sky and then went into the kitchen. Food didn't sound appetizing, nor did the thought of booze. He found himself staring out a second portal - memories flashing back to the last time he stood in this spot. He could still hear her screams - plain as day. He wondered if he moved faster if he could've changed the outcome of it all. He flipped to lean against the sink now, hands rubbed over his face. He didn't inspect the kitchen too thoroughly, in fear that he would see more of Ellie's blood or a phantom image of her. He was scared shitless of seeing some piece of evidence that the police left behind - scared shitless of the moment he'd see her around his house.

He knew if he continued to think this way, he'd drive himself mad. He needed to stop thinking about Ellie and the neighbor - they were dead, and he was alive. He wondered what the death toll was up to, and he wondered how in the hell he was still kicking. He moved to the small TV and once again flicked on the stations, all of which had fallen quiet in a matter of days. He flicked until he found one - a room that was once filled with news anchors now having dwindled to one brave soul.

Even then, he could sense the scripts that ran through her bones - the way her eyes stared past the camera as opposed to looking into it. He watched the way they darted just slightly, almost to the point that she was robotic in her line delivery, her words not reaching him.

"Military has yet to get involved, and deaths are skyrocketing for no rhyme or reason. Hospital beds are limited, and 911 calls are starting to get over-whelming. Police are unable to keep up with the in-flux of criminal activity, prisons being overcrowded and those with lesser convictions are being released from holding. We still aren't sure if there is an end in sight to any of this, or if a cure is what we should be searching for."

A cure. A cure for insanity. Tatum couldn't help but chuckle at the thought. Human on human mur-der had been happening for thousands of years, and now they expect a poke of a needle to stop it? How many people would line up, person after person, to get a needle stuck in their arm to cure the incurable? No, this was going to be survival of the fittest. There was no military propaganda, no population control. Merely surviving. Hell, he could go his entire life without encountering another human, he would be safe. He laughed at the ignorance of humans - the ignorance in the thought of needing human touch to survive. He let out another chuckle, to the point that his stomach shook, and his throat rattled. He wasn't sure the last time he laughed, or let a chuckle stumble past his drunken lips, but here he stood. He stood in the window frame, a mere ghost among the stretches of darkness. His neighborhood was shown real fear, the things that only haunted video games and cheesy movies. These were the things people wrote about and he stood amongst it all. He stood within the madness and could only hope that the world would work itself out. Survival of the fittest and all that, and Tatum assumed he would do just fine on his own, he's made it this far.

"There has been talk about shutting down the borders to prevent the spread of whatever this is. Local authorities are trying to keep people put, but they are stressing that there is no reason to panic."

No need to panic his ass. He had nearly been slaughtered by his best friend and was almost strangled to death by his nurse. The hospital was on the verge of being burned to the ground when he left, and he could only imagine it was going to get worse. He knew there were security officers and the like at that hospital, but not even they could save all the people in that huge hospital. Tatum still wasn't sure how he got out alive.

He moved towards the living room and sat on the couch, now two separate televisions on, playing a different channel. Both voices mingled together, and he acted as if his right ear listened to one while the left listened to the other. It was nothing but nonsense to him, nonsense that he truly didn't care about or care for, he was just along for the ride. The one thing worse than an idiot was an uncultured idiot, one that had no clue what was going on in the world. He needed to be aware, but that didn't mean he was going to like it. No one was holding a gun to his head. No one was forcing him to stay up to date, but here he sat. Was it too soon to talk about being held at gunpoint? Would there ever be a time in which he could talk about that stuff flippantly? He wasn't 'sure as he moved into his bedroom and laid out on his bed, hands moving to rub his face.

For the first time in many nights, he didn't need to completely blackout to sleep. He didn't need to smoke himself into oblivion. He just drifted off into a faraway land. He didn't dream - his mind was a blank slate. There was a part of him that still didn't feel refreshed, a part of him that always felt as if he had run a marathon only to get run over by a dump truck, but it was what he needed to push through the day. He must've not been the most aware, as he was suddenly holding a cup of coffee in his hands, the steam rising, and the bold smell drifting into his nose. He looked down at the liquid, surrounded by a dark blue cup, making the coffee a black pit in appearance. He watched as the steam rose, the cup hotter to hold than the handle. He felt the burn at his fingertips, wondering just how much it would take to burn them off. He sat for a minute, wondering when he made this cup of coffee.

That was whenever he started to wonder when Ellie made her cups of coffee the other night. Was it last night or the night before that? He couldn't remember. What he did remember was her several cups, all strewn about but ready to be drank out of. Some were colder than the others, sure, but he also knew that Ellie wasn't in a sound state of mind. He knew that the girl was somewhat clean, somewhat orderly. No, she wasn't a neat freak, but she also didn't live in piles of garbage like he did. The thought prompted him to look at his shoulder, bone protruding from his skin exposed by the shirt that was too large for him, and his eyes scanned the surface of his countertops. He moved quickly now, the cup still burning off his hands, and his eyes landed in the sink.

The pot, crusted over with Alfredo sauce and two noodles, still sat in the sink. He watched as the flies crawled over the rounded parts, and he couldn't help but fear what other creatures lived in the garbage disposal or in the areas below the pot. In the sink, he didn't notice any signs warning him that he was losing his mind. Fresh cups of coffee didn't line the bottom of the sink with steam rising from them. He carefully lifted the mug that was in there, but it wasn't a fresh cup. No, that shit was crusted over and chunks of what he assumed to be mold floated. The dishes weren't fresh and new, they were dirty - filthy, even. Part of him considered calling up the hospital to tell them a side effect may be making too many cups of coffee. No, they wouldn't believe him. He'd be accused of not taking this whole thing seriously and he'd just made out to be an ass. He couldn't afford bad press or a knock to his reputation. Tatum Hyland wasn't going to go down for an insensitive comment. No, he'd keep to himself. He wasn't going to lose his mind. He knew the symptoms now. Too many cups of coffee, distant stare, the cough, and dropping things unexpectedly.

His eyes scanned the countertops, his coffee pot, the Keurig that Ellie bought him three Christmases ago. The coffee pot had a crack in it and hasn't been used in months, not since he let it run only to discover brown liquid spreading through all the crevices of his tile flooring. Tatum was sure that there were probably still brown stains from the incident in his kitchen. The Keurig was still plugged in, so he assumed that was what he used to get his caffeinated beverage, but he wasn't sure what flavor he put in or if any sweetener was dumped into it. The coffee didn't resemble that of milk, so he could only assume that it was black.

With the cup lifted to his lips he ignored the steam's familiar burn and welcomed in the bold flavor. The liquid assaulted his tongue, bringing familiar boils to it, and he could feel the lava as it burned down his throat and didn't cool down until it reached down past his sternum.

"Our president still hasn't made an official statement on the things taking place worldwide."

"Do we take that as a good sign or a bad one?"

A bad one, obviously. Tatum figured that they were probably scrambling, trying to find the reasoning behind it all before they spoke. The president couldn't fuck up, not when the entire world was going up in flames. Tatum took to Twitter next, scrolling through the thousands of tweets and retweets.

My best friend was murdered today. You probably won't see much of me anymore. RIP

Is it time to sell my bonds and take all my cash? #ImpendingApocalypse?

Tatum's fingers hesitated over the words and he watched as the world started to fall into a panic. He wondered just how many people have died, how many of his followers were affected. He didn't know the usernames or their profile pictures, most of these people he probably followed in some kind of writer's lift. He tried to put reasoning behind only what he assumed to be their insanity, but he came up empty.

Fuck, was their world coming to an end? Was one of the last pieces of advice that he offered up to Ellie a lie? No, the world wasn't ending. There was already talk about a vaccine. Sure, he was just shitting on it five minutes ago, but if it ultimately meant he could publish his book without a problem, what harm could it do? There would probably be no way to tell if the stupid thing worked, as murders would forever occur. Did that mean that every murderer put on trial could say it was the virus that did this? That they were in no control? How many people would get off on a ruse like that one? Tatum tucked the thought away for safekeeping, but if he wasn't infected now, would he ever be? Three people, all of whom have presumably had this virus, have physically touched him. Two even had their hands around his throat. If physical contact didn't give it to him, what would? Was he immune?

"Stop it," he said aloud as he moved through the house and into the bathroom. He stood over the sink and his fingers clutched the porcelain marble. He held it like a lifeline before he flicked the faucet on, and his eyes watched as the water made its appearance. He cupped some of the water in his hand and threw it onto his face, most of the liquid hitting his chin and chest instead. With the relaxation of the water that hit him, he wondered what was happening outside the safety of his bathroom. Part of him wanted to wander into the world, to walk on the streets, and experience the tragedy around him. At least then, he would have his content handed to him. The material for his book would be there, but did he want to put himself at risk? Did he want to put his life at risk in order to get content? Or should he just stay behind, lock himself in, and brave this storm? At the thought, he knew he was ill-prepared. People were dying and here he stood moronically, not an object in place for protection. If someone were to come into his house right now, he would be caught with his pants down. The thought sprung him into action, feet moving across the tile flooring and into his bedroom.

He never owned a gun, no less fired one, so his choice of weaponry was limited. He got on his hands and knees and knelt next to his bed, eyes scanning its surface. Dust flew up into his nostrils and tickled the insides of his nose, but he managed to spot what he was looking for. He was surprised it had been there, one of the only objects having survived his previous tumultuous relationship with his father. The bat was heavy in his hands, probably weighing more than his right arm as he gave it a few practice swings. It wasn't ideal, as it would only incapacitate any enemy for a few short minutes, but he didn't know if he had it in him to kill someone by bashing their heads in. He assumed maybe he was more like Chelsea than he thought - only a survivor to a certain extent.

He set the bat near his bedroom door then wandered out into the kitchen, fingers grabbing the handles to his cupboards. He pulled each of them open, sometimes only finding cups and pots. He opened the others, eyes landing on things like stale crackers, left out of their packaging, or some boxes of cereal he had forgotten he had. He couldn't remember the last time he sat and had a bowl of cereal, hence the boxes left to collect dust in the cupboard. He couldn't survive merely on this shit alone, but he didn't want to brave the grocery stores. He was insane, but not that insane. He'd just have to hold up with what he had.

Loneliness had never bothered Tatum before, but why did he feel the ache in his heart. Was that once filled with Ellie, and now that she was gone, he had nothing? There was a gnawing in his chest, a deep feeling in his bones that reminded him he might just end up in the world alone. He might end up dying in the corner, bat in his hand, with no one left to find him. He might end up a skeleton, propped against a wall, waiting for the looters to come and discover his bones. Loneliness was something Tatum thrived on. He needed it to write and to function. He needed his bed to himself and he didn't need another body to fulfill him. He could say he was all he needed in this world, but without Ellie, who would fill the void? The void would so eagerly take him in, never spit him out again. Loneliness would become him slowly but surely, but maybe that was the key to survival. He knew, ultimately, that another person would be someone else to worry about. It would be someone else who would hold emotional baggage over his head, someone he'd have to protect every day. Tatum ultimately didn't like the thought, but who wouldn't want someone like Spencer around in an apocalypse?

He looked at the time and he knew that it was better late than never. He had his meeting with Jackie-his only light in the darkened tunnel of his life.

He and Jackie were going to create something great. He and Jackie were going to be the last book put out before the world ended. He and Jackie were going to do this.

The world would end knowing Tatum Hyland. He'd be the poster man of a life that once was and Chelsea and Spencer would be the images of survival, the images of hope.

He could do this. He needed to do this.

CHAPTER THIRTEEN

Tatum didn't have much else to show for the time between when he spoke to Jackie on the phone and right at this moment. He had written another chapter, but he forwarded it to her email already. He merely wasted precious paper to present his work to her. He had a list of prompts to give her for when she inevitably told him that they were talking about pushing back all projects until things resumed to normal. If he got through to her that they were going to thrive off their current timing, they'd be golden. There would be nothing they couldn't do, and people would chew up the mere thought of carrying around his book in their apocalyptic world. Their branding would be the last book ever. His tweets and promotion would read:

If you're going to be stuck in a room, surviving the apocalypse, you may as well be reading a good book!

It would sell. It would be high in demand. The kind of book people wouldn't want to lose in the mail. If his books were the only pieces of mail being delivered in a time like this, it would be a success story.

In a time where the world had nothing, they had his book.

He gave them one thing to look forward to.

The once full parking lot was now empty. He used to remember a time where he'd have to drive circles around the lot until he found a spot that wasn't too far away. Now he pulled up three spots back from the handicapped parking, and he moved inside the building. There was no security to buzz him in, and there was no one to check his bag or tell him he could go up to the fourth floor. There was no one to hold his laptop like it was some sort of explosive, and the one rounder security guard wasn't here to give him grief over the allowance of his devices. There was no one to stop him and demand that she call Jackie before allowing him up, the place was just a ghost town. Even more so than the last time he was here. What was that, like two days ago? If that? Nothing looked out of place, the building had yet to be ransacked, so maybe the world wasn't as bad as the news made it out to be. Maybe the world as he knew it wasn't coming to an end and this was merely a blip. Merely a string of convenient hostile aggressions. Something that could be tied to the weather, the moon's gravitational pull, or something stupid like that. They'd receive answers and all the believers would be made fools of.

But what about Ellie? She wasn't an aggressive person. The girl couldn't hurt anyone even if she needed to, and she would hear out anyone's side of the story. She was the kind of girl to sit and listen to anyone talking, and she would go out of her way to help others. He couldn't help but question why she had to die, and he got to live. Why would the earth take her? Why would the void choose to suck her in and not spit her out? Why did the universe choose her? He didn't want to die, he had too much to offer. But, when it came to Ellie living and him dying, would he have responded differently? He knew he was the one that drove a knife through her chin and killed her, of course he knew this, but she didn't leave him any other choice. He begged her not to make him do this, but she kept stepping forward. She wouldn't stop. Ellie was dead and he was alive, and while he still wondered why, he knew someone bigger and stronger was calling the shots, and he was kept here for a reason. That reason was to publish books. To be a beacon of hope.

He moved into Jackie's office, unlocked and open for anyone to come in. He assumed that Jackie was already in, but when he moved into the back room, she still wasn't there. He paced, looking at her tank of fishes until he saw the Nemo looking fish floating on its back. His face twisted at the smell that came from the tank, and he stepped away quickly, moving to distract himself with her desk. He moved through

the various knick knacks and objects, the things
nearly child and toylike in nature. He smoked a cigarette as he looked at the multiple awards that hung on
the wall, and next, he looked at the degree that was
proudly put in the middle of it. He wondered when
she walked the stage and got that degree if she knew
the amount of success she'd acclaim by fifty. He wondered if she had her sights set on this position, this
office. He wondered if her parents were proud.

His fingers touched the plaque cut out of the cover
of *The Devil's Bride* that also had the pesky #1 *New York
Times* Bestseller on the bottom. He smiled gently
at the accomplishment, thinking back to when he
found out. He was young, innocent, and he didn't
know how much his life would change back then.
Whenever this happened, he felt unstoppable, and
now he knew that life didn't slow down for anyone.
There was always someone bigger and better, someone hungrier and more willing to do anything to get
on top. He's since lost his spunk and he noticed that
the cover for *The Devil's Child* didn't make it onto her
makeshift hall of fame - as the title only made it to
the top ten spots on the bestseller list.

It was then his phone rang and he noticed Jackie
fifteen minutes late. It was Jackie that always lectured him on timeliness. Jackie was the one always
fifteen minutes early for meetings, and an hour early
for events. Jackie was never late.

"Jackie, where are you?" The first time they met,
Tatum was twenty minutes early and Jackie nearly
turned him away at the door. At that time, she told

him if he wasn't at the very least thirty minutes early, then he must not really be that serious about his writing. Since then, he was always absurdly early. It was a nasty habit she instilled under his bones, sometimes having to pay an additional thirty minutes on parking due to being too early to events. Sometimes having to suffer through tickets to ease his time-related anxiety. Now it was his turn to question her and demand to know what was so important in her life that made her waste his time. It was his turn to push for answers, to raise an eyebrow at her once she came through the door.

"Tatum, I have some bad news," she said to him.

The drop in his chest appeared, a stunt in his breathing. Bad things didn't exist in Jackie's world. The woman only knew success. She only knew greatness and wonders.

"We're closing up shop. This is over."

CHAPTER FOURTEEN

"What... what do you mean this is over?" he asked her, mouth dry. "I thought you liked what I had to offer," he breathed out to her, the feeling of sickness rising to his body. This wasn't merely a breakup between friends or a boyfriend and a girlfriend. This was something more. His livelihood being ripped away from him. Was it him, or was it Jackie? Was she going to let him know? Was she going to give him a list of things? Tell him that if he needed references, he could ask?

"I love what you have, it's not that, Tatum." There was a shake in her voice, something that sounded like desperation.

"Then what is it?" he finally asked, grip tightening on his phone and his teeth grinding together to the point that they ached at the pressure.

"The world, Tatum. We have to close up for good."

"Why?" he asked her.

"Because we aren't essential. No one is going to buy a book in the condition we are in now," she replied to him. "Are you going to be okay?" she finally asked after a long silence.

"We can do this, Jackie. Imagine how much attention we'd get if we were the last book to be published before the world ended! We don't need publishers or graphic designers. We can do it on our own... old school," he pleaded as he started to pace.

"I'm sorry, Tatum. I wish there were another way, some kind of alternative," Jackie said to him, "They're shutting us down. We aren't legally allowed to do anything."

"No, this is bullshit." Tatum gripped onto his phone, fists tight and teeth grinding.

"It's not bullshit, Tatum. This is serious. Our world may be in some trouble," she nearly lectured him through the phone. "The world doesn't want to be buying any kind of entertainment. Not whenever everything is breaking into pieces. The banks are crashing, people are pulling out of contract agreements, stores are closing to prevent them from being looted. No one is going to be buying books right now."

"The world is going to be fine. We're going to be fine." Tatum paced back and forth now, shoes scuffing against the carpet as he walked quicker. He stumbled as the tip of his shoe hit the carpet, falling forward slightly before he balanced himself.

"Tatum. It's over. Maybe someday we can come back to this. But that time... isn't right now. You need to take care of yourself, and you need to keep safe. People are crazy these days."

Tatum didn't need to hear it from Jackie. He didn't need to hear how the world was ending, how it was coming to a close. He didn't need to hear about how he would go down in history known as the romance guy. If he could do it all over again, he would. He wouldn't have written a sappy love story. He would've written a story about survival and getting through whatever was needed to make it. He would've been a different kind of big and a different type of success. He would've been the ruler of this world, and he would've been the best that the world had ever seen. Now he was going to die like the rest of the world - as some nobody. As a has-been.

Tatum's hands found the surface of Jackie's desk before he could balance the pros and cons of his actions. His forearm made contact with the computer first, and he watched as he swiped the entirety of their contents onto the floor. It crashed and it clanged, and with each sound of something breaking, he felt relief. He let out a scream, his vocal cords ripped and tugging as he pulled out one of the file cabinet drawers. It popped out and joined everything else on the floor, breaking and splattering from one side of the room to the other. Pens and papers joined in heaps and puddles on the floor, cabinet drawers and computers fought for dominance, one trying to reach the top before the other one. He watched as the

Rubix cube sat as King on top, a name plaque falling under it - where it belonged, in Tatum's eyes.

His foot moved to kick the desk next, his toenail splintering into the tip of his shoe. He felt the cool crackle of the nail, and the desk hardly budged under the pressure. He moved now to press the heels of his hands into the corners, the strain and the pull of his lower back urging him forward. The desk flipped on its side and crushed all the objects under its weight.

"Fuck!" he yelled out as he pushed his fingers through his hair. He fought back the tears of anger and the frustration as he kicked the carnage at his feet. His hands ripped through his hair now, hands balling and holding locks of brown. "No!" he yelled, teeth-gritting. "No, no, no, no." He pulled until small locks were plucked from his head, and until strands added to the piles of shit on the floor. For good measure, he delivered another kick, feeling a burning sensation in his toes. "No," he declared again as he rolled out his spine and then his shoulders. No, Tatum Hyland didn't break things in rage. He didn't kick or punch things. This wasn't him. He needed to get back to who he was all those years ago. All he wanted was to re-brand himself, but maybe the romance guy was what people wanted.

He didn't need Jackie to get what he wanted. No, that was what independent and private publishers were for. It wouldn't be hard to finish his book and come up with a simple cover, right? Hell, he's seen books that had nothing more than a title and a name on a plain colored background. It wouldn't be hard to upload it, do this whole damn thing himself. He had the following, he'd promote endlessly, make sure people knew he was back, and he would be a success story again. He would be known as the guy who couldn't be told no - who stopped at nothing. How great would it be to say that he could publish his own book, even in the apocalypse? That he was able to fight the odds, write for the people who couldn't write and get his work out there? People would see him as a determined man, one that stopped at nothing. They'd title him as hard-working, a man who truly cared for the entertainment of those left in a cruel world. People would want to thank him for his tireless efforts to get his art out there. He'd be known for stopping at nothing to get it out. He'd inspire others to write and to do what they wanted, despite the world ending.

He moved into the lobby area again and pulled his hood up over his head. He moved with a limp in his leg, his right foot hurting more than the left one. He moved as quickly as he could, down to his car, and drove home as fast as possible. Before he knew it, he was back at his house, everything in a similar condition as he left it. He moved to sweep up his laptop off the ground, the thing not yet broken into pieces like the rest of his life. He picked it up and opened it, the computer cracking and croaking. It was on his last leg, much like Tatum was. It peeled open and he balanced the machine in the palm of his left hand, kicking his shoes off to the best of his ability. Red splotches stained the tip of his big toe, and the irrational part of his brain warned him not to take his socks off. If he did and his toenail peeled off, he would pass out, no doubt about it. If he wasn't into something right here, right now, part of him would hope he'd hit his head on the way down. But no, he had a book to write. He had a book to publish. He was reinventing himself, without a manager in his corner. He was selling his soul to the indie publishers now and he didn't see any shame in it. He plopped onto the couch, put the laptop on the edge of his kneecaps, and started his search. He searched through the lists of agents, the self-publishing agencies, and what all his options were.

He scratched at the stubble on his chin as he weighed his options. He could finish his book as early as tomorrow, have it up for review, and the eBook could potentially be up by tomorrow night. The only issue was if people were worried about an apocalypse, they probably wouldn't bring an eReader around with them, and they certainly wouldn't use their phone battery to read his stuff. He shook his head as he knew he couldn't think like this, he just needed to focus on getting the content out. If he focused and got this done, the paperback would be ready to go within two days. He knew that was faster than Jackie could've only dreamed of. He would do this himself. All it would take was a few google searches to get the information he didn't have. He'd use a few apps to come up with a decent enough cover, and that should only take fifteen minutes. He'd come up with a simple book description, some tags, and the thing would be up. The sooner he got it under review, the better, he knew this, but could he truly write a book in a matter of twenty-four hours - at that? He wasn't sure if he had it in him, as he knew the requirements for any kind of modern novel. It all came down to word counts and he started to dabble in the idea of whether a short story would be better. Gauge interest, see who likes it, if it does well, or if it flops. A short story eliminates the potential of wasted time.

Yes, that was it. He wouldn't have to pay a graphic designer. Jackie wouldn't tell him to make changes so that she could take half of his earnings. He didn't need to pay an editor. Shit, why didn't he do this sooner? The world was his baby, and everything he could have wanted is right here in front of him. It was him against the world, how it should have always been. He couldn't help but feel the grin as it spread against his face, fingers starting to type faster - starting to move more quickly. He could write what he wanted to write for once in his life, and he didn't have to worry about overusing words like fuck and shit. He could probably use the word whore if he wanted to. He could do whatever the fuck he wanted. He didn't know why he had never considered it before. Maybe it was because those around him made him feel that those who didn't publish traditionally weren't truly published.

Jesus, how much of his life had been wasted doing what everyone else had told him? How much of his life did he waste feeling as if his best moves had to be

motivated by financial things and popularity standards? His world was ending, he knew this, but all he
had was his writing. It was survival of the fittest, and
he'd survive. Whenever the world moved into post-
apocalypse, whenever groups of survivors made cities and safe houses, he'd sell his book. He wasn't going
anywhere. Tatum wasn't going anywhere. Tatum Hyland was here to stay.

He had his account set up now. He had his tags set
up. He had age restrictions put in, despite the short
story not overusing the words fuck and whore like he
originally intended. If he had time, he'd edit out most
swear words to fit a younger audience. Yes, he could
sell this to those under the age of eighteen. Young
adult would fit well, really well. Whenever their
world ended, teens left behind in bunkers would read
it and look up to characters like Chelsea and Spencer.
Maybe this was the book he was meant to write all
along - a story of survival - a tale of hope. Young adult
apocalyptic was what he wanted. He'd pay for an
ISBN, merely because it was required, not because
he thought he needed to guarantee a string of digits
to his name. He was sure that at the end of the day,
nobody would be trying to steal his shit. Jackie was
right when she said that entertainment in the forms
of books probably aren't at the top of anyone's radar.
He'd use this to his advantage.

Now the ISBN was assigned randomly, he needed
to pick a title. His fingers tapped a few times on the
keyboard, his brain rattled with thoughts. He considered the end of their world - his refusal to believe

it. He thought of Ellie and his neighbors. He thought about the kids across the street that may be dead by the end of the month, if they weren't already. He thought about the people in the car accidents. He thought about his world and the world Chelsea and Spencer lived it. It was poetic that their world had ended and his was on the brink of it.

Yes, that was the thought he needed. The string that pulled everything together.

Cessation.

Maybe it would be hard to pronounce, and maybe they wouldn't know what the word even meant - but the story would speak for itself. It would speak for the end of their world. To come to an end. That is what cessation means, after all. The word never carried much weight until now, until he lived within cessation. His world was ending as he knew it. Those who were meant to be left on this earth will still be wandering tomorrow. Those who were too weak have already perished. This was the start of Tatum's new livelihood. One where he would be a beacon of hope. Within Cessation, people would find him. They'd adore him. He just needed to get the book out.

He moved into the makeshift online studio and put together the first things the readers would see. The cover, he decided, was grey with black lettering. He had to admit that it looked nice having his name on the front of a book again. Yes, this is what was meant to happen.

The description was easy. Not ideal, but not the worst he's ever written.

"A young mother left alone with her four year-old-daughter fight through the realm of flesh-eating monsters known as "The Bodies." They live in a world fueled by survival and doing whatever it takes to see another day. What will happen when they are introduced to a stranger with an intimidating presence?"

Okay, maybe it was terrible. But he could always change it once he makes it big. That is what he would do. Right now, his story would merely be a work in progress, nothing more. Once the world got stable again, once people stopped dying by the thousands, he would fix it. He'd straighten and polish. He'd make the description better. Right now, though? He just needed to get his baby ready so that he could publish the damn thing. Microsoft Word and other free programs would have to do for now. There was no time for beta readers or for professional editors. Part of him preferred it this way, as he had no time to stress over the small details. He had no time to change a sentence eighteen times before it pleased him. He was going to do this thing. He was living right now, he was breathing, and he was going to do it.

Now he just needed to finish the damn book.

CESSATION CHAPTER SIX

Chelsea didn't know whether to cry or to pee herself. Surely, she couldn't just lay in the grass and listen to Spencer experience whatever the hell she was about to go through. Jillian wasn't going to last another sixty seconds, no less however long they'd be stuck frozen with fear. How would she explain this to Jillian? Ultimately, she didn't want her child to grow up with immense trust issues, but when two people disappear from her life, how would she react? What would she think? How would Chelsea tell her daughter that Spencer was a nice woman that probably sacrificed her life for a couple of strangers? Chelsea knew that when it came down to it, she was never going to leave her daughter or put her in any danger. She knew that she had a little girl to care for, love, and ensure that she got every piece of food and water that could be given her way. Chelsea didn't sacrifice her rations to win some mother of the year award. She did it because her child deserved a life. Deserved to live, to breathe, and to exist like she did. Her daughter would never have an ideal life, but Chelsea always fought for her to be comfortable. But Chelsea also couldn't let her new friend, one who has saved her, she couldn't let her give herself up. Everything about Spencer spoke of survival. She was the living and breathing image of a badass, one that didn't take any shit. Spencer could've shot her in the back, left Jillian in the ceiling to rot, but she gave her a chance. They had barely scratched the surface of their potential, but Chelsea wasn't about to give it up. Not yet. She couldn't let her go.

"Wait," Chelsea stood up. She instantly cursed her knee jerk reaction as it was Jillian that poked her head up next. The grass just reached her neck, only allowing her small head to pop up.

"We're right here," Chelsea breathed out, arms up. Whenever she died in the apocalypse, she never anticipated it this way. She and John always agreed that they'd rather go out in a badass way, like getting bitten in the neck by a body, as opposed to being taken out by a group of strangers, by a group of humans.

Their guns were raised, pointed at them, and Chelsea's hands rose, much like they did when she met Spencer. This wasn't going to be the same situation, though, Chelsea knew that much. These people were mean to their core, wrinkles around their heads due to years of scowling and showing nothing but anger. They looked dirty, their skin the color of rust. Most had missing teeth and tattered clothing, even worse than the usual victims of an apocalypse. Chelsea could almost smell their stench from here.

"You killed our friends," one of them said, a gun pointed directly at Chelsea.

"They tried to kill us," Chelsea said lowly, a heartbeat rising into her throat and pulsing the blood in her neck.

"You broke into our homes," the same face replied.

"Oh, shut the hell up," Spencer scoffed. "This is the apocalypse, y'all. There are no rules. No rights to possessions." Chelsea looked at Spencer as she spoke, realizing now that the girl probably didn't care whether she lived or died. But to take the option away from Chelsea? Her blood pulsed. There was a streak of red that fell into her eyelids, a push of anger she tried not to show.

"Spencer," Chelsea breathed out to the woman lowly, Chelsea's hands still up, but Spencer stood on the defensive side.

Spencer whipped her head around to look at Chelsea, irritation flooding her system. "What?"

she asked her. "You gonna let a bunch of creepy nobodies run us out of their little safe house? After they would've killed you and Jillian?" She asked as she crossed her arms. "Sorry, Chelsea, but I'm not just gonna go out like some little bitch," she said before she looked back at the group.

They were outnumbered and the others had more weapons. The trio didn't stand a chance, and Spencer was going to be the one that put them in their grave if she kept the stupid stuff up. Chelsea swallowed and rubbed her ring finger into the center of her palm and she then looked at the group standing before them.

"What do we have to do to walk out of here?" she asked after a moment, her arms crossed in front of her chest and her voice holding a slight shake.

"Return the stuff-" a younger male piped up from the back, but their makeshift leader held up a fist of silence.

"Be quiet, Tyler. We can't let these people come in and take what they want and expect them to get away with it," the leader said as he looked Spencer up and down and then Chelsea. "You're going to come with us, and from there, we are going to decide what we wanna do with ya," he said as he tucked his gun into his pants. "They aren't going to hurt you, right guys?" He turned to look at the group, a grin on his face that revealed most, if not all, of his teeth were long gone. Chelsea shuddered at the sight of him, and she knew that even before the apocalypse, these guys probably weren't the best to be around. She could tell by how they carried themselves that they were always eyesores, but the kind that nobody messed with - the type that would throw a punch at any given time. She knew better than to test this guy. She looked over at Spencer who was now looking at her, jaw locked, and arms still crossed.

"And if we say no?" Spencer looked back at the man.

"We kill you where you stand," he replied shortly. "The child we will keep," he said as he looked at Jillian next. "She does have quite the innocent and cute little face." He grinned as he opened his arms up in some kind of grand gesture.

"We can keep you safe here. We take turns guarding the perimeter. We have food, drinks, toys for the little one," he said as he looked around the gated community with a proud smirk.

"Oh yeah, you did a real good job watching the perimeter yesterday," Spencer said lowly as she looked at the man with another shake of her head, red tendrils slipping into her face. "Listen, asshole, me and my friends here were just needing a place to sleep. The place looked abandoned, so we chose to stop. It was your friends that fucked it up for you. Can we go now?" she asked.

"You seem to be doing a lot of talking, but we haven't heard from your very passive and very kind friend over there." The man pointed towards Chelsea as he looked over her body once more.

"She doesn't have anything to say to you," Spencer replied. "Now, are you going to let us through?" she asked with a huff.

"Or what?" the man asked her with a laugh.

"I'll shoot you," Spencer replied as she moved to grab the bow in her hand but everyone in the group in front of her panicked, lifting their guns into position.

"You don't stand a chance, pretty lady," the leader said as he looked at her through her scope. Chelsea knew, deep down, that they weren't getting out of here alive. This wasn't like the time that Spencer stumbled upon her and chose to let her live. These guys weren't sitting ducks, and it wasn't two against two. In the spare chance that Spencer could fire off one arrow, the other five would be on top of them in a few seconds. It was moments like these in which Chelsea wished she still had her ammo and that they had gotten to Spencer's uncle's place a lot sooner. Would they have faced a different fate had they not stopped here last night? Chelsea took in another long breath as she looked at Spencer and the group in front of them.

"Just let us go," Chelsea begged. "We will give you what we took, and we will ensure that you never see our faces again, okay?" she said to them.

"You took away that opportunity when you tried to rob us and whenever you killed our friends," the same man replied, the rest of the group still seeming to be on guard.

"Your friend tried to attack us." Chelsea felt the repetitive cycle, one that couldn't be ended. The man would always seem to know more, would always seem to have the answers as to why he couldn't let the two girls go. Chelsea chewed on her lips and then her cheek. "I have a little girl." She said to them with a sigh. "She has done nothing wrong." She begged them as she watched the gun get raised in her direction.

"Mmmhm, and where is the baby daddy?" the man asked them with a smirk on his face. She held her hand up as she could sense Spencer starting to fire up. Ultimately and truthfully, it wasn't any of this man's business, Chelsea knew this, but getting angry over every little thing wasn't going to help. The truth was that her boyfriend left them behind and she had no idea where he was. She could lie, say that her boyfriend died tragically in attempts to save his daughter. Chelsea could go into an elaborate story talking about the grief, how much they've starved over these past few weeks without him. She also knew that if Jillian paid too much attention, she'd just ask questions. She would call her bluff with the facts, those facts being her boyfriend left her high and dry. The facts were that her boyfriend said their daughter was holding him back. The truth was that her boyfriend tried to convince her to leave Jillian behind one night, saying they'd all be dead soon by the end of the week, anyway. It didn't make any difference though, and it didn't change anything. The fact of the matter was that Chelsea was probably going to die today. She didn't die yesterday like she was supposed to, so it only made sense that it came back around to bite them. Would she live with knowing that she caused the death of a stranger and her daughter, too? She knew that once that bullet was fired, she'd find out if there was a thing such as eternal life or rebirth. She would find out in a few moments whether there was heaven or hell.

"Riley. Stand down," a voice called out from the side.

"But-" the man who Chelsea assumed to be the leader objected, all attention moved towards the new voice.

"Riley," the voice was stern and to the point, and Chelsea could pick it out of a crowd. She knew that they were truly done for as Jillian heard it, too.

"Daddy!" Jillian yelled as she took off running, Chelsea having just missed the younger girl's body. Chelsea watched as Jillian ran into the arms of the man that betrayed them without a second thought. She watched as her child wrapped her arms around his thick neck and her legs around his sternum. Chelsea bet that the guy probably smelled the same he always did, despite the apocalypse taking place.

"They're with me and they're fine," he finally spoke as his eyes met Chelsea's and he had the audacity to smirk at her and Spencer. "Go clear

Oliver and Ethan out of the house and clean it up for my girls here. I want you all to clean it well and ensure they have clean sheets put on the bed." He said and the group didn't stand and gawk, they all moved into action, a pep in their step.

"You really need to work on keeping your perimeter secure," Spencer said flatly as she crossed her arms. "We aren't staying in this stupid place. You all are nothing short of a bunch of idiots. I don't know how you've made it this far."

"Spence, it's okay," Chelsea said as she looked over at him, the man she used to run around with for all these years. "You're an idiot, you know that?" Chelsea asked as she looked at him, arms crossed.

"Just... come and talk to me and let me explain. If you don't want to stay after that, then we will give you all the supplies you want and get you on your way," he said as he looked at her for a long moment. "You owe me this much," he spoke lowly.

"I owe you shit," Chelsea replied just as quick. "You left us, remember?" she asked him.

"Member, daddy?" Jillian pulled away to look at him as a hand moved to touch the grown-in beard that lined his face.

"Let me explain it to you," he said as he looked to Chelsea and then to Spencer. "What's your story?" He took a few steps backward.

"Her story is none of your business. If you wanna talk, she is coming with me," Chelsea said as she pulled her hair out of its ponytail and looked at him, arms crossed.

"Alright. Let's go talk."

CHAPTER FIFTEEN

Tatum truly didn't want to bring the baby daddy in like this. No, he wanted Chelsea to find his corpse hanging from a tree, or maybe he just wanted to bring him in as some kind of crazy cannibal. But his heart panged with sadness. Not bringing the dad in wasn't an option. Not whenever Ellie expected him to come back at the end. Would this be the way that Ellie wanted it? He could envision her as she read it now, her green eyes lit up and a grin on her face. She would hold his manuscript and dance around the room like a child. She would chant and holler about how she "knew it" and "saw it coming." On social media, she would've promoted his book, telling them that she knew the twist and that the readers would never see it coming. The reality was that the introduction of the baby daddy was a cheap move. But if he wanted to make this a short story, publish this, and call it quits, now would be the perfect time to do so. If he got feedback from everyone who lived through this, and if they said they hated it, he could just have the dad kill everyone. That seemed to be the best course of action, and he knew that he would be one of the first people to get book reviews in a post-apocalyptic world. The thought made him smile as he closed out of the Word document and take in a deep breath.

The most satisfying part of the writing process was to write the two words that every writer craved, the words that read **THE END**. That feeling was always a burden lifted off any writer's shoulders, despite the endless revisions that would follow afterward. The end was never really the end, but it was just the start of a different journey. He knew that if this book were to have happened three years ago or even a month ago, he'd feel prouder of his work. It would probably be seventy-thousand words and two hundred pages long, it'd go through multiple editors and multiple line by line discussions, but it wasn't their world right now.

He was certain that the thing was riddled with spelling errors, mistakes, and verb issues, but he never dwelled on simple things. In his mind, if someone was distracted by a simple comma, he felt sorry for that person. He felt as if that person didn't deserve to read his shit, as they would be too bent out of shape over the technicalities. In his eyes, art was art, and if everyone could read what he was saying, he was content with it.

He also couldn't help but smile at how it felt, knowing that the book that was written during the apocalypse would be the most expensive thing on the market once everything got under control. Once the world was stabilized, he could sell extended versions of his book, he could sell second editions with the spelling errors fixed, but the first edition would be what survived it all.

He knew he needed to format the damn thing and then get it all uploaded up and ready to go. It made him sad knowing that he was probably never going to hold a physical copy of his book in his hands, not yet anyway, but these were the prices he had to pay for writing in an apocalyptic world. He needed to do what was necessary, some sacrifices needed to be made, and that was what contact information was for. Those that were still on his newsletter would get fifty percent off the book if they survived the apocalypse, and then he would have a post-apocalyptic book sale for those poor, unfortunate people who didn't read his shit before the world turned to... well, shit.

When things were back to normal, he'd create a real book cover. He would do things traditionally and charge out the ass for these things. When his book was being made into what would more than likely be a short TV series, he would be set for life. He'd dedicate an episode to Ellie, and he'd find a person that looked like her to play one of his characters. It wasn't the best, but it was what he could do with what he's been given.

"Focus," he finally said as he looked at his screen for a long moment. All he would have to do was left indent each page, give each chapter a title and a number, come up with a dedication and an about the author page, and have the book up for review. By tomorrow he would be the guy who wrote the last modern-day apocalypse novel before the world turned into its own apocalyptic story.

He couldn't focus, no matter how hard he tried. Not whenever his chest thudded a little harder with depression. It was a sadness that festered and hadn't been dealt with. Ellie, his Ellie, was dead. The only girl he had ever loved was gone. He dedicated books to her in the past, mainly because he had no one else in his life to dedicate his books to, but this time would be different. There would be no tabloids to stir the pot or to ask him whether that was his girlfriend. There wouldn't be any speculations - not because Ellie was dead, but because the press wasn't going to be concerned with dedications and acknowledgments. No, they'd turn past the dedications, the acknowledgements, and they'd turn past the prologue. Tatum knew, ultimately, that this is what was going to happen. It would be worth it, he knew, but it wouldn't happen if he didn't just write the damn thing and get it over with.

To Ellie - Love you forever and a day.

He bit on his knuckle as his right hand slowly typed the words. Despite the flash of the stupid cursor, none of it felt real. There was a part of him that wanted to wake up from a horrible nightmare, hope that the memories of this book and everything else would come with him, but he wanted to find Ellie alive. Maybe once he woke up, he'd marry her, raise a child with her, have some of his own. The thought had a nice ring to it, but with the way his teeth tried to gnaw through flesh, he knew that he was in reality. There was no waking up from this point - he was in it for the long haul, whether he wanted to be or not. He'd have to shut up, put his eyes forward, and get through this book.

All he wanted was for the world to see his brilliance. Was that too much to ask? Too much to expect? He knew the idea was a good one - Jackie had said so. He already had his cast in mind for the movie deal he would inevitably get. He knew that the world would see it, love it, eat it up, and praise him for it. He just needed to get the book up. He couldn't wait anymore. As long as he got something up, he could later edit and rework. Hell, with his world ending, he'd have all the time in the world. He just needed to get it up. The sooner, the better, as people were dying by the hundreds, and that would affect the number of potential readers. If he got it up now, he could promote it and he could get the word out. He would sell it with taglines like *"If Chelsea and Jillian can survive the apocalypse, so can you!"* When things were more normalized, they could see guns that looked like Chelsea's. Jillian would be the new most popular name. Things were looking up, this he knew.

His eyes strained as he stared at the screen. For-matting was something he never had to dabble in be-fore. Formatting was something he paid other people to do - but if the apocalypse taught him anything it was that the only person you could rely on was your-self. Ultimately, he was the only one that could get this shit done and get it done right, even though this made him want to off himself. One wrong click sent everything in the wrong direction. He had to try to make sure things were as correct as possible. Certain words needed italicized, to which he thanked Tatum Hyland of the past for not overdoing it. The phras-ing and words were simple - nothing to get excited over. He found a few wrong commas, a few backward parentheses, and he stared at the darkened words at the end of the manuscript with triumph. He felt his body shake with excitement as he moved to format his author page and used a photo that Ellie had taken of him at their coffee shop. It was a quintessential au-thor photo - his glasses and white mug in front of him, his elbows folded and rested on the table. If he had the right editing software, he'd remove the glare of Ellie's reflection in his glasses, but that would be part of him forever. He stopped for a long time to look at the photo, to try to make out her small nose, to try to make out her long brunette hair. He sighed as he tried to eliminate any and all memory of her.

He moved to delete the photo he had previously chosen, and he selected a new one. He looked younger, his hair less disheveled, no glasses on his face, and a few pounds heavier. This one taken in a studio with a legitimate camera, no signs of Ellie in his eyes. He deleted that one next, as it was Ellie that forced him to go to a professional for his author photos. He let out a grunt of frustration as he couldn't decide on a photo. The photo of him outside a brick wall, also taken by Ellie, the photo of him on some random beach had Ellie originally cropped out of it. It was always her. It was her in his eyes, a memory that followed with him, and a piece of her that would show up everywhere.

He swiped part of the laptop away from him, the object clicking and groaning at the rough behavior. The right corner pulled up off the table before it fell back down, the open screen staring right back at him. Everything burned as he pulled the laptop closer and looked at the screen yet again. He didn't need an author photo for the stupid page, did he? No, he needed it. He needed to be the face of the apocalypse. He needed to be the face that all the new single moms would hold in their bunker, and he needed to be the face people hoped to come across in the streets.

Without thinking, his fingers started to move on his phone screen, the phone tapping with eagerness before he placed it against his ear. He smiled whenever he heard her voice on the other end.

"Jackie, I've decided I'm gonna do this without ya," he grinned triumphantly as he moved into the kitchen, his hands fumbling to find a new bottle of booze. He found the Smirnoff and chugged it down as he listened to the silence that came on the other end.

"What?" Jackie asked him, confusion ringing in her voice.

"I said," Tatum pulled the bottle from his lips, "I'm gonna do this without you. Once I get the last part of formatting done, I'm gonna post it up for review, and you're going to watch my face as it rises on the charts. No thanks to you," He chugged down more booze, eager to feel the buzz of the alcohol.

"Tatum, you can't do that," Jackie replied on the other end.

"Watch me," Tatum laughed as he shook his head and slammed the bottle down on the countertop. "Me publishing online just skipped over the hundreds of hoops you woulda made me jump through, and I get to keep all my royalties." He smiled to himself as he paced through the kitchen, his feet crunching papers and trash.

"Tatum, they're closing it all down. Nobody is going to be able to approve your review," Jackie said bluntly. "Can you listen to me for once? You need to put this to rest for now and ge-"

Tatum threw his phone across the room, and he watched as it collided with the wall, the screen popping off and clattering to the floor. He let out a scream as he pulled his hands through his hair, his fist moving to punch the next available object, his knuckles crunching and snapping on impact. He screamed again as his hands found his laptop and swiped that, too. He watched as the lid got its long-awaited release, cracking off and crashing onto the floor. His fist grabbed the alcohol bottle and chugged down more of the contents, feeling the bitter liquid swirl around his empty stomach. Blood dripped down his hand, over the still open wound on his arm. He screamed and yelled, knocking whatever he could off the walls. There were always reminders of Ellie, of the life that he wasted. He screamed at the fact that he lived while the others died. Innocent people, people who deserved to live - they were dying by the hundreds. He screamed for them until his vocal cords were raw. He trashed the house that had been his safe place for so long. He trashed the place that was once a refuge from all socialization, a place where no one would bother him. *The Devils* saga wasn't born in this house, but it was the first 'big boy 'purchase he had made with his money that he should've tucked into savings. He had fucked up, he knew this. He didn't deserve any of this. The thought drove him mad, forced him to move through the house, a new determination in mind.

His hands didn't fumble for a predetermined zombie apocalypse bag. He didn't grab for his guns or his knives, he didn't clean his kitchen of its contents, and he didn't fill up a water bottle for the road. He didn't get one cup of coffee as he stormed out, the rain falling in thick sheets and blankets, making the bottoms of his feet slick. He slipped and moved towards his car, his knee hitting against the ground and his hand gripping the handle for support. The bottle swooshed and mingled with the rain as he gained his balance and pulled the door open, nearly taking himself out with the door.

He turned his keys in the ignition harder than necessary, the engine struggling to turn over. The rain pelted the car and the visibility was low - sky grey and unwelcoming. He knew that if he was going to die a single man, as a loser, he might as well do so on his own accord instead of the insanity of others.

He chewed on his fingernails that belonged to the swollen and bleeding fist. He pulled his fingers away from his mouth, the digits moving to tap on the wheel to an imaginary beat. At the thought, he flicked on the radio and he waited to hear the ray of hope that he longed for. He waited to hear a closure to this wild story, and he wanted this all to be put to rest. He wanted to wake up from this nightmare coated in frustration and murder. He wanted to lay Ellie to rest, and for her body not to be the start to a pile in a morgue somewhere. He didn't want her to be a body in a ditch, a body without a proper home. How over-crowded would the hospitals be? How long until he got blamed for all of this?

No, the murders were happening before they reached him. The murders were something that had reached the news, had been in other cities and states before they closed his down. No, they couldn't arrest him due to some coincidences.

With this thought in mind, his hand moved to flick on the radio, thumbing through the stations. He wanted to hear something - anything. He could no longer suffer the ticks of the rain and the ending world. He could no longer sit and let the silence become him. He needed something - whether it be heavy metal or jazz. He needed to hear something that would give him hope.

But it was all static. Endless and relentless static, some of it being louder than the one before it. He listened to the whispers and the crackles in the madness, the rain mixed in to create a somber lullaby. That was when he heard it, the voice of hope.

"The undead... or the dead... or the living... or whatever the fuck they are, got to my boyfriend and cohost, and they're both beating at the studio door..." a woman's voice said. "I'm on my last bottle of booze, or I'd invite some of you to come up and enjoy this life with me." Tatum listened as she took in a deep breath, "This will be my last song, and then I'm signing off. Stay alive out there and do some good."

The woman's last dying wish, Tatum assumed, was to have her probable favorite song play on the radio. Was she walking to the door now, ready to let the murderers into the studio? Who started the infection in her studio to begin with? He wondered if they were going to find the body or if they were the cause. Her last words were that she wanted the humans, even if it was just Tatum, to do some good. Tatum knew her real last wish, though, was to hear her song one last time. He listened, and he anticipated, he wondered what song spoke the most to her in a moment of destruction. What song would be the thing that brought her peace and carried her into the night? How long until she gave in and opened the door herself? How long until she starved? If it came down to it, he wasn't sure what song he would've wanted to play last. As he waited for the woman to pick her song, silently hoping he didn't drive out of range, and he listened. He wondered what song spoke to her most - he wondered if it was going to be Bieber or something obscure. He wondered if he'd even know it, or if he was about to go into his apocalypse not knowing the song name or artist. The familiar upbeat cut through his thoughts, though. He felt the car buzz and he felt the mood get a bit lighter, despite it only being him in the car, and he started to drive in the darkness. He listened as *Everybody Wants to Rule the World* played into the darkness of the night. He watched as the music danced to the yellow stripes on the dark road. He tapped to the familiar beat, wishing now, more than ever, that he could've ruled the world. Maybe then he could've saved Ellie, and maybe then he wouldn't have to do all this other side work.

With this thought in mind, he continued to drive, letting Curt Smith's voice carry him into the night. All he wanted was to rule the world, to be the new face of the apocalypse.

All Tatum wanted was to reinvent himself, to be something more than the hopeless romantic he was all those years ago. There was a time where he had nothing but hope for the world – a happiness for the fictional characters he created. For a long time, he was proud of the life he had breathed into the pages. For a long time, he thought he was the next Stephen King. Part of him wanted nothing more than to go back to that shitty dorm room. The room where his initial idea came to him, the room where his shirt stuck to his skin with sweat, the room where the rustiness of the window screen rubbed off on his fingers. He wanted to go back to a time where Ellie would sit on his bed and would run to the dinner hall to get him coffee, when they had nothing else to worry about. While his writing was horrendous and trite, his life was simpler. He didn't feel the pressure he does now to be the next best thing. Back then he was merely a small-town guy, nothing strange or unique about him, who wrote a story about a devil falling in love with a human. Things were different now. He had years of success under his belt, several writing seminars and classes attended, and he had a story that would take off. He wanted to put his old life to rest. He wanted to be bigger and better, but the world wasn't letting him. He wanted to prove more than anything else that he was talented - that it wasn't just a lucky break.

As he drove, his vision stretched the world in straight pinpoint lines, his eyes heavy and his car veering off the road each time he tried to focus harder. The remainder of the bottle sat to his right, and his head rested on his hand as he drove, no location in his mind. The radio had died down to static and he had yet to hear the woman's voice again. He tried to listen and make sense of it all. He tried to wonder why he never continued writing. He tried to understand the mysteries of life and understand why his idea wasn't given to him sooner. He wanted to grab God by the shoulders and shake him - ask him why he did this to him. He wanted to know why God took Ellie first and why he waited so long to plant the idea in his head. He wanted to ask him if this was an ultimate punishment for all his wrongdoings. For all the times he cheated on his fiancé or for all the times he stole a few snacks from the gas station. He wondered if it was for all the times he had to drag himself to hang out with Ellie, for all the times he pretended to be sick to avoid her.

The apocalypse was supposed to be what sparked him to reinvent himself. It was supposed to be the thing that pushed him to the top of the world. There was always hope that the world would turn around, but he had too many sins to drag him into the pits of hell. He didn't deserve to have his brilliance shown. No, he deserved to be known as the romance guy. He deserved to be known as a one-hit-wonder, one of the guys who had fifteen minutes of fame.

Now here he was, drunk driving, alone, a nobody. He was a mere blip in the universe that was eagerly being chewed up and sucked into a black hole. He left no indentation, no book to be read and studied in school. He left no prodigy, no human to carry on the family name. The universe simply didn't care about him. He realized this now. He realized that they were showing no mercy on him, no mercy on Ellie, his neighbor, the kids across the street, the car accident people, or those in the hospital. They were a bump in the road of something awful, something darker that brewed and turned like the sky above his head.

He was never meant to be special. He realized this now. He was nothing more than a stubborn artist who got his agent super rich one time ten years ago. He was never meant to be a brilliant writer, one that deserved to have his work digested and read repeatedly. People weren't going to get Chelsea and

Spencer tattooed on their bodies and they weren't going to name their kids after his Jillian. He wasn't special - he was nothing more than another living and breathing skeleton - ready to be taken back. He wasn't special.

No, he was merely Tatum Hyland. A blip. A defect. A sellout. Another mindless drone in the void that didn't care for him.

The thought prompted a hard jerk of the wheel to the right. He heard the car's tires as they screeched, trying to save his life. The tires lifted and they slid around the landslide of rocks and pebbles alike. The fight or flight kicked in as his head smashed up against the driver's side window, his hand still trying to gain control over the wheel. He felt as if he was spinning out forever, and it wasn't until his car smashed like an accordion that he realized he was done moving. The scent of gas filled his nostrils, smoke beginning to flood out from the sides of the engine, but Tatum didn't care. He managed to close his eyes, both from defeat and from injury, and he tried his best to drift off into a sleep he would hopefully never wake from.

CHAPTER SIXTEEN

He woke up to the scent of fire and his engine burning. Whenever he pulled his head up, he felt the warmth that dripped down his face and into his eyes. He felt the blood as it fell off his chin, and he pulled the mirror down to look at his reflection. His once smooth and pimple-free face had a deep gash across his forehead, his flesh covered with cuts and scrapes from the glass. He was certain he could see his skull through the laceration, part of him uncertain as to why he didn't see his own brain. His hands shook as he lifted them, knuckles cut and arm limp as he tried to free himself from the restraints of his seatbelt. He felt the splinters of his broken ribcage with each time he tried to roll free, he wanted to adjust himself and get to standing. He kicked at the windshield and watched the glass shatter like he had taken a hammer to it. He drug his knees across the shards, red coating his eyesight as he moved forward. A part of him was certain that his legs and wrist were broken, as they lay in awkward and bent angles, limp and lifeless as they moved.

He dragged himself across the cement now as his car groaned at him. As he moved, he didn't have his intentions clearly set. He scooted until he reached a tree - his fingers touching the grooves and valleys of the object stronger than him. He didn't know how hard and how fast he hit the thing, but it looked good as new. It looked firm in its ways, not even slightly wayward. His car no longer looked like a car, but he glanced at the tree - much like the one that grew in his backyard. It was the kind of tree that he at one point searched so fervently for ideas. When did he last do that? A week ago? A month ago? How much time has passed since his first meeting with Jackie? He couldn't be sure anymore. When the world was ending, time had no meaning. The tick of the clock no longer existed and there were no deadlines to be met. Tatum realized now that every relationship, every embarrassing moment, every accomplishment, and every certificate or medal...it had no purpose. None of it mattered as he dragged himself amongst the black pit of cement, amongst the shimmer of glass from his windshield.

He leaned on the trunk and despite the darkness, he stared into the drop off ahead of him. He could hear the trees as they swayed and the tick of the rain against the ground around him. There was no yelling of a child, and there were no dogs barking. It was a deadly silence of the world that had lost its mind, and he knew he was soon to join them. Tatum wiped more of the red substance on the back of his wrist and watched as it streaked in a line down his forearm. He was going to die here, this he knew. The world would never know Chelsea. They wouldn't know Spencer or Jillian. The world would never have a glimmer of survival and a glimmer of hope. He would die as the romance guy. He would die as a nobody.

At the thought - he opened his mouth and screamed. He screamed into the void. He screamed into the world that took everything from him without mercy. He screamed, even though nobody would hear him, and despite the fact nobody was listening.

THE END

NOIR HAYES

While always awkward and uncomfortable, Noir Hayes spends her days trying to create worlds and characters bigger than herself. Writing anything from the dark and gritty world of New York to the softest of romances, Noir finds a love for it all. Outside of writing, Noir is a full-time student and teaches ballet to younger adults, teens, and children.

Other works by Noir Hayes:

Razor Blades

ABOUT THE AUTHOR

Noir Hayes

Noir isn't done telling stories yet..
Follow her on her social media accounts!
Instagram: @Noir_hayes
Twitter: @Noirhayes
Facebook: Noir Hayes
Want exclusive content? Noir is creating stories on Patreon!

Made in the USA
Monee, IL
04 October 2021